ANIMAL STORIES

ANIMAL STORIES

TALES OF THE OLD PLANTATION

BY JOEL CHANDLER HARRIS

ILLUSTRATIONS BY EZRA JACK KEATS

JUNIOR DELUXE EDITIONS

GARDEN CITY, NEW YORK

INTRODUCTION

I am advised by my publishers that this book is to be included in their catalogue of humorous publications, and this friendly warning gives me an opportunity to say that however humorous it may be in effect, its intention is perfectly serious; and even if it were otherwise, it seems to me that a volume written wholly in dialect must have its solemn, not to say melancholy, features. With respect to the Folk-Lore series, my purpose has been to preserve the legends themselves in their original simplicity, and to wed them permanently to the quaint dialect—if, indeed, it can be called a dialect—through the medium of which they have become a part of the domestic history of every Southern family; and I have endeavored to give to the whole a genuine flavor of the old plantation.

Each legend has its variants, but in every instance I have retained that particular version which seemed to me to be the most characteristic, and have given it without embellishment and without exaggeration.

If the reader not familiar with plantation life will imagine that the myth-stories of Uncle Remus are told night after night to a little boy by an old Negro who appears to be venerable enough to have lived during the period which he describes—who has nothing but pleasant memories of the discipline of slavery—and who has all the prejudices of caste and pride of family that were the natural results of the system; if the reader can imagine all this, he will find little difficulty in appreciating and sympathizing with the air of affectionate superiority which Uncle Remus assumes as he proceeds to unfold the mysteries of plantation lore to a little child who is the product of that practical reconstruction which has been going on to some extent since the war in spite of the politicians.

J.C.H.

1880

CONTENTS

ANIMAL STORIES

One evening recently, the lady whom Uncle Remus calls "Miss Sally" missed her little seven-year-old. Making search for him through the house and through the yard, she heard the sound of voices in the old man's cabin, and, looking through the window, saw the child sitting by Uncle Remus. His head rested against the old man's arm, and he was gazing with an expression of the most intense interest into the rough, weather-beaten face, that beamed so kindly upon him. This is what "Miss Sally" heard:

"Bimeby, one day, arter Brer Fox bin doin' all dat he could fer ter ketch Brer Rabbit, en Brer Rabbit bin doin' all he could fer ter keep 'im fum it, Brer Fox say to hisse'f dat he'd put up a game on Brer Rabbit, en he ain't mo'n got de wuds out'n his mouf twel Brer Rabbit come a lopin' up de big road, lookin' des ez plump, en ez fat, en ez sassy ez a Moggin hoss in a barley-patch.

" 'Hol' on dar, Brer Rabbit,' sez Brer Fox, sezee.

" 'I ain't got time, Brer Fox,' sez Brer Rabbit, sezee, sorter mendin' his licks.

" 'I wanter have some confab wid you, Brer Rabbit,' sez Brer Fox, sezee.

" 'All right, Brer Fox, but you better holler fum whar you stan'. I'm monstus full er fleas dis mawnin',' sez Brer Rabbit, sezee.

" 'I seed Brer B'ar yistiddy,' sez Brer Fox, sezee, 'en he sorter rake me over de coals kaze you en me ain't make frens en live naberly, en I tole 'im dat I'd see you.'

"Den Brer Rabbit scratch one year wid his off hinefoot sorter jub'usly, en den he ups en sez, sezee:

" 'All a settin', Brer Fox. Spose'n you drap roun' termorrer en take dinner wid me. We ain't got no great doin's at our house, but I speck

de ole 'oman en de chilluns kin sorter scramble roun' en git up sump'n fer ter stay yo' stummuck.'

" 'I'm 'gree'ble, Brer Rabbit,' sez Brer Fox, sezee.

" 'Den I'll 'pen' on you,' sez Brer Rabbit, sezee.

"Nex' day, Mr. Rabbit an' Miss Rabbit got up soon, 'fo' day, en raided on a gyarden like Miss Sally's out dar, en got some cabbiges, en some roas'n years, en some sparrer-grass, en dey fix up a smashin' dinner. Bimeby one er de little Rabbits, playin' out in de back-yard, come runnin' in hollerin', 'Oh, ma! Oh, ma! I seed Mr. Fox a comin'!' En den Brer Rabbit he tuck de chilluns by der years en make um set down, en den him en Miss Rabbit sorter dally roun' waitin' for Brer Fox. En dey keep on waitin', but no Brer Fox ain't come. Atter 'while Brer Rabbit goes to de do', easy like, en peep out, en dar, stickin' out frum behime de cornder, wuz de tip-een' er Brer Fox tail. Den Brer Rabbit shot de do' en sot down, en put his paws behime his years en begin fer ter sing:

" 'De place wharbouts you spill de grease,
  Right dar youer boun' ter slide,
 An' whar you fine a bunch er ha'r,
  You'll sholy fine de hide.'

"Nex' day, Brer Fox sont word by Mr. Mink, en skuze hisse'f kaze he wuz too sick fer ter come, en he ax Brer Rabbit fer ter come en take dinner wid him, en Brer Rabbit say he wuz 'gree'ble.

"Bimeby, w'en de shadders wuz at der shortes', Brer Rabbit he sorter brush up en santer down ter Brer Fox's house, en w'en he got dar, he yer somebody groanin', en he look in de do' en dar he see Brer Fox settin' up in a rockin' cheer all wrop up wid flannil, en he look mighty weak. Brer Rabbit look all 'roun', he did, but he ain't see no dinner. De dish-pan wuz settin' on de table, en close by wuz a kyarvin' knife.

" 'Look like you gwineter have chicken fer dinner, Brer Fox,' sez Brer Rabbit, sezee.

" 'Yes, Brer Rabbit, deyer nice, en fresh, en tender,' sez Brer Fox, sezee.

"Den Brer Rabbit sorter pull his mustarsh, en say: 'You ain't got no calamus root, is you, Brer Fox? I done got so now dat I can't eat no chicken 'ceppin she's seasoned up wid calamus root.' En wid dat Brer Rabbit lipt out er de do' and dodge 'mong de bushes, en sot dar watchin' fer Brer Fox; en he ain't watch long, nudder, kaze Brer Fox flung off de flannil en crope out er de house en got whar he could cloze in on Brer Rabbit, en bimeby Brer Rabbit holler out: 'Oh, Brer Fox! I'll des put yo' calamus root out yer on dish yer stump. Better come git it while hit's fresh,' and wid dat Brer Rabbit gallop off home. En Brer Fox ain't never kotch 'im yit, en w'at's mo', honey, he ain't gwineter."

"Didn't the fox *never* catch the rabbit, Uncle Remus?" asked the little boy the next evening.

"He come mighty nigh it, honey, sho's you bawn—Brer Fox did. One day atter Brer Rabbit fool 'im wid dat calamus root, Brer Fox went ter wuk en got 'im some tar, en mix it wid some turkentime, en fix up a contrapshun wat he call a Tar-Baby, en he tuck dish yer Tar-Baby en he sot 'er in de big road, en den he lay off in de bushes fer ter see wat de news wuz gwineter be. En he didn't hatter wait long, nudder, kaze bimeby here come Brer Rabbit pacin' down de road—lippity-clippity, clippity-lippity—dez ez sassy ez a jay-bird. Brer Fox, he lay low. Brer Rabbit come prancin' 'long twel he spy de Tar-Baby, en den he fotch up on his behime legs like he wuz 'stonished. De Tar-Baby, she sot dar, she did, en Brer Fox, he lay low.

" 'Mawnin'!' sez Brer Rabbit, sezee. 'Nice wedder dis mawnin',' sezee.

"Tar-Baby ain't sayin' nuthin', en Brer Fox, he lay low.

" 'How duz yo' sym'tums seem ter segashuate?' sez Brer Rabbit, sezee.

"Brer Fox, he wink his eye slow, en lay low, en de Tar-Baby, she ain't sayin' nuthin'.

" 'How you come on, den? Is you deaf?' sez Brer Rabbit, sezee. 'Kaze if you is, I kin holler louder,' sezee.

"Tar-Baby stay still, en Brer Fox, he lay low.

" 'Youer stuck up, dat's w'at you is,' says Brer Rabbit, sezee, 'en I'm gwineter kyore you, dat's w'at I'm a gwineter do,' sezee.

"Brer Fox, he sorter chuckle in his stummuck, he did, but Tar-Baby ain't sayin' nuthin'.

" 'I'm gwineter larn you howter talk ter 'specttubble fokes ef hit's

de las' ack,' sez Brer Rabbit, sezee. 'Ef you don't take off dat hat en tell me howdy, I'm gwineter bus' you wide open,' sezee.

"Tar-Baby stay still, en Brer Fox, he lay low.

"Brer Rabbit keep on axin' 'im, en de Tar-Baby, she keep on sayin' nuthin', twel present'y Brer Rabbit draw back wid his fis', he did, en blip he tuck 'er side er de head. Right dar's whar he broke his merlasses jug. His fis' stuck, en he can't pull loose. De tar hilt 'im. But Tar-Baby, she stay still, en Brer Fox, he lay low.

" 'Ef you don't lemme loose, I'll knock you agin,' sez Brer Rabbit, sezee, en wid dat he fotch 'er a wipe wid de udder han', en dat stuck. Tar-Baby, she ain't sayin' nuthin', en Brer Fox, he lay low.

" 'Tu'n me loose, fo' I kick de natal stuffin' outen you,' sez Brer Rabbit, sezee, but de Tar-Baby, she ain't sayin' nuthin'. She des hilt on, en den Brer Rabbit lose de use er his feet in de same way. Brer Fox, he lay low. Den Brer Rabbit squall out dat ef de Tar-Baby don't tu'n 'im loose he butt 'er cranksided. En den he butted, en his head got stuck. Den Brer Fox, he sa'ntered fort', lookin' des ez innercent ez wunner yo' mammy's mockin'-birds.

" 'Howdy, Brer Rabbit,' sez Brer Fox, sezee. 'You look sorter stuck up dis mawnin',' sezee, en den he rolled on de groun', en laft en laft twel he couldn't laff no mo'. 'I speck you'll take dinner wid me dis time, Brer Rabbit. I done laid in some calamus root, en I ain't gwineter take no skuse,' sez Brer Fox, sezee."

Here Uncle Remus paused, and drew a two-pound yam out of the ashes.

"Did the fox eat the rabbit?" asked the little boy to whom the story had been told.

"Dat's all de fur de tale goes," replied the old man. "He mout, en den agin he moutent. Some say Jedge B'ar come 'long en loosed 'im—some say he didn't. I hear Miss Sally callin'. You better run 'long."

"One night," said Uncle Remus—taking Miss Sally's little boy on his knee, and stroking the child's hair thoughtfully and caressingly—"one night Brer Possum call by fer Brer Coon, 'cordin' ter 'greement, en atter gobblin' up a dish er fried greens en smokin' a seegyar, dey rambled fort' fer ter see how de ballunce er de settlement wuz gittin' 'long. Brer Coon, he wuz wunner deze yer natchul pacers, en he racked 'long same ez Mars John's bay pony, en Brer Possum he went in a han'-gallup; en dey got over heap er groun', mon. Brer Possum, he got his belly full er 'simmons, en Brer Coon, he scoop up a 'bunnunce er frogs en tadpoles. Dey amble 'long, dey did, des ez soshubble ez a baskit er kittens, twel bimeby dey hear Mr. Dog talkin' ter hisse'f way off in de woods.

" 'Spozen he runs up on us, Brer Possum, w'at you gwineter do?' sez Brer Coon, sezee. Brer Possum sorter laff 'round de cornders un his mouf.

" 'Oh, ef he come, Brer Coon, I'm gwineter stan' by you,' sez Brer Possum. 'W'at you gwineter do?' sezee.

" 'Who? Me?' sez Brer Coon. 'Ef he run up onter me, I lay I give 'im one twis',' sezee."

"Did the dog come?" asked the little boy.

"Go 'way, honey!" responded the old man, in an impressive tone. "Go way! Mr. Dog, he come en he come a zoonin'. En he ain't wait fer ter say howdy, nudder. He des sail inter de two un um. De ve'y fus pas he make Brer Possum fetch a grin fum year ter year, en keel over like he wuz dead. Den Mr. Dog, he sail inter Brer Coon, en right dar's whar he drap his munnypus, kaze Brer Coon wuz cut out fer dat kinder bizness, en he fa'rly wipe up de face er de earf wid 'im. You better b'leeve dat w'en Mr. Dog got a chance to make hisse'f

skase he tuck it, en w'at der wuz lef' un him went skaddlin' thoo de
woods like hit wuz shot outen a muskit. En Brer Coon, he sorter
lick his cloze inter shape en rack off, en Brer Possum, he lay dar like
he wuz dead, twel bimeby he raise up sotter keerful like, en w'en he
fine de coas' cle'r he scramble up en scamper off like sumpin was
atter 'im."

Here Uncle Remus paused long enough to pick up a live coal
of fire in his fingers, transfer it to the palm of his hand, and thence
to his clay pipe, which he had been filling—a proceeding that was
viewed by the little boy with undisguised admiration. The old man
then proceeded:

"Nex' time Brer Possum meet Brer Coon, Brer Coon 'fuse ter
'spon' ter his howdy, en dis make Brer Possum feel mighty bad,
seein' ez how dey useter make so many 'scurshuns tergedder.

" 'W'at make you hol' yo' head so high, Brer Coon?' sez Brer Possum, sezee.

" 'I ain't runnin' wid cowerds deze days,' sez Brer Coon. 'W'en I wants you I'll sen' fer you,' sezee.

"Den Brer Possum git mighty mad.

" 'Who's enny cowerd,' sezee.

" 'You is,' sez Brer Coon, 'dat's who. I ain't soshatin' wid dem w'at lies down on de groun' en plays dead w'en dar's a free fight gwine on,' sezee.

"Den Brer Possum grin en laff fit to kill hisse'f.

" 'Lor', Brer Coon, you don't speck I done dat kaze I wuz 'feared, duz you?' sezee. 'W'y I want no mo' 'feared dan you is dis minnit. W'at wuz dey fer ter be skeered un?' sezee. 'I know'd you'd git away wid Mr. Dog ef I didn't, en I des lay dar watchin' you shake him, waitin' fer ter put in w'en de time come,' sezee.

"Brer Coon tu'n up his nose.

" 'Dat's a mighty likely tale,' sezee, 'w'en Mr. Dog ain't mo'n tech you 'fo' you keel over, en lay dar stiff,' sezee.

" 'Dat's des w'at I wuz gwineter tell you 'bout,' sez Brer Possum, sezee. 'I want no mo' skeer'd dan you is right now, en' I wuz fixin' fer ter give Mr. Dog a sample er my jaw,' sezee, 'but I'm de most ticklish chap w'at you ever laid eyes on, en no sooner did Mr. Dog put his nose down yer 'mong my ribs dan I got ter laffin, en I laft twel I ain't had no use er my lim's,' sezee, 'en it's a mussy unto Mr. Dog dat I wuz ticklish, kaze a little mo' en I'd e't 'im up,' sezee. 'I don't mine fightin', Brer Coon, no mo' dan you duz,' sezee, 'but I declar' ter grashus ef I kin stan' ticklin'. Git me in a row whar dey ain't no ticklin' 'lowed, en I'm your man,' sezee.

"En down ter dis day," continued Uncle Remus, watching the smoke from his pipe curl upward over the little boy's head, "down ter dis day, Brer Possum's bound ter s'render w'en you tech him in de short ribs, en he'll laff ef he knows he's gwineter be smashed fer it."

"Uncle Remus," said the little
boy one evening, when he had found the old man with little or nothing to do, "did the fox kill and eat the rabbit when he caught him
with the Tar-Baby?"

"Law, honey, ain't I tell you 'bout dat?" replied the old darkey,
chuckling slyly. "I 'clar ter grashus I ought er tole you dat, but ole
man Nod wuz ridin' on my eyeleds 'twel a leetle mo'n I'd a dis'member'd my own name, en den on to dat here come yo' mammy hollerin'
atter you.

"W'at I tell you w'en I fus' begin? I tole you Brer Rabbit wuz a
monstus soon beas'; leas'ways dat's w'at I laid out fer ter tell you.
Well, den, honey, don't you go en make no udder kalkalashuns, kaze
in dem days Brer Rabbit en his fambly wuz at de head er de gang
w'en enny racket wuz on han', en dar dey stayed. 'Fo' you begins
fer ter wipe yo' eyes 'bout Brer Rabbit, you wait en see whar'bouts
Brer Rabbit gwineter fetch up at. But dat's needer yer ner dar.

"W'en Brer Fox fine Brer Rabbit mixt up wid de Tar-Baby, he feel
mighty good, en he roll on de groun' en laff. Bimeby he up'n say,
sezee:

" 'Well, I speck I got you dis time, Brer Rabbit,' sezee; 'maybe I
ain't, but I speck I is. You been runnin' roun' here sassin' atter me a
mighty long time, but I speck you done come ter de een' er de row.
You bin cuttin' up you' capers en bouncin' 'roun' in dis naberhood
ontwel you come ter b'leeve yo'se'f de boss er de whole gang. En den
youer allers some'rs whar you got no bizness,' sez Brer Fox, sezee.
'Who ax you fer ter come en strike up a 'quaintence wid dish yer
Tar-Baby? En who stuck you up dar whar you iz? Nobody in de
roun' worril. You des tuck en jam yo'se'f on dat Tar-Baby widout
waitin' fer enny invite,' sez Brer Fox, sezee, 'en dar you is, en dar

you'll stay twel I fixes up a bresh-pile and fires her up, kaze I'm gwineter bobbycue you dis day, sho,' sez Brer Fox, sezee.

"Den Brer Rabbit talk mighty 'umble.

" 'I don't keer w'at you do wid me, Brer Fox,' sezee, 'so you don't fling me in dat brier-patch. Roas' me, Brer Fox,' sezee, 'but don't fling me in dat brier-patch,' sezee.

" 'Hit's so much trouble fer ter kindle a fier,' sez Brer Fox, sezee, 'dat I speck I'll hatter hang you,' sezee.

" 'Hang me des ez high as you please, Brer Fox,' sez Brer Rabbit, sezee, 'but do fer de Lord's sake don't fling me in dat brier-patch,' sezee.

" 'I ain't got no string,' sez Brer Fox, sezee, 'en now I speck I'll hatter drown you,' sezee.

" 'Drown me des ez deep ez you please, Brer Fox,' sez Brer Rabbit, sezee, 'but do don't fling me in dat brier-patch,' sezee.

" 'Dey ain't no water nigh,' sez Brer Fox, sezee, 'en now I speck I'll atter skin you,' sezee.

" 'Skin me, Brer Fox,' sez Brer Rabbit, sezee, 'snatch out my eyeballs, t'ar out my years by de roots, en cut off my legs,' sezee, 'but do please, Brer Fox, don't fling me in dat brier-patch,' sezee.

"Co'se Brer Fox wanter hurt Brer Rabbit bad ez he kin, so he cotch 'im by de behime legs en slung 'im right in de middle er de brier-patch. Dar wuz a considerbul flutter whar Brer Rabbit struck de bushes, en Brer Fox sorter hang 'roun' fer ter see w'at wuz gwineter happen. Bimeby he hear somebody call 'im, en way up de hill he see Brer Rabbit settin' cross-legged on a chinkapin log koamin' de pitch outen his har wid a chip. Den Brer Fox know dat he bin swop off mighty bad. Brer Rabbit wuz bleedzed fer ter fling back some er his sass, en he holler out:

" 'Bred en bawn in a brier-patch, Brer Fox—bred en bawn in a brier-patch!' En wid dat he skip out des ez lively ez a cricket in de embers."

THE STORY OF THE DELUGE
AND HOW IT CAME ABOUT

"One time," said Uncle Remus —adjusting his spectacles so as to be able to see how to thread a large darning-needle with which he was patching his coat—"one time, way back yander, 'fo' you wuz borned, honey, en 'fo' Mars John er Miss Sally wuz borned—way back yander 'fo' enny un us wuz borned, de anemils en de beasteses sorter 'lecshuneer roun' 'mong deyselves, twel at las' dey' greed fer ter have a 'sembly. In dem days," continued the old man, observing a look of incredulity on the little boy's face, "in dem days creeturs had lots mo' sense dan dey got now; let 'lone dat, dey had sense same like folks. Hit was tech en go wid um, too, mon, en w'en dey make up dere mines w'at hatter be done, 'twant mo'n menshun'd 'fo' hit wuz done. Well, dey 'lected dat dey hatter hole er 'sembly fer ter sorter straighten out marters en yer de complaints, en w'en de day come dey wuz on han'. De Lion, he wuz dere, kaze he wuz de king, en de hatter be dere. De Rhynos-syhoss, he wuz dere, en de Elephent, he wuz dere, en de Cammils, en de Cows, en plum down ter de Crawfishes, dey wuz dere. Dey wuz all dere. En w'en de Lion shuck his mane, en tuck his seat in de big cheer, den de sesshun begun fer ter commence."

"What did they do, Uncle Remus?" asked the little boy.

"I kin skacely call to mine 'zackly wa't dey did do, but dey spoke speeches, en hollered, en cusst, en flung der langwidge 'roun' des like w'en yo' daddy wuz gwineter run fer de legislater en got lef'. Howsomever, dey 'ranged der 'fairs, en splained der bizness. Bimeby, w'ile dey wuz 'sputin' 'longer wunner nudder, de Elephent tromped on wunner de Crawfishes. Co'se w'en dat creetur put his foot down, w'atsumever's under dere's bound fer ter be squshed, en dey wuzn't nuff er dat Crawfish lef' fer ter tell dat he'd bin dar.

"Dis make de udder Crawfishes mighty mad, en dey sorter

swawmed tergedder en draw'd up a kinder peramble wid some wharfo'es in it, en read her out in de 'sembly. But, bless grashus! sech a racket wuz a gwine on dat nobody ain't hear it, 'ceppin may be de Mud Turkle en de Spring Lizzud, en dere enfloons wuz pow'-ful lackin'.

"Bimeby, w'iles de Nunicorn wuz 'sputin' wid de Lion, en w'ile de Hyener wuz a laffin ter hisse'f, de Elephent squshed anudder one er de Crawfishes, en a little mo'n he'd er ruint de Mud Turkle. Den de Crawfishes, w'at dey wuz lef' un um, swawmed tergedder en draw'd up anudder peramble wid sum mo' wharfo'es; but dey might ez well er sung Ole Dan Tucker ter a harrycane. De udder creeturs wuz too bizzy wid der fussin' fer ter 'spon' unto de Crawfishes. So dar dey wuz, de Crawfishes, en dey didn't know w'at minnit wuz gwineter be de nex'; en dey kep' on gittin madder en madder en skeerder en skeerder, twel bimeby dey gun de wink ter de Mud Turkle en de Spring Lizzud, en den dey bo'd little holes in de groun' en went down outer sight."

"Who did, Uncle Remus?" asked the little boy.

"De Crawfishes, honey. Dey bo'd inter de groun' en kep' on bo'in twel dey onloost de fountains er de earf; en de waters squirt out, en riz higher en higher twel de hills wuz kivvered, en de creeturs wuz all drownded; en all bekaze dey let on 'mong deyselves dat dey wuz bigger dan de Crawfishes."

Then the old man blew the ashes from a smoking yam, and pro-ceeded to remove the peeling.

"Where was the ark, Uncle Remus?" the little boy inquired, presently.

"W'ich ark's dat?" asked the old man, in a tone of well-feigned curiosity.

"Noah's ark," replied the child.

"Don't you pester wid ole man Noah, honey. I boun' he tuck keer

er dat ark. Dat's w'at he wuz dere fer, en dat's w'at he done. Leas'-ways, dat's w'at dey tells me. But don't you bodder longer dat ark, 'ceppin' your mammy fetches it up. Dey mout er bin two deloojes, en den agin dey moutent. Ef dey wuz enny ark in dish yer w'at de Crawfishes brung on, I ain't heern tell un it, en w'en dey ain't no arks 'roun, I ain't got no time fer ter make um en put um in dere. Hit's gittin' yo' bedtime, honey."

One evening when the little boy, whose nights with Uncle Remus are as entertaining as those Arabian ones of blessed memory, had finished supper and hurried out to sit with his venerable patron, he found the old man in great glee. Indeed, Uncle Remus was talking and laughing to himself at such a rate that the little boy was afraid he had company. The truth is, Uncle Remus had heard the child coming, and, when the rosy-cheeked chap put his head in at the door, was engaged in a monologue, the burden of which seemed to be—

"Ole Molly Har',
  W'at you doin' dar,
  Settin' in de cornder
  Smokin' yo' seegyar?"

As a matter of course this vague allusion reminded the little boy of the fact that the wicked Fox was still in pursuit of the Rabbit, and he immediately put his curiosity in the shape of a question.

"Uncle Remus, did the Rabbit have to go clean away when he got loose from the Tar-Baby?"

"Bless grashus, honey, dat he didn't. Who? Him? You dunno nuthin' 'tall 'bout Brer Rabbit ef dat's de way you puttin' 'im down. W'at he gwine 'way fer? He mouter stayed sorter close twel de pitch rub off'n his ha'r, but tweren't menny days 'fo' he wuz lopin' up en down de naberhood same ez ever, en I dunno ef he wern't mo' sassier dan befo'.

"Seem like dat de tale 'bout how he got mixt up wid de Tar-Baby got 'roun' 'mongst de nabers. Leas'ways, Miss Meadows en de gals got win' un' it, en de nex' time Brer Rabbit paid um a visit Miss Meadows tackled 'im 'bout it, en de gals sot up a monstus gigglement.

Brer Rabbit, he sot up des ez cool ez a cowcumber, he did, en let 'em run on."

"Who was Miss Meadows, Uncle Remus?" inquired the little boy.

"Don't ax me, honey. She wuz in de tale, Miss Meadows en de gals wuz, en de tale I give you like hi't wer' gun ter me. Brer Rabbit, he sot dar, he did, sorter lam' like, en den bimeby he cross his legs, he did, and wink his eye slow, en up en say, sezee:

" 'Ladies, Brer Fox wuz my daddy's ridin'-hoss fer thirty year; maybe mo', but thirty year dat I knows un,' sezee; en den he paid um his 'specks, en tip his beaver, en march off, he did, des ez stiff en ez stuck up ez a fire-stick.

"Nex' day, Brer Fox cum a callin', and w'en he gun fer ter laff 'bout Brer Rabbit, Miss Meadows en de gals, dey ups en tells 'im 'bout w'at Brer Rabbit say. Den Brer Fox grit his toof sho' nuff, he did, en he look mighty dumpy, but w'en he riz fer ter go he up en say, sezee:

" 'Ladies, I ain't 'sputin' w'at you say, but I'll make Brer Rabbit chaw up his words en spit um out right yer whar you kin see 'im,' sezee, en wid dat off Brer Fox marcht.

"En w'en he got in de big road, he shuck de dew off'n his tail, en made a straight shoot fer Brer Rabbit's house. W'en he got dar, Brer Rabbit wuz spectin' un 'im, en de do' wuz shet fas'. Brer Fox knock. Nobody ain't ans'er. Brer Fox knock. Nobody ans'er. Den he knock agin—blam! blam! Den Brer Rabbit holler out mighty weak:

" 'Is dat you, Brer Fox? I want you ter run en fetch de doctor. Dat bait er pusly w'at I e't dis mawnin' is gittin' 'way wid me. Do, please, Brer Fox, run quick,' sez Brer Rabbit, sezee.

" 'I come atter you, Brer Rabbit,' sez Brer Fox, sezee. 'Dere's gwineter be a party up at Miss Meadows's, sezee. 'All de gals 'll be dere, en I promus' dat I'd fetch you. De gals, dey 'lowed dat hit wouldn't be no party 'ceppin' I fotch you,' sez Brer Fox, sezee.

"Den Brer Rabbit say he wuz too sick, en Brer Fox say he wuzzent, en dar dey had it up and down, 'sputin' en contendin'. Brer Rabbit say he can't walk. Brer Fox say he tote 'im. Brer Rabbit say how? Brer Fox say in his arms. Brer Rabbit say he drap 'im. Brer Fox 'low he won't. Bimeby Brer Rabbit say he go ef Brer Fox tote 'im on his back. Brer Fox say he would. Brer Rabbit say he can't ride widout a saddle. Brer Fox say he git de saddle. Brer Rabbit say he can't set in saddle less he have bridle fer ter hol' by. Brer Fox say he git de bridle. Brer Rabbit say he can't ride widout bline bridle, kaze Brer Fox be shyin' at stumps 'long de road, en fling 'im off. Brer Fox say he git bline bridle. Den Brer Rabbit say he go. Den Brer Fox say he ride Brer Rabbit mos' up ter Miss Meadows's, en den he could git down en walk de balance er de way. Brer Rabbit 'greed, en den Brer Fox lipt out atter de saddle en de bridle.

"Co'se Brer Rabbit know de game dat Brer Fox wuz fixin' fer ter play, en he 'termin' fer ter outdo 'im, en by de time he koam his ha'r en twis' his mustarsh, en sorter rig up, yer come Brer Fox, saddle en bridle on, en lookin' ez peart ez a circus pony. He trot up ter de do' en stan' dar pawin' de ground en chompin' de bit same like sho 'nuff hoss, en Brer Rabbit he mount, he did, en dey amble off. Brer Fox can't see behime wid de bline bridle on, but bimeby he feel Brer Rabbit raise one er his foots.

" 'W'at you doin' now, Brer Rabbit?' sezee.

" 'Short'nin' de lef stir'p, Brer Fox,' sezee.

"Bimeby Brer Rabbit raise up de udder foot.

" 'W'at you doin' now, Brer Rabbit?' sezee.

" 'Pullin' down my pants, Brer Foz,' sezee.

"All de time, bless grashus, honey, Brer Rabbit wer puttin' on his spurrers, en w'en dey got close to Miss Meadows's, whar Brer Rabbit wuz to git off, en Brer Fox made a motion fer ter stan' still, Brer Rabbit slap de spurrers inter Brer Fox flanks, en you better b'leeve he got over groun'. W'en dey got ter de house, Miss Meadows en all de gals wuz settin' on de peazzer, en stidder stoppin' at de gate, Brer Rabbit rid on by, he did, en den come gallopin' down de road en up ter de hoss-rack, w'ich he hitch Brer Fox at, en den he santer inter de house, he did, en shake han's wid de gals, en set dar, smokin' his seegyar same ez a town man. Bimeby he draw in long puff, en den let hit out in a cloud, en squar hisse'f back en holler out, he did:

" 'Ladies, ain't I done tell you Brer Fox wuz de ridin'-hoss fer our fambly? He sorter losin' his gait now, but I speck I kin fetch 'im all right in a mont' er so,' sezee.

"En den Brer Rabbit sorter grin, he did, en de gals giggle, en Miss Meadows, she praise up de pony, en dar wuz Brer Fox hitch fas' ter de rack, en couldn't he'p hisse'f."

"Is that all, Uncle Remus?" asked the little boy as the old man paused.

"Dat ain't all, honey, but 'twon't do fer ter give out too much cloff fer ter cut one pa'r pants," replied the old man sententiously.

When "Miss Sally's" little boy went to Uncle Remus the next night to hear the conclusion of the adventure in which the rabbit made a riding-horse of the Fox to the great enjoyment and gratification of Miss Meadows and the girls, he found the old man in a bad humor.

"I ain't tellin' no tales ter bad chilluns," said Uncle Remus curtly.

"But, Uncle Remus, I ain't bad," said the little boy plaintively.

"Who dat chunkin' dem chickens dis mawnin'? Who dat knockin' out fokes's eyes wid dat Yallerbammer sling des 'fo' dinner? Who dat sickin' dat pinter puppy atter my pig? Who dat scatterin' my ingun sets? Who dat flingin' rocks on top er my house, w'ich a little mo' en one un em would er drap spang on my head?"

"Well, now, Uncle Remus, I didn't go to do it. I won't do so any more. Please, Uncle Remus, if you will tell me, I'll run to the house and bring you some teacakes."

"Seein' um's better'n hearin' tell un um," replied the old man, the severity of his countenance relaxing somewhat; but the little boy darted out, and in a few minutes came running back with his pockets full and his hands full.

"I lay yo' mammy 'll 'spishun dat de rats' stummucks is widenin' in dis naberhood w'en she come fer ter count up 'er cakes," said Uncle Remus, with a chuckle. "Deze," he continued, dividing the cakes into two equal parts—"deze I'll tackle now, en deze I'll lay by fer Sunday."

"Lemme see. I mos' dis'member wharbouts Brer Fox en Brer Rabbit wuz."

"The rabbit rode the fox to Miss Meadows's, and hitched him to the horse-rack," said the little boy.

"W'y co'se he did," said Uncle Remus. "Co'se he did. Well, Brer

Rabbit rid Brer Fox up, he did, en tied 'im to de rack, en den sot out in de peazzer wid de gals a smokin' er his seegyar wid mo' proudness dan wa't you mos' ever see. Dey talk, en dey sing, en dey play on de peanner, de gals did, twel bimeby hit come time fer Brer Rabbit fer to be gwine, en he tell um all good-by, en strut out to de hoss-rack same's ef he wuz de king er de patter-rollers,[1] en den he mount Brer Fox en ride off.

"Brer Fox ain't sayin' nuthin 'tall. He des rack off, he did, en keep his mouf shet, en Brer Rabbit know'd der wuz bizness cookin' up fer him, en he feel monstus skittish. Brer Fox amble on twel he git in de long lane, outer sight er Miss Meadows's house, en den he tu'n loose, he did. He rip en he r'ar, en he cuss, en he swar; he snort en he cavort."

"What was he doing that for, Uncle Remus?" the little boy inquired.

"He wuz tryin' fer ter fling Brer Rabbit off'n his back, bless yo' soul! But he des might ez well er rastle wid his own shadder. Every time he hump hisse'f Brer Rabbit slap de spurrers in 'im, en dar dey had it, up en down. Brer Fox fa'rly to' up de groun', he did, en he jump so high en he jump so quick dat he mighty nigh snatch his own tail off. Dey kep' on gwine on dis way twel bimeby Brer Fox lay down en roll over, he did, en dis sorter onsettle Brer Rabbit, but by de time Brer Fox got back on his footses agin, Brer Rabbit wuz gwine thoo de underbresh mo' samer dan a race-hoss. Brer Fox he lit out atter 'im, he did, en he push Brer Rabbit so close dat it wuz 'bout all he could do fer ter git in a holler tree. Hole too little fer

---

[1] Patrols. In the country districts, order was kept on the plantations at night by the knowledge that they were liable to be visited at any moment by the patrols. Hence a song current among the Negroes, the chorus of which was:
"Run, nigger, run; patter-roller ketch you—
Run, nigger, run; hit's almos' day."

Brer Fox fer ter git in, en he hatter lay down en res' en gedder his mine tergedder.

"While he wuz layin' dar, Mr. Buzzard come floppin' long, en seein' Brer Fox stretch out on de groun', he lit en view de premusses. Den Mr. Buzzard sorter shake his wing, en put his head on one side, en say to hisse'f like, sezee:

"'Brer Fox dead, en I so sorry,' sezee.

"'No I ain't dead, nudder,' sez Brer Fox, sezee. 'I got ole man Rabbit pent up in yer,' sezee, 'en I'm a gwineter git 'im dis time ef it take twel Chris'mus,' sezee.

"Den, atter some mo' palaver, Brer Fox make a bargain dat Mr. Buzzard wuz ter watch de hole, en keep Brer Rabbit dar wiles Brer Fox went atter his axe. Den Brer Fox, he lope off, he did, en Mr. Buzzard, he tuck up his stan' at de hole. Bimeby, w'en all git still, Brer Rabbit sorter scramble down close ter de hole, he did, en holler out:

"'Brer Fox! Oh! Brer Fox!'

"Brer Fox done gone, en nobody say nuthin'. Den Brer Rabbit squall out like he wuz mad; sezee:

"'You needn't talk less you wanter,' sezee; 'I knows youer dar, en I ain't keerin',' sezee. 'I des wanter tell you dat I wish mighty bad Brer Tukkey Buzzard wuz here,' sezee.

"Den Mr. Buzzard try ter talk like Brer Fox:

"'W'at you want wid Mr. Buzzard?' sezee.

"'Oh, nuthin' in 'tickler, 'cep' dere's de fattes' gray squir'l in yer dat ever I see,' sezee, 'en ef Brer Tukkey Buzzard wuz 'roun' he'd be mighty glad fer ter git 'im,' sezee.

"'How Mr. Buzzard gwine ter git 'im?' sez de Buzzard, sezee.

"'Well, dars a little hole roun' on de udder side er de tree,' sez Brer Rabbit, sezee, 'en ef Brer Tukkey Buzzard wuz here so he could take up his stan' dar,' sezee, 'I'd drive dat squir'l out,' sezee.

"'Drive 'im out, den,' sez Mr. Buzzard, sezee, 'en I'll see dat Brer Tukkey Buzzard gits 'im,' sezee.

"Den Brer Rabbit kick up a racket, like he wer' drivin' sumpin' out, en Mr. Buzzard he rush 'roun' fer ter ketch de squir'l, en Brer Rabbit, he dash out, he did, en he des fly fer home."

At this point Uncle Remus took one of the tea-cakes, held his head back, opened his mouth, dropped the cake in with a sudden motion, looked at the little boy with an expression of astonishment, and then closed his eyes, and begun to chew, mumbling as an accompaniment the plaintive tune of "Don't you Grieve atter Me."

The *séance* was over; but, before the little boy went into the "big house," Uncle Remus laid his rough hand tenderly on the child's shoulder, and remarked, in a confidential tone:

"Honey, you mus' git up soon Chris'mus mawnin' en open de do'; kase I'm gwineter bounce in on Marse John en Miss Sally, en holler Chris'mus gif' des like I useter endurin' de fahmin' days fo' de war, w'en ole Miss wuz 'live. I boun' dey don't fergit de ole nigger, nudder. W'en you hear me callin' de pigs, honey, you des hop up en onfassen de do'. I lay I'll give Marse John wunner deze yer 'sprize parties."

"Ef I don't run inter no mistakes," remarked Uncle Remus, as the little boy came tripping in to see him after supper, "Mr. Tukkey Buzzard wuz gyardin' de holler whar Brer Rabbit went in at, en w'ich he come out un."

The silence of the little boy verified the old man's recollection.

"Well, Mr. Buzzard, he feel mighty lonesome, he did, but he done prommust Brer Fox dat he'd stay, en he 'termin' fer ter sorter hang 'roun' en jine in de joke. En he ain't hatter wait long, nudder, kase bimeby yer come Brer Fox gallopin' thoo de woods wid his axe on his shoulder.

"'How you speck Brer Rabbit gittin' on, Brer Buzzard?' sez Brer Fox, sezee.

"'Oh, he in dar,' sez Brer Buzzard, sezee. 'He mighty still, dough. I speck he takin' a nap,' sezee.

"'Den I'm des in time fer ter wake 'im up,' sez Brer Fox, sezee. En wid dat he fling off his coat, en spit in his han's, en grab de axe. Den he draw back en come down on de tree—pow! En eve'y time he come down wid de axe—pow!—Mr. Buzzard, he step high, he did, en holler out:

"'Oh, he in dar, Brer Fox. He in dar, sho.'

"En eve'y time a chip ud fly off, Mr. Buzzard, he'd jump, en dodge, en hole his head sideways, he would, en holler:

"'He in dar, Brer Fox. I done heerd 'im. He in dar, sho.'

"En Brer Fox, he lammed away at dat holler tree, he did, like a man maulin' rails, twel bimeby, atter he done got de tree mos' cut thoo, he stop fer ter ketch his bref, en he seed Mr. Buzzard laffin' behime his back, he did, en right den en dar, widout gwine enny

fudder, Brer Fox, he smelt a rat. But Mr. Buzzard, he keep on holler'n:

"'He in dar, Brer Fox. He in dar, sho. I done seed 'im.'

"Den Brer Fox, he make like he peepin' up de holler, en he say, sezee:

"'Run yer, Brer Buzzard, en look ef dis ain't Brer Rabbit's foot hanging down yer.'

"En Mr. Buzzard, he come steppin' up, he did, same ez ef he wer treddin' on kurkle-burrs, en he stick his head in de hole; en no sooner did he done dat dan Brer Fox grab 'im. Mr. Buzzard flap his wings, en scramble 'roun' right smartually, he did, but 'twant no use. Brer Fox had de 'vantage er de grip, he did, en he hilt 'im right down ter de groun'. Den Mr. Buzzard squall out, sezee:

"'Lemme 'lone, Brer Fox. Tu'n me loose,' sezee; 'Brer Rabbit'll git out. Youer gittin' close at 'im,' sezee, 'en leb'm mo' licks'll fetch 'im,' sezee.

"'I'm nigher ter you, Brer Buzzard,' sez Brer Fox, sezee, 'dan I'll be ter Brer Rabbit dis day,' sezee. 'W'at you fool me fer?' sezee.

"'Lemme 'lone, Brer Fox,' sez Mr. Buzzard, sezee; 'my ole 'oman waitin' fer me. Brer Rabbit in dar,' sezee.

"'Dar's a bunch er his fur on dat black-be'y bush,' sez Brer Fox, sezee, 'en dat ain't de way he come,' sezee.

"Den Mr. Buzzard up'n tell Brer Fox how 'twuz, en he low'd, Mr. Buzzard did, dat Brer Rabbit wuz de low-downest w'atsizname w'at he ever run up wid. Den Brer Fox say, sezee:

"'Dat's needer here ner dar, Brer Buzzard,' sezee. 'I lef' you yer fer ter watch dish yer hole, en I lef' Brer Rabbit in dar. I comes back en I fines you at de hole en Brer Rabbit ain't in dar,' sezee. 'I'm gwineter make you pay fer't. I done bin tampered wid twel plum' down ter de sap sucker'll set on a log en sassy me. I'm gwineter fling you in a bresh-heap en burn you up,' sezee.

" 'Ef you fling me on der fier, Brer Fox, I'll fly 'way,' sez Mr. Buzzard, sezee.

" 'Well, den, I'll settle yo' hash right now,' sez Brer Fox, sezee, en wid dat he grab Mr. Buzzard by de tail, he did, en make fer ter dash 'im 'gin de groun', but des 'bout dat time de tail fedders come out, en Mr. Buzzard sail off like wunner dese yer berloons; en ez he riz, he holler back:

" 'You gimme good start, Brer Fox,' sezee, en Brer Fox sot dar en watch 'im fly outer sight."

"But what became of the Rabbit, Uncle Remus?" asked the little boy.

"Don't you pester 'longer Brer Rabbit, honey, en don't you fret 'bout 'im. You'll year whar he went en how he come out. Dish yer cole snap rastles wid my bones, now," continued the old man, putting on his hat and picking up his walking-stick. "Hit rastles wid me monstus, en I gotter rack 'roun' en see if I kin run up agin some Chris'mus leavin's."

"Uncle Remus,"
said the little boy, "what became of the Rabbit after he fooled
the Buzzard, and got out of the hollow tree?"

"Who? Brer Rabbit? Bless yo' soul, honey, Brer Rabbit went skippin' 'long home, he did, des ez sassy ez a jay-bird at a sparrer's nes'.
He went gallopin' 'long, he did, but he feel mighty tired out, en
stiff in his jints, en he wuz mighty nigh dead for sumpin fer ter
drink, en bimeby, wen he got mos' home, he spied ole Miss Cow
feedin' roun' in a fiel', he did, en he 'termin' fer ter try his han' wid
'er. Brer Rabbit know mighty well dat Miss Cow won't give 'im no
milk, kaze she done 'fuse 'im mo'n once, en w'en his ole 'oman wuz
sick, at dat. But never mind dat. Brer Rabbit sorter dance up 'long
side er de fence, he did, en holler out:

" 'Howdy, Sis Cow,' sez Brer Rabbit, sezee.

" 'W'y, howdy, Brer Rabbit,' sez Miss Cow, sez she.

" 'How you fine yo'se'f deze days, Sis Cow?' sez Brer Rabbit,
sezee.

" 'I'm sorter toler'ble, Brer Rabbit; how you come on?' sez Miss
Cow, sez she.

" 'Oh, I'm des toler'ble myse'f, Sis Cow; sorter linger'n' twix' a
bauk en a break-down,' sez Brer Rabbit, sezee.

" 'How yo' fokes, Brer Rabbit?' sez Miss Cow, sez she.

" 'Dey er des middlin', Sis Cow; how Brer Bull gittin' on?' sez
Brer Rabbit, sezee.

" 'Sorter so-so,' sez Miss Cow, sez she.

" 'Dey er some mighty nice 'simmons up dis tree, Sis Cow,' sez
Brer Rabbit, sezee, 'en I'd like mighty well fer ter have some un um,'
sezee.

" 'How you gwineter git um, Brer Rabbit?' sez she.

"'I 'low'd maybe dat I might ax you fer ter butt 'gin de tree, en shake some down, Sis Cow,' sez Brer Rabbit, sezee.

"C'ose Miss Cow don't wanter diskommerdate Brer Rabbit, en she march up ter de 'simmon tree, she did, en hit it a rap wid'er hawns —blam! Now, den," continued Uncle Remus, tearing off the corner of a plug of tobacco and cramming it into his mouth—"now, den, dem 'simmons wuz green ez grass, en na'er one never drap. Den Miss Cow butt de tree—blim! Na'er 'simmon drap. Den Miss Cow sorter back off little, en run agin de tree—blip! No 'simmons never drap. Den Miss Cow back off little fudder, she did, en hi'st her tail on 'er back, en come agin de tree, kerblam! En she come so fas', en she come so hard, twel wunner her hawns went spang thoo de tree, en dar she wuz. She can't go forreds, en she can't go backerds. Dis zackly w'at Brer Rabbit waitin' fer, en he no sooner seed ole Miss Cow all fas'en'd up dan he jump up, he did, en cut de pidjin-wing.

"'Come he'p me out, Brer Rabbit,' sez Miss Cow, sez she.

"'I can't clime, Sis Cow,' sez Brer Rabbit, sezee, 'but I'll run'n tell Brer Bull,' sezee: en wid dat Brer Rabbit put out fer home, en 'twan't long 'fo here he come wid his ole 'oman en all his chilluns, en

de las' wunner de fambly wuz totin' a pail. De big uns had big pails, en de little uns had little pails. En dey all s'roundid ole Miss Cow, dey did, en you hear me, honey, dey milk't 'er dry. De ole uns milk't en de young uns milk't, en den w'en dey done got nuff, Brer Rabbit, he up'n say, sezee:

"'I wish you mighty well, Sis Cow. I 'low'd bein's how dat you'd hatter sorter camp out all night dat I'd better come en swaje yo' bag,' sezee."

"Do which, Uncle Remus?" asked the little boy.

"Go 'long, honey! Swaje 'er bag. W'en cows don't git milk't, der bag swells, en youk'n hear um a moanin' en a beller'n des like dey wuz gittin' hurtid. Dat's w'at Brer Rabbit done. He 'sembled his fambly, he did, en he swaje ole Miss Cow's bag.

"Miss Cow, she stood dar, she did, en she study en study, en strive fer ter break loose, but de hawn done bin jam in de tree so tight dat twuz way 'fo day in de mornin' 'fo' she loose it. Ennyhow hit wuz endurin' er de night, en atter she git loose she sorter graze 'roun', she did, fer ter jestify 'er stummuck. She 'low'd, ole Miss Cow did, dat Brer Rabbit be hoppin' 'long dat way fer ter see how she gittin' on, en she tuck'n lay er trap fer 'im; en des 'bout sunrise wat'd ole Miss Cow do but march up ter de 'simmon tree en stick er hawn back in de hole? But, bless yo' soul, honey, w'ile she wuz croppin' de grass, she tuck one moufull too menny, kaze w'en she hitch on ter de 'simmon tree again, Brer Rabbit wuz settin' in de fence cornder a watchin' un 'er. Den Brer Rabbit he say ter hisse'f:

"'Heyo,' sezee, 'w'at dis yer gwine on now? Hole yo' hosses, Sis Cow, twel you hear me comin',' sezee.

"En den he crope off down de fence, Brer Rabbit did, en bimeby here he come—lippity-clippity, clippity-lippity—des a sailin' down de big road.

" 'Mawnin', Sis Cow,' sez Brer Rabbit, sezee, 'how you come on dis mawnin'?' sezee.

" 'Po'ly, Brer Rabbit, po'ly,' sez Miss Cow, sez she. 'I ain't had no res' all night,' sez she. 'I can't pull loose,' sez she, 'but ef you'll come en ketch holt er my tail, Brer Rabbit,' sez she, 'I reckon may be I kin fetch my hawn out,' sez she. Den Brer Rabbit, he come up little closer, but he ain't gittin' too close.

" 'I speck I'm nigh nuff, Sis Cow,' sez Brer Rabbit, sezee. 'I'm a mighty puny man, en I might git trompled,' sezee. 'You do de pullin', Sis Cow,' sezee, 'en I'll do de gruntin',' sezee.

Den Miss Cow, she pull out 'er hawn, she did, en tuck atter Brer Rabbit, en down de big road dey had it, Brer Rabbit wid his years laid back, en Miss Cow wid 'er head down en 'er tail curl. Brer Rabbit kep' on gainin', en bimeby he dart in a brier-patch, en by de time Miss Cow come 'long he had his head stickin' out, en his eyes look big ez Miss Sally's chany sassers.

" 'Heyo, Sis Cow! Whar you gwine?' sez Brer Rabbit, sezee.

" 'Howdy, Brer Big-Eyes,' sez Miss Cow, sez she. 'Is you seed Brer Rabbit go by?'

" 'He des dis minit pass,' sez Brer Rabbit, sezee, 'en he look mighty sick,' sezee.

"En wid dat, Miss Cow tuck down de road like de dogs wuz atter 'er, en Brer Rabbit, he des lay down dar in de brier-patch en roll en laff twel his sides hurtid 'im. He bleedzd ter laff. Fox atter 'im, Buzzard atter 'im, en Cow atter 'im, en dey ain't kotch 'im yit."

"Miss Sally's" little boy again occupying the anxious position of auditor, Uncle Remus took the shovel and "put de noses er de chunks tergedder," as he expressed it, and then began:

"One day, atter Sis Cow done run pas' 'er own shadder tryin' fer ter ketch 'im, Brer Rabbit tuck'n 'low dat he wuz gwineter drap in en see Miss Meadows en de gals, en he got out his piece er lookin'-glass en primp up, he did, en sot out. Gwine canterin' 'long de road, who should Brer Rabbit run up wid but ole Brer Tarrypin—de same ole one-en-sixpunce. Brer Rabbit stop, he did, en rap on de roof er Brer Tarrypin house."

"On the roof of his house, Uncle Remus?" interrupted the little boy.

"Co'se honey, Brer Tarrypin kare his house wid 'im. Rain er shine, hot er cole, strike up wid ole Brer Tarrypin w'en you will en w'ilst you may, en whar you fine 'im, dar you'll fine his shanty. Hit's des like I tell you. So den! Brer Rabbit he rap on de roof er Brer Tarrypin's house, he did, en ax wuz he in, en Brer Tarrypin 'low dat he wuz, en den Brer Rabbit, he ax 'im howdy, en den Brer Tarrypin likewise 'spon' howdy, en den Brer Rabbit he say whar wuz Brer Tarrypin gwine, en Brer Tarrypin, he say w'ich he wern't gwine nowhar skasely. Den Brer Rabbit 'low he wuz on his way fer ter see Miss Meadows en de gals, en he ax Brer Tarrypin ef he won't jine in en go long, en Brer Tarrypin 'spon' he don't keer ef he do, en den dey sot out. Dey had plenty er time fer confabbin' 'long de way, but bimeby dey got dar, en Miss Meadows en de gals dey come ter de do', dey did, en ax um in, en in dey went.

"W'en dey got in, Brer Tarrypin wuz so flat-footed dat he wuz too low on de flo', en he wern't high nuff in a cheer, but while they wuz all scramblin' 'roun' tryin' fer ter git Brer Tarrypin a cheer, Brer Rabbit, he pick 'im up en put 'im on de shelf whar de water-bucket sot, en ole Brer Tarryin, he lay back up dar, he did, des es proud ez a nigger widder cook 'possum.

"Co'se de talk fell on Brer Fox, en Miss Meadows en de gals make a great 'miration 'bout w'at a gaily ridin'-hoss Brer Fox wuz, en dey make lots er fun, en laff en giggle same like gals duz deze days. Brer Rabbit, he sot dar in de cheer smokin' his seegyar, en he sorter kler up his th'oat, en say, sezee:

"'I'd er rid 'im over dis mawnin', ladies,' sezee, 'but I rid 'im so hard yistiddy dat he went lame in de off fo' leg, en I speck I'll hatter swop 'im off yit,' sezee.

"Den Brer Tarryin, he up'n say, sezee:

"'Well, ef you gwineter sell 'im Brer Rabbit,' sezee, 'sell him some'rs outen dis naberhood, kase he done bin yer too long now,' sezee. 'No longer'n day 'fo' yistiddy,' sezee, 'Brer Fox pass me on de road, en whatter you reckin he say?' sezee:

"'Law, Brer Tarrypin,' sez Miss Meadows, sez she, 'you don't mean ter say he cust?' sez she, en den de gals hilt der fans up 'fo' der faces.

"'Oh, no, ma'm,' sez Brer Tarryin, sezee, 'he didn't cust, but he holler out—"Heyo Stinkin' Jim!"' sezee.

"'Oh, my! You hear dat, gals?' sez Miss Meadows, sez she; 'Brer Fox call Brer Tarryin Stinkin' Jim,' sez she, en den Miss Meadows en de gals make great wonderment how Brer Fox kin talk dat a way 'bout nice man like Brer Tarryin.

"But bless grashus, honey! w'ilst all dis gwine on, Brer Fox wuz stannin' at de back do' wid one year at de cat-hole lissenin.' Eave-drappers don't hear no good er deyse'f, en de way Brer Fox wuz 'bused dat day wuz a caution.

"Bimeby Brer Fox stick his head in de do', en holler out:

" 'Good evenin', fokes, I wish you mighty well,' sezee, en wid dat he make a dash fer Brer Rabbit, but Miss Meadows en de gals dey holler en squall, dey did, en Brer Tarrypin he got ter scramblin' roun' up dar on de shelf, en off he come, en blip he tuck Brer Fox on de back er de head. Dis sorter stunted Brer Fox, en w'en he gedder his 'membunce de mos' he seed wuz a pot er greens turnt over in de fireplace, en a broke cheer. Brer Rabbit wuz gone, en Brer Tarry-pin wuz gone, en Miss Meadows en de gals wuz gone."

"Where did the Rabbit go, Uncle Remus?" the little boy asked, after a pause.

"Bless yo' soul, honey! Brer Rabbit he skint up de chimbly—dats w'at turnt de pot er greens over. Brer Tarrypin, he crope under de bed, he did, en got behime de cloze-chist, en Miss Meadows en de gals, dey run out in de yard.

"Brer Fox, he sorter look roun' en feel er de back er his head, whar Brer Tarrypin lit, but he don't see no sine er Brer Rabbit. But de smoke en de ashes gwine up de chimbly got de best er Brer Rabbit, en bimeby he sneeze—*huckychow!*

" 'Aha!' sez Brer Fox, sezee: 'youer dar, is you?' sezee. 'Well, I'm gwineter smoke you out, ef it takes a mont'. Youer mine dis time,' sezee. Brer Rabbit ain't sayin' nuthin'.

" 'Ain't you comin' down?' sez Brer Fox, sezee. Brer Rabbit ain't sayin' nuthin'. Den Brer Fox, he went out atter some wood, he did, en w'en he come back he hear Brer Rabbit laffin'.

" 'W'at you laffin' at, Brer Rabbit?' sez Brer Fox, sezee.

" 'Can't tell you, Brer Fox,' sez Brer Rabbit, sezee.

" 'Better tell, Brer Rabbit,' sez Brer Fox, sezee.

" ' 'Taint nuthin' but a box er money somebody done gone en lef' up yer in de chink er de chimbly,' sez Brer Rabbit, sezee.

" 'Don't b'leeve you,' sez Brer Fox, sezee.

" 'Look up en see,' sez Brer Rabbit, sezee, en w'en Brer Fox look up, Brer Rabbit spit his eyes full er terbarker joose, he did, en Brer Fox, he make a break fer de branch, en Brer Rabbit he come down en tole de ladies good-by.

" 'How you git 'im off, Brer Rabbit?' sez Miss Meadows, sez she.

" 'Who? Me?' sez Brer Rabbit, sezee; 'w'y I des tuck en tole 'im dat ef he didn't go 'long home en stop playin' his pranks on spectubble fokes, dat I'd take 'im out and th'ash 'im,' sezee."

"And what became of the Terrapin?" asked the little boy.

"Oh, well den!" exclaimed the old man. "Chilluns can't speck ter know all 'bout eve'ything 'fo' dey git some res'. Dem eyeleds er yone wanter be propped wid straws dis minnit."

"I lay yo' ma got comp'ny," said Uncle Remus, as the little boy entered the old man's door with a huge piece of mince-pie in his hand, "en ef she aint got comp'ny, den she done gone en drap de cubberd key som'ers whar you done run up wid it."

"Well, I saw the pie lying there, Uncle Remus, and I just thought I'd fetch it out to you."

"Tooby sho, honey," replied the old man, regarding the child with admiration. "Tooby sho, honey; dat changes marters. Chrismus doin's is outer date, en dey aint got no bizness layin' roun' loose. Dish yer pie," Uncle Remus continued, holding it up and measuring it with an experienced eye, "will gimme strenk fer ter persoo on atter Brer Fox en Brer Rabbit en de udder beastesses w'at dey roped in 'long wid um."

Here the old man paused, and proceeded to demolish the pie— a feat accomplished in a very short time. Then he wiped the crumbs from his beard and began:

"Brer Fox feel so bad, en he git so mad 'bout Brer Rabbit, dat he dunno w'at ter do, en he look mighty downhearted. Bimeby, one day wiles he wuz gwine 'long de road, ole Brer Wolf come up wid 'im. W'en dey done howdyin' en axin' atter one nudder's fambly kunnexshun, Brer Wolf, he 'low, he did, dat der wuz sump'n wrong wid Brer Fox, en Brer Fox, he 'low'd der wern't, en he went on en laff en make great ter-do kaze Brer Wolf look like he spishun sump'n. But Brer Wolf, he got mighty long head, en he sorter broach 'bout Brer Rabbit's kyar'ns on, kaze de way dat Brer Rabbit 'ceive Brer Fox done got ter be de talk er de naberhood. Den Brer Fox en Brer Wolf dey sorter palavered on, dey did, twel bimeby Brer Wolf he up'n say dat he done got plan fix fer ter trap Brer Rabbit. Den Brer

Fox say how. Den Brer Wolf up'n tell 'im dat de way fer ter git de drap on Brer Rabbit wuz ter git 'im in Brer Fox house. Brer Fox dun know Brer Rabbit uv ole, en he know dat sorter game done wo' ter a frazzle, but Brer Wolf, he talk mighty 'swadin'.

" 'How you gwine git 'im dar?' sez Brer Fox, sezee.

" 'Fool 'im dar,' sez Brer Wolf, sezee.

" 'Who gwine do de foolin'?' sez Brer Fox, sezee.

" 'I'll do de foolin',' sez Brer Wolf, sezee, 'ef you'll do de gamin',' sezee.

" 'How you gwine do it?' sez Brer Fox, sezee.

" 'You run 'long home, en git on de bed, en make like you dead, en don't you say nuthin' twel Brer Rabbit come en put his han's onter you,' sez Brer Wolf, sezee, 'en ef we don't git 'im fer supper, Joe's dead en Sal's a widder,' sezee.

"Dis look like mighty nice game, en Brer Fox 'greed. So den he amble off home, en Brer Wolf, he march off ter Brer Rabbit house. W'en he got dar, hit look like nobody at home, but Brer Wolf he walk up en knock on de do'—blam! Blam! Nobody come. Den he lam aloose en knock 'gin—blim! Blim!

" 'Who dar?' sez Brer Rabbit, sezee.

" 'Fr'en',' sez Brer Wolf.

" 'Too menny fr'en's spiles de dinner,' sez Brer Rabbit, sezee; 'w'ich un's dis?' sezee.

" 'I fetch bad news, Brer Rabbit,' sez Brer Wolf, sezee.

" 'Bad news is soon tole,' sez Brer Rabbit, sezee.

"By dis time Brer Rabbit done come ter de do', wid his head tied up in a red hankcher.

" 'Brer Fox died dis mawnin',' sez Brer Wolf, sezee.

" 'Whar yo' mo'nin' gown, Brer Wolf?' sez Brer Rabbit, sezee.

" 'Gwine atter it now,' sez Brer Wolf, sezee. 'I des call by fer ter bring de news. I went down ter Brer Fox house little bit 'go, en dar I foun' 'im stiff,' sezee.

"Den Brer Wolf lope off. Brer Rabbit sot down en scratch his head, he did, en bimeby he say ter hisse'f dat he b'leeve he sorter drap 'roun' by Brer Fox house fer ter see how de lan' lay. No sooner said'n done. Up he jump, en out he went. W'en Brer Rabbit got close ter Brer Fox house, all look lonesome. Den he went up nigher. Nobody stirrin'. Den he look in, en dar lay Brer Fox stretch out on de bed des ez big ez life. Den Brer Rabbit make like he talkin' to hisse'f.

" 'Nobody 'roun' fer ter look atter Brer Fox—not even Brer Tukkey Buzzard ain't come ter de funer'l,' sezee. 'I hope Brer Fox ain't dead, but I speck he is,' sezee. 'Even down ter Brer Wolf done en lef' 'im. Hit's de busy season wid me, but I'll set up wid 'im. He seem like he dead, yit he mayn't be,' sez Brer Rabbit, sezee. 'W'en a man go ter see dead fokes, dead fokes allers raises up der behime leg en hollers, *wahoo!*' sezee.

"Brer Fox he stay still. Den Brer Rabbit he talk little louder:

" 'Mighty funny. Brer Fox look like he dead, yit he don't do like he dead. Dead fokes hists der behime leg en hollers *wahoo!* w'en a man come ter see um,' sez Brer Rabbit, sezee.

"Sho' nuff, Brer Fox lif' up his foot en holler *wahoo!* en Brer Rabbit he tear out de house like de dogs wuz atter 'im. Brer Wolf mighty smart, but nex' time you hear fum 'im, honey, he'll be in trouble. You des hole yo' breff'n wait."

"One day," said Uncle Remus, sharpening his knife on the palm of his hand—"one day Brer Fox strike up wid Brer Tarrypin right in de middle er de big road. Brer Tarrypin done heerd 'im comin', en he 'low ter hisse'f dat he'd sorter keep one eye open; but Brer Fox wuz monstus perlite, en he open up de confab, he did, like he ain't see Brer Tarrypin sence de las' freshit.

"'Heyo, Brer Tarrypin, whar you bin dis long-come-short?' sez Brer Fox, sezee.

"'Lounjun 'roun', Brer Fox, lounjun 'roun',' sez Brer Tarrypin.

"'You don't look sprucy like you did, Brer Tarrypin,' sez Brer Fox, sezee.

"'Lounjun 'roun' en suffer'n',' sez Brer Tarrypin, sezee.

"Den de talk sorter run on like dis:

"'W'at ail you, Brer Tarrypin? Yo' eye look mighty red,' sez Brer Fox, sezee.

"'Lor', Brer Fox, you dunner w'at trubble is. You ain't bin lounjun 'roun' en suffer'n',' sez Brer Tarrypin, sezee.

"'Bofe eyes red, en you look like you mighty weak, Brer Tarrypin,' sez Brer Fox, sezee.

"'Lor', Brer Fox, you dunner w'at trubble is,' sez Brer Tarrypin, sezee.

"'W'at ail you now, Brer Tarrypin?' sez Brer Fox, sezee.

"'Tuck a walk de udder day, en man come 'long en sot de fiel' a-fier. Lor', Brer Fox, you dunner w'at trubble is,' sez Brer Tarrypin, sezee.

"'How you git out de fier, Brer Tarrypin?' sez Brer Fox, sezee.

"'Sot en tuck it, Brer Fox,' sez Brer Tarrypin, sezee. 'Sot en tuck it, en de smoke sif' in my eye, en de fier scorch my back,' sez Brer Tarrypin, sezee.

" 'Likewise hit bu'n yo' tail off,' sez Brer Fox, sezee.

" 'Oh, no, dar's de tail, Brer Fox,' sez Brer Tarrypin, sezee, en wid dat he oncurl his tail fum under de shell, en no sooner did he do dat dan Brer Fox grab it, en holler out:

" 'Oh, yes, Brer Tarrypin! Oh, yes! En so youer de man w'at lam me on de head at Miss Meadows's is you? Youer in wid Brer Rabbit, is you? Well, I'm gwineter out you.'

"Brer Tarrypin beg en beg, but 'twan't no use. Brer Fox done bin fool so much dat he look like he 'termin' fer ter have Brer Tarrypin haslett. Den Brer Tarrypin beg Brer Fox not fer ter drown 'im, but Brer Fox ain't makin' no prommus, en den he beg Brer Fox fer ter bu'n 'im, kaze he done useter fier, but Brer Fox don't say nuthin'. Bimeby Brer Fox drag Brer Tarrypin off little ways b'low de spring-'ouse, en souze 'im under de water. Den Brer Tarrypin begin fer ter holler:

" 'Tu'n loose dat stump root en ketch holt er me—tu'n loose dat stump root en ketch holt er me.'

"Brer Fox he holler back:

" 'I ain't got holt er no stump root, en I is got holt er you.'

"Brer Tarrypin he keep on holler'n:

" 'Ketch holt er me—I'm a drownin'—I'm a drownin'—tu'n loose de stump root en ketch holt er me.'

"Sho nuff, Brer Fox tu'n loose de tail, en Brer Tarrypin, he went down ter de bottom—kerblunkity-blink!"

No typographical combination or description could do justice to the guttural sonorousness—the peculiar intonation—which Uncle Remus imparted to this combination. It was so peculiar, indeed, that the little boy asked:

"How did he go to the bottom, Uncle Remus?"

"Kerblunkity-blink!"

"Was he drowned, Uncle Remus?"

"Who? Ole man Tarrypin? Is you drowndid w'en yo' ma tucks you in de bed?"

"Well, no," replied the little boy, dubiously.

"Ole man Tarrypin wuz at home I tell you, honey. Kerblinkity-blunk!"

Uncle Remus was half-soling one of his shoes, and his Miss Sally's little boy had been handling his awls, his hammers, and his knives to such an extent that the old man was compelled to assume a threatening attitude; but peace reigned again, and the little boy perched himself on a chair, watching Uncle Remus driving in pegs.

"Folks w'at's allers pesterin' people, en bodderin' 'longer dat w'at ain't dern, don't never come ter no good eend. Dar wuz Brer Wolf; stidder mindin' un his own bizness, he hatter take en go in pardnerships wid Brer Fox, en dey want skacely a minnit in de day dat he want atter Brer Rabbit, en he kep' on en kep' on twel fus' news you knowed he got kotch up wid—en he got kotch up wid monstus bad."

"Goodness, Uncle Remus! I thought the Wolf let the Rabbit alone, after he tried to fool him about the Fox being dead."

"Better lemme tell dish yer my way. Bimeby hit'll be yo' bed time, en Miss Sally'll be a hollerin' atter you, en you'll be a whimplin' roun', en den Mars John'll fetch up de re'r wid dat ar strop w'at I made fer 'im."

The child laughed, and playfully shook his fist in the simple, serious face of the venerable old darkey, but said no more. Uncle Remus waited awhile to be sure there was to be no other demonstration, and then proceeded:

"Brer Rabbit ain't see no peace w'atsumever. He can't leave home 'cep' Brer Wolf 'ud make a raid en tote off some er de fambly. Brer Rabbit b'ilt 'im a straw house, en hit wuz tored down; den he made a house outen pine-tops, en dat went de same way; den he made 'im a bark house, en dat wuz raided on, en eve'y time he los' a house he los' wunner his chilluns. Las' Brer Rabbit got mad, he did, en cust, en den he went off, he did, en got some kyarpinters, en dey b'ilt 'im a plank house wid rock foundashuns. Atter dat he could have some peace en quietness. He could go out en pass de time er day wid his nabers, en come back en set by de fier, en smoke his pipe, en read de newspapers same like enny man w'at got a fambly. He made a hole, he did, in de cellar whar de little Rabbits could hide out w'en dar wuz much uv a racket in de naberhood, en de latch er de front do' kotch on de inside. Brer Wolf, he see how de lan' lay, he did, en he lay low. De little Rabbits wuz mighty skittish, but hit got so dat cole chills ain't run up Brer Rabbit's back no mo' w'en he heerd Brer Wolf go gallopin' by.

"Bimeby, one day w'en Brer Rabbit wuz fixin' fer ter call on Miss Coon, he heerd a monstus fuss en clatter up de big road, en 'mos' 'fo' he could fix his years fer ter lissen, Brer Wolf run in de do'. De little Rabbits dey went inter dere hole in de cellar, dey did, like blowin' out a cannle. Brer Wolf wuz far'ly kivver'd wid mud, en mighty nigh outer win'.

"'Oh, do pray save me, Brer Rabbit!' sez Brer Wolf, sezee. 'Do please, Brer Rabbit! De dogs is atter me, en dey'll t'ar me up. Don't you year um comin'? Oh, do please save me, Brer Rabbit! Hide me some'rs whar de dogs won't git me.'

"No quicker sed dan done.

"'Jump in dat big chist dar, Brer Wolf,' sez Brer Rabbit, sezee. 'Jump in dar en make yo'se'f at home.'

"In jump Brer Wolf, down come de led, en inter de hasp went de hook, en dar Mr. Wolf wuz. Den Brer Rabbit went ter de lookin'-glass, he did, en wink at hisse'f, en den he drawd de rockin'-cheer in front er de fier, he did, en tuck a big chaw terbarker."

"Tobacco, Uncle Remus?" asked the little boy, incredulously.

"Rabbit terbarker, honey. You know dis yer life ev'lastin' w'at Miss Sally puts 'mong de cloze in de trunk; well, dat's rabbit terbarker. Den Brer Rabbit sot dar long time, he did, turnin' his mine over en wukken his thinkin' masheen. Bimeby he got up, en sorter stir 'roun'. Den Brer Wolf open up:

" 'Is de dogs all gone, Brer Rabbit?'

" 'Seem like I hear one un um smellin' roun' de chimbly-cornder des now.'

"Den Brer Rabbit git de kittle en fill it full er water, en put it on de fier.

" 'W'at you doin' now, Brer Rabbit?'

" 'I'm fixin' fer ter make you a nice cup er tea, Brer Wolf.'

"Den Brer Rabbit went ter de cubberd en git de gimlet, en commence for ter bo' little holes in de chist-led.

" 'W'at you doin' now, Brer Rabbit?'

" 'I'm a bo'in' little holes so you kin get bref, Brer Wolf.'

"Den Brer Rabbit went out en git some mo' wood, en fling it on de fier.

" 'W'at you doin' now, Brer Rabbit?'

" 'I'm a chunkin' up de fier so you won't git cole, Brer Wolf.'

"Den Brer Rabbit went down inter de cellar en fotch out all his chilluns.

" 'W'at you doin' now, Brer Rabbit?'

" 'I'm a tellin' my chilluns w'at a nice man you is, Brer Wolf.'

"En de chilluns, dey had ter put der han's on der moufs fer ter keep fum laffin'. Den Brer Rabbit he got de kittle en commenced fer to po' de hot water on de chist-lid.

" 'W'at dat I hear, Brer Rabbit?'

" 'You hear de win' a blowin', Brer Wolf.'

"Den de water begin fer ter sif' thoo.

" 'W'at dat I feel, Brer Rabbit?'

" 'You feels de fleas a bitin', Brer Wolf.'

" 'Dey er bitin' mighty hard, Brer Rabbit.'

" 'Tu'n on de udder side, Brer Wolf.'

" 'W'at dat I feel now, Brer Rabbit?'

" 'Still you feels de fleas, Brer Wolf.'

" 'Dey er eatin' me up, Brer Rabbit,' en dem wuz de las' words er Brer Wolf, kase de scaldin' water done de bizness.

"Den Brer Rabbit call in his nabers, he did, en dey hilt a reg'lar juberlee; en ef you go ter Brer Rabbit's house right now, I dunno but w'at you'll fine Brer Wolf's hide hangin' in de back-po'ch, en all bekaze he wuz so bizzy wid udder fo'kses doin's."

When the little boy
ran in to see Uncle Remus the night after he had told him of the
awful fate of Brer Wolf, the only response to his greeting was:

"I-doom-er-ker-kum-mer-ker!"

No explanation could convey an adequate idea of the intonation
and pronunciation which Uncle Remus brought to bear upon this
wonderful word. Those who can recall to mind the peculiar gur-
gling, jerking, liquid sound made by pouring water from a large jug,
or the sound produced by throwing several stones in rapid succession
into a pond of deep water, may be able to form a very faint idea of the
sound, but it can not be reproduced in print. The little boy was as-
tonished.

"What did you say, Uncle Remus?"

"I-doom-er-ker-kum-mer-ker! I-doom-er-ker-kum-mer-ker!"

"What is that?"

"Dat's Tarrypin talk, dat is. Bless yo' soul, honey," continued the
old man, brightening up, "w'en you git ole ez me—w'en you see w'at
I sees, en year w'at I years—de creeturs dat you can't talk wid 'll be
mighty skase—dey will dat. W'y, ders er old gray rat w'at uses 'bout
yer, en time atter time he comes out w'en you all done gone ter bed
en sets up dar in de cornder en dozes, en me en him talks by de 'our;
en w'at dat ole rat dunno ain't down in de spellin' book. Des now,
w'en you run in and broke me up, I wuz fetchin' inter my mine
w'at Brer Tarrypin say ter Brer Fox w'en he turn 'im loose in de
branch."

"What did he say, Uncle Remus?"

"Dat w'at he said—I-doom-er-ker-kum-mer-ker! Brer Tarrypin wuz
at de bottom er de pon', en he talk back, he did, in bubbles—I-doom-
er-ker-kum-mer-ker! Brer Fox, he ain't sayin' nuthin', but Brer Bull-

Frog, settin' on de bank, he hear Brer Tarrypin, he did, en he holler back:

"'Jug-er-rum-kum-dum! Jug-er-rum-kum-dum!'

"Den n'er Frog holler out:

"'Knee-deep! Knee-deep!'

"Den ole Brer Bull-Frog, he holler back:

"'Don't-you-berlieve-'im! Don't-you-berlieve-'im!'

"Den de bubbles come up fum Brer Tarrypin:

"'I-doom-er-ker-kum-mer-ker!'

"Den n'er Frog sing out:

"'Wade in! Wade in!'

"Den ole Brer Bull-Frog talk thoo his ho'seness:

"'Dar-you'll-fine-yo'-brudder! Dar-you'll-fine-yo'-brudder!'

"Sho nuff, Brer Fox look over de bank, he did, en dar wuz n'er Fox lookin' at 'im outer de water. Den he retch out fer ter shake han's, en in he went, heels over head, en Brer Tarrypin bubble out:

"'I-doom-er-ker-kum-mer-ker!' "

"Was the Fox drowned, Uncle Remus?" asked the little boy.

"He wern't zackly drowndid, honey," replied the old man, with an air of cautious reserve. "He did manage fer ter scramble out, but a little mo' en de Mud Turkle would er got 'im, en den he'd bin made hash un worril widout een'."

MR. FOX GOES A-HUNTING,
BUT MR. RABBIT BAGS THE GAME

"Atter Brer Fox hear 'bout how Brer Rabbit done Brer Wolf," said Uncle Remus, scratching his head with the point of his awl, "he 'low, he did, dat he better not be so brash, en he sorter let Brer Rabbit 'lone. Dey wuz all time seein' one nudder, en 'bunnunce er times Brer Fox could er nab Brer Rabbit, but eve'y time he got de chance, his mine 'ud sorter rezume 'bout Brer Wolf, en he let Brer Rabbit 'lone. Bimeby dey 'gun ter git kinder familious wid wunner nudder like dey useter, en it got so Brer Fox'd call on Brer Rabbit, en dey'd set up en smoke der pipes, dey would, like no ha'sh feelin's 'd ever rested 'twixt um.

"Las', one day Brer Fox come 'long all rig out, en ax Brer Rabbit fer ter go huntin' wid 'im, but Brer Rabbit, he sorter feel lazy, en he tell Brer Fox dat he got some udder fish fer ter fry. Brer Fox feel mighty sorry, he did, but he say he b'leeve he try his han' enny how, en off he put. He wuz gone all day, en he had a monstus streak er luck, Brer Fox did, en he bagged a sight er game. Bimeby, to'rds de shank er de evenin', Brer Rabbit sorter stretch hisse'f, he did, en 'low hit's mos' time fer Brer Fox fer ter git 'long home. Den Brer Rabbit, he went'n mounted a stump fer ter see if he could year Brer Fox comin'. He ain't bin dar long, twel sho' nuff, yer come Brer Fox thoo de woods, singing like a nigger at a frolic. Brer Rabbit, he lipt down off'n de stump, he did, en lay down in de road en make like he dead. Brer Fox he come 'long, he did, en see Brer Rabbit layin' dar. He tu'n 'im over, he did, en 'zamine 'im, en say, sezee:

" 'Dish yer rabbit dead. He look like he bin dead long time. He dead, but he mighty fat. He de fattes' rabbit w'at I ever see, but he bin dead too long. I feard ter take 'im home,' sezee.

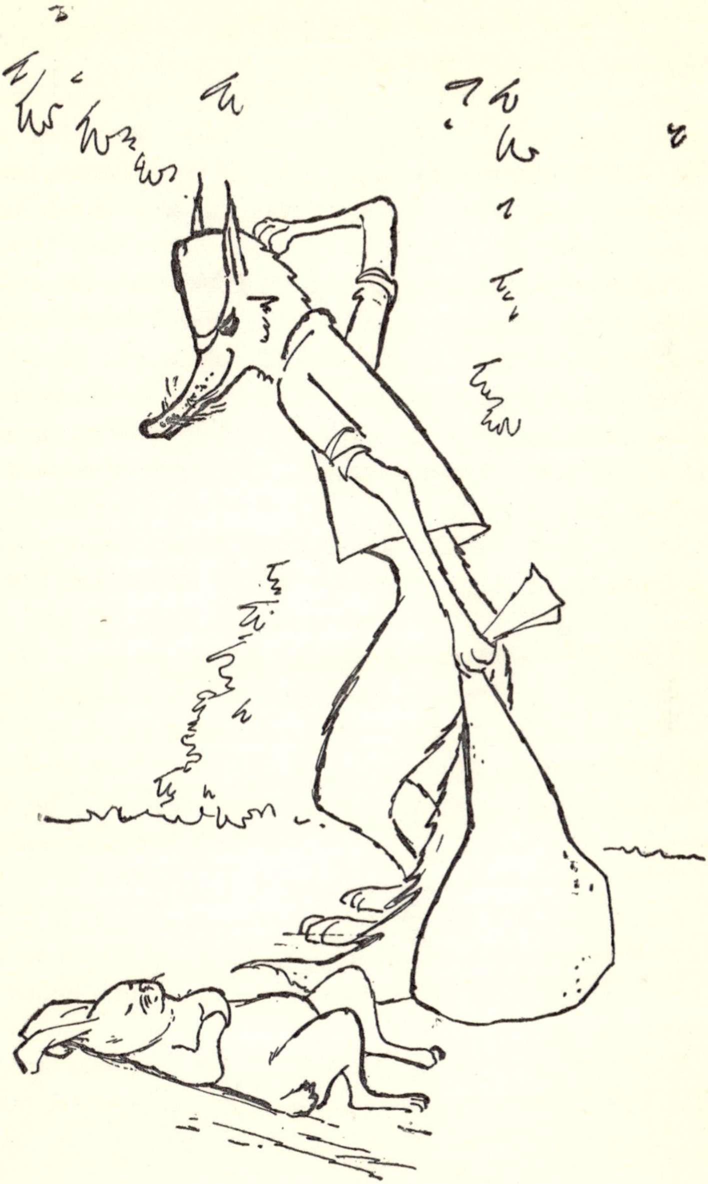

"Brer Rabbit ain't sayin' nuthin'. Brer Fox, he sorter lick his chops, but he went on en lef' Brer Rabbit layin' in de road. Dreckly he wuz outer sight, Brer Rabbit, he jump up, he did, en run roun' thoo de woods en git befo Brer Fox agin. Brer Fox, he come up, en dar lay Brer Rabbit, periently cole en stiff. Brer Fox, he look at Brer Rabbit, en he sorter study. Atter while he onslung his game-bag, en say ter hisse'f, sezee:

" 'Deze yer rabbits gwine ter was'e. I'll des 'bout leave my game yer, en I'll go back'n git dat udder rabbit, en I'll make fokes b'leeve dat I'm ole man Hunter fum Huntsville,' sezee.

"En wid dat he drapt his game en loped back up de road atter de udder rabbit, en w'en he got outer sight, ole Brer Rabbit, he snatch up Brer Fox game en put out fer home. Nex' time he see Brer Fox, he holler out:

" 'What you kill de udder day, Brer Fox?' sezee.

"Den Brer Fox, he sorter koam his flank wid his tongue, en holler back:

" 'I kotch a han'ful er hard sense, Brer Rabbit,' sezee.

"Den ole Brer Rabbit, he laff, he did, en up en 'spon,' sezee:

" 'Ef I'd a know'd you wuz atter dat, Brer Fox, I'd a loant you some er mine,' sezee."

OLD MR. RABBIT, HE'S A GOOD FISHERMAN

"Brer Rabbit en Brer Fox wuz like some chilluns w'at I knows un," said Uncle Remus, regarding the little boy, who had come to hear another story, with an affectation of great solemnity. "Bofe un um wuz allers atter wunner nudder, a prankin' en a pester'n 'roun', but Brer Rabbit did had some peace, kaze Brer Fox done got skittish 'bout puttin' de clamps on Brer Rabbit.

"One day, w'en Brer Rabbit, en Brer Fox, en Brer Coon, en Brer B'ar, en a whole lot un um wuz clearin' up a new groun' fer ter plant a roas'n'year patch, de sun 'gun ter git sorter hot, en Brer Rabbit he got tired; but he didn't let on, kaze he 'fear'd de balance un um'd call 'im lazy, en he keep on totin' off trash en pilin' up bresh, twel bimeby he holler out dat he gotter brier in his han', en den he take'n slip off, en hunt fer cool place fer ter res'. Atter w'ile he come 'crosst a well wid a bucket hangin' in it.

"'Dat look cool,' sez Brer Rabbit, sezee, 'en cool I speck she is. I'll des 'bout git in dar en take a nap,' en wid dat in he jump, he did, en he ain't no sooner fix hisse'f dan de bucket 'gun ter go down."

"Wasn't the Rabbit scared, Uncle Remus?" asked the little boy.

"Honey, dey ain't bin no wusser skeer'd beas' sence de worril begin dan dish yer same Brer Rabbit. He far'ly had a ager. He know whar he cum fum, but he dunner whar he gwine. Dreckly he feel de bucket hit de water, en dar she sot, but Brer Rabbit he keep mighty still, kaze he dunner w'at minnit gwineter be de nex'. He des lay dar en shuck en shiver.

"Brer Fox allers got one eye on Brer Rabbit, en w'en he slip off fum de new groun', Brer Fox he sneak atter 'im. He know Brer Rabbit wuz atter some projick er nudder, en he tuck'n crope off, he did, en watch 'im. Brer Fox see Brer Rabbit come to de well en stop, en den he see 'im jump in de bucket, en den, lo en beholes, he see 'im go down outer sight. Brer Fox wuz de mos' 'stonish Fox dat you ever laid eyes on. He sot off dar in de bushes en study en study, but he don't make no head ner tails ter dis kinder bizness. Den he say ter hisse'f, sezee:

" 'Well, ef dis don't bang my times,' sezee, "den Joe's dead en Sal's a widder. Right down dar in dat well Brer Rabbit keep his money hid, en ef 'tain't dat den he done gone en 'skiver'd a gole-mine, en ef 'tain't dat, den I'm a gwineter see w'at's in dar,' sezee.

"Brer Fox crope up little nigher, he did, en lissen, but he don't year no fuss, en he keep on gittin' nigher, en yit he don't year nuthin'. Bimeby he git up close en peep down, but he don't see nuthin' en he don't year nuthin'. All dis time Brer Rabbit mighty nigh skeer'd outen his skin, en he fear'd fer ter move kaze de bucket might keel over en spill him out in de water. W'ile he sayin' his pra'rs over like a train er kyars runnin', ole Brer Fox holler out:

" 'Heyo, Brer Rabbit! Who you wizzitin' down dar?' sezee.

" 'Who? Me? Oh, I'm des a fishin', Brer Fox,' sez Brer Rabbit, sezee. 'I des say ter myse'f dat I'd sorter sprize you all wid a mess er fishes fer dinner, en so here I is, en dar's de fishes. I'm a fishin' fer suckers, Brer Fox,' sez Brer Rabbit, sezee.

" 'Is dey many un um down dar, Brer Rabbit?' sez Brer Fox, sezee.

" 'Lot's un um, Brer Fox; scoze en scoze un um. De water is natally live wid um. Come down en he'p me haul um in, Brer Fox,' sez Brer Rabbit, sezee.

" 'How I gwineter git down, Brer Rabbit?'

" 'Jump inter de bucket, Brer Fox. Hit'll fetch you down all safe en soun'.'

"Brer Rabbit talk so happy en talk so sweet dat Brer Fox he jump in de bucket, he did, en, ez he went down, co'se his weight pull

68

Brer Rabbit up. W'en dey pass one nudder on de half-way groun', Brer Rabbit he sing out:

" 'Good-by, Brer Fox, take keer yo' cloze,
  Fer dis is de way de worril goes;
  Some goes up en some goes down,
  You'll git ter de bottom all safe en soun'.' [1]

"W'en Brer Rabbit got out, he gallop off en tole de fokes w'at de well b'long ter dat Brer Fox wuz down in dar muddyin' up de drinkin' water, en den he gallop back ter de well, en holler down ter Brer Fox:

" 'Yer come a man wid a great big gun—
  W'en he haul you up, you jump en run.' "

"What then, Uncle Remus?" asked the little boy, as the old man paused.

"In des 'bout half n'our, honey, bofe un um wuz back in de new groun' wukkin des like dey never heer'd er no well, ceppin' dat eve'y now'n den Brer Rabbit'd bust out in er laff, en ole Brer Fox, he'd git a spell er de dry grins."

[1] As a Northern friend suggests that this story may be somewhat obscure, it may be as well to state that the well is supposed to be supplied with a rope over a wheel, or pulley, with a bucket at each end.

MR. RABBIT NIBBLES UP THE BUTTER

"De animils en de beastesses," said Uncle Remus, shaking his coffee around in the bottom of his tin-cup, in order to gather up all the sugar, "dey kep' on gittin' mo' en mo' familious wid wunner nudder, twel bimeby, 'twan't long 'fo' Brer Rabbit, en Brer Fox, en Brer Possum got ter sorter bunchin' der perwishuns tergedder in de same shanty. Atter wile de roof sorter 'gun ter leak, en one day Brer Rabbit, en Brer Fox, en Brer Possum, 'semble fer ter see ef dey can't kinder patch her up. Dey had a big day's work in front un um, en dey fotch der dinner wid um. Dey lump de vittles up in one pile, en de butter w'at Brer Fox brung, dey goes en puts in de spring-'ouse fer ter keep cool, en den dey went ter wuk, en 'twan't long 'fo' Brer Rabbit stummuck 'gun ter sorter growl en pester 'im. Dat butter er Brer Fox sot heavy on his mine, en his mouf water eve'y time he 'member 'bout it. Present'y he say ter hisse'f dat he bleedzd ter have a nip at dat butter, en den he lay his plans, he did. Fus' news you know, w'ile dey wuz all wukkin' 'long, Brer Rabbit raise his head quick en fling his years forrerd en holler out:

"'Here I is. W'at you want wid me?' en off he put like sump'n wuz atter 'im.

"He sallied 'roun', ole Brer Rabbit did, en atter he make sho dat nobody ain't foller'n un 'im, inter de spring-'ouse he bounces, en dar he stays twel he git a bait er butter. Den he santer on back en go to wuk.

"'Whar you bin?' sez Brer Fox, sezee.

"'I hear my chilluns callin' me,' sez Brer Rabbit, sezee, 'en I hatter go see w'at dey want. My ole 'oman done gone en tuck mighty sick,' sezee.

"Dey wuk on twel bimeby de butter tas'e so good dat ole Brer

Rabbit want some mo'. Den he raise up his head, he did, en holler out:

"'Heyo! Hole on! I'm a comin'!' en off he put.

"Dis time he stay right smart w'ile, en w'en he git back Brer Fox ax him whar he bin.

"'I bin ter see my ole 'oman, en she's a sinkin',' sezee.

"Dreckly Brer Rabbit hear um callin' 'im ag'in en off he goes, en dis time, bless yo' soul, he gits de butter out so clean dat he kin see hisse'f in de bottom er de bucket. He scrape it clean en lick it dry, en den he go back ter wuk lookin' mo' samer dan a nigger w'at de patter-rollers bin had holt un.

"'How's yo' ole 'oman dis time?' sez Brer Fox, sezee.

"'I'm oblije ter you, Brer Fox,' sez Brer Rabbit, sezee, 'but I'm fear'd she's done gone by now,' en dat sorter make Brer Fox en Brer Possum feel in moanin' wid Brer Rabbit.

"Bimeby, w'en dinner-time come, dey all got out der vittles, but Brer Rabbit keep on lookin' lonesome, en Brer Fox en Brer Possum dey sorter rustle roun' fer ter see ef dey can't make Brer Rabbit feel sorter splimmy."

"What is that, Uncle Remus?" asked the little boy.

"Sorter splimmy-splammy, honey—sorter like he in a crowd—sorter like his ole 'oman ain't dead ez she mout be. You know how fokes duz w'en dey gits whar people's a moanin'.'"

The little boy didn't know, fortunately for him, and Uncle Remus went on:

"Brer Fox en Brer Possum rustle roun', dey did, gittin out de vittles, en bimeby Brer Fox, he say, sezee:

"'Brer Possum, you run down ter de spring en fetch de butter, en I'll sail 'roun' yer en set de table,' sezee.

"Brer Possum, he lope off atter de butter, en dreckly here he come lopin' back wid his years a trimblin' en his tongue a hangin' out. Brer Fox, he holler out:

" 'W'at de matter now, Brer Possum?' sezee.

" 'You all better run yer, fokes,' sez Brer Possum, sezee. 'De las' drap er dat butter done gone!'

" 'Whar she gone?' sez Brer Fox, sezee.

" 'Look like she dry up,' sez Brer Possum, sezee.

"Den Brer Rabbit, he look sorter sollum, he did, en he up'n say, sezee:

" 'I speck dat butter melt in somebody mouf,' sezee.

"Den dey went down ter de spring wid Brer Possum, en sho nuff de butter done gone. W'iles dey wuz sputin' over der wunderment, Brer Rabbit say he see tracks all 'roun' dar, en he p'int out dat ef dey'll all go ter sleep, he kin ketch de chap w'at stole de butter. Den dey all lie down en Brer Fox en Brer Possum dey soon drapt off ter sleep, but Brer Rabbit he stay 'wake, en w'en de time come he raise up easy en smear Brer Possum mouf wid de butter on his paws, en den he run off en nibble up de bes' er de dinner w'at dey lef' layin' out, en den he come back en wake up Brer Fox, en show 'im de butter on Brer Possum mouf. Den dey wake up Brer Possum, en tell 'im 'bout it, but c'ose Brer Possum 'ny it ter de las'. Brer Fox, dough, he's a kinder lawyer, en he argafy dis way—dat Brer Possum wuz de fus one at de butter, en de fus one fer ter miss it, en mo'n dat, dar hang de signs on his mouf. Brer Possum see dat dey got 'im jammed up in a cornder, en den he up en say dat de way fer ter ketch de man w'at stole de butter is ter b'il' a big bresh-heap en set her afier, en all han's try ter jump over, en de one w'at fall in, den he de chap w'at stole de butter. Brer Rabbit en Brer Fox dey bofe 'gree, dey did, en dey whirl in en b'il' de bresh-heap, en dey b'il' her high en dey b'il' her wide, en den dey totch her off. W'en she got ter blazin' up good, Brer Rabbit, he tuck de fus turn. He sorter step back, en look 'roun' en giggle, en over he went mo' samer dan a bird flyin'. Den come Brer Fox. He got back little fudder, en spit on his han's, en lit out en made de jump, en he come so nigh gittin' in dat de een' er his tail kotch afier. Ain't you never see no fox, honey?" inquired Uncle Remus, in a tone that implied both conciliation and information.

The little boy thought probably he had, but he wouldn't commit himself.

"Well, den," continued the old man, "nex' time you see one un um, you look right close en see ef de een' er his tail ain't w'ite. Hit's des like I tell you. Dey b'ars de skyar er dat bresh-heap down ter dis day. Dey er marked—dat's w'at dey is—dey er marked."

"And what about Brother Possum?" asked the little boy.

"Ole Brer Possum, he tuck a runnin' start, he did, en he come lumberin' 'long, en he lit—kerblam!—right in de middle er de fier, en dat wuz de las' er ole Brer Possum."

"But, Uncle Remus, Brother Possum didn't steal the butter after all," said the little boy, who was not at all satisfied with such summary injustice.

"Dat w'at make I say w'at I duz, honey. In dis worril, lots er fokes is gotter suffer fer udder fokes sins. Look like hit's mighty onwrong; but hit's des dat away. Tribbalashun seem like she's a waitin' roun' de cornder fer ter ketch one en all un us, honey."

"Hit look like ter me dat I let on de udder night dat in dem days w'en de beastesses wuz santer'n 'roun' same like fokes, none un um wuz brash nuff fer ter ketch up wid Brer Rabbit," remarked Uncle Remus, reflectively.

"Yes," replied the little boy, "that's what you said."

"Well, den," continued the old man with unction, "dar's whar my 'membunce gin out, kaze Brer Rabbit did git kotched up wid, en hit cool 'im off like po'in' spring water on one er deze yer biggity fices."

"How was that, Uncle Remus?" asked the little boy.

"One day w'en Brer Rabbit wuz gwine lippity-clippitin' down de road, he meet up wid ole Brer Tarrypin, en atter dey pass de time er day wid wunner nudder, Brer Rabbit, he 'low dat he wuz much 'blije ter Brer Tarrypin fer de han' he tuck in de rumpus dat day down at Miss Meadows's."

"When he dropped off of the water-shelf on the Fox's head," suggested the little boy.

"Dat's de same time, honey. Den Brer Rabbit 'low dat Brer Fox run mighty fas' dat day, but dat ef he'd er bin atter 'im stidder Brer Rabbit, he'd er kotch 'im. Brer Rabbit say he could er kotch 'im hisse'f but he didn't keer 'bout leavin' de ladies. Dey keep on talkin', dey did, twel bimeby dey gotter 'sputin' 'bout w'ich wuz de swif'es'. Brer Rabbit, he say he kin outrun Brer Tarrypin, en Brer Tarrypin, he des vow dat he kin outrun Brer Rabbit. Up en down dey had it, twel fus news you know Brer Tarrypin say he got a fifty-dollar bill in de chink er de chimbly at home, en dat bill done tole 'im dat he could beat Brer Rabbit in a fa'r race. Den Brer Rabbit say he got a fifty-dollar bill w'at say dat he kin leave Brer Tarrypin so fur behime, dat he could sow barley ez he went 'long en hit 'ud be ripe nuff fer ter cut by de time Brer Tarrypin pass dat way.

"Enny how dey make de bet en put up de money, en ole Brer Tukky Buzzard, he wuz summonzd fer ter be de jedge, en de stakeholder; en 'twan't long 'fo' all de 'rangements wuz made. De race wuz a five-mile heat, en de groun' wuz medjud off, en at de een' er ev'ey mile a pos' wuz stuck up. Brer Rabbit wuz ter run down de big road, en Brer Tarrypin, he say he'd gallup thoo de woods. Fokes tole 'em he could git long faster in de road, but ole Brer Tarrypin, he know w'at he doin'. Miss Meadows en de gals en mos' all de nabers got win' er de fun, en w'en de day wuz sot dey 'termin' fer ter be on han'. Brer Rabbit he train hisse'f ev'ey day, en he skip over de groun' des ez gayly ez a June cricket. Ole Brer Tarrypin, he lay low in de swamp. He had a wife en th'ee chilluns, ole Brer Tarrypin did, en dey wuz all de ve'y spit en image er de ole man. Ennybody what know one fum de udder gotter take a spy-glass, en den dey er li'ble fer ter git fooled.

"Dat's de way marters stan' twel de day er de race, en on dat day, ole Brer Tarrypin, en his ole 'oman, en his th'ee chilluns, dey got up 'fo' sun-up, en went ter de place. De ole 'oman, she tuck 'er stan' nigh de fus' mile-pos' she did, en de chilluns nigh de udders, up ter de las', en dar ole Brer Tarrypin, he tuck his stan'. Bimeby, here come de fokes: Jedge Buzzard, he come, en Miss Meadows en de gals, dey come, en den yer come Brer Rabbit wid ribbins tied 'roun' his neck en streamin' fum his years. De fokes all went ter de udder een' er de track fer ter see how dey come out. W'en de time come Jedge Buzzard strut 'roun' en pull out his watch, en holler out:

" 'Gents, is you ready?'

"Brer Rabbit, he say 'yes,' en ole Miss Tarrypin holler 'go' fum de aidge er de woods. Brer Rabbit, he lit out on de race, en ole Miss Tarrypin, she put out for home. Jedge Buzzard, he riz en skimmed 'long fer ter see dat de race wuz runned fa'r. W'en Brer Rabbit got ter de fus mile-pos' wunner de Tarrypin chilluns crawl out de woods, he did, en make fer de place. Brer Rabbit, he holler out:

" 'Whar is you, Brer Tarrypin?'

" 'Yer I come a bulgin',' sez de Tarrypin, sezee.

"Brer Rabbit so glad he's ahead dat he put out harder dan ever, en de Tarrypin, he make fer home. W'en he come ter de nex' pos', nudder Tarrypin crawl out er de woods.

" 'Whar is you, Brer Tarrypin?' sez Brer Rabbit, sezee.

" 'Yer I come a bilin',' sez de Tarrypin, sezee.

"Brer Rabbit, he lit out, he did, en come ter nex' pos', en dar wuz de Tarrypin. Den he come ter nex', en dar wuz de Tarrypin. Den he had one mo' mile fer ter run, en he feel like he gittin' bellust. Bimeby, ole Brer Tarrypin look way off down de road en he see Jedge Buzzard sailin' 'long en he know hit's time fer 'im fer ter be up. So he scramble outen de woods, en roll 'cross de ditch, en shuffle thoo de crowd er folks en git ter de mile-pos' en crawl behime it. Bimeby, fus' news you know, yer come Brer Rabbit. He look 'roun' en he don't see Brer Tarrypin, en den he squall out:

" 'Gimme de money, Brer Buzzard! Gimme de money!'

"Den Miss Meadows en de gals, dey holler and laff fit ter kill deyse'f, en ole Brer Tarrypin, he raise up fum behime de pos' en sez, sezee:

" 'Ef you'll gimme time fer ter ketch my breff, gents en ladies, one en all, I speck I'll finger dat money myse'f,' sezee, en sho nuff, Brer Tarrypin tie de pu's 'roun' his neck en skaddle[1] off home."

"But, Uncle Remus," said the little boy, dolefully, "that was cheating."

"Co'se, honey. De beastesses 'gun ter cheat, en den fokes tuck it up, en hit keep on spreadin'. Hit mighty ketchin', en you mine yo' eye, honey, dat somebody don't cheat you 'fo' yo' ha'r git gray ez de ole nigger's."

[1] It may be interesting to note here that in all probability the word "skedaddle," about which there was some controversy during the war, came from the Virginia Negro's use of "skaddle," which is a corruption of "scatter." The matter, however, is hardly worth referring to.

"You'll tromple on dat bark twel hit won't be fitten fer ter fling 'way, let 'lone make hoss-collars out'n," said Uncle Remus, as the little boy came running into his cabin out of the rain. All over the floor long strips of "wahoo" bark were spread, and these the old man was weaving into horse-collars.

"I'll sit down, Uncle Remus," said the little boy.

"Well, den, you better, honey," responded the old man, "kaze I 'spizes fer ter have my wahoo trompled on. Ef 'twuz shucks, now, hit mout be diffunt, but I'm a gittin' too ole fer ter be projickin' longer shuck collars."

For a few minutes the old man went on with his work, but with a solemn air altogether unusual. Once or twice he sighed deeply, and the sighs ended in a prolonged groan, that seemed to the little boy to be the result of the most unspeakable mental agony. He knew by experience that he had done something which failed to meet the approval of Uncle Remus, and he tried to remember what it was, so as to frame an excuse; but his memory failed him. He could think of nothing he had done calculated to stir Uncle Remus's grief. He was not exactly seized with remorse, but he was very uneasy. Presently Uncle Remus looked at him in a sad and hopeless way, and asked:

"W'at dat long rigmarole you bin tellin' Miss Sally 'bout yo' little brer dis mawnin?"

"Which, Uncle Remus?" asked the little boy, blushing guiltily.

"Dat des w'at I'm a axin' un you now. I hear Miss Sally say she's a gwineter stripe his jacket, en den I knowed you bin tellin' on 'im."

"Well, Uncle Remus, he was pulling up your onions, and then he went and flung a rock at me," said the child, plaintively.

"Lemme tell you dis," said the old man, laying down the section of horse-collar he had been plaiting, and looking hard at the little boy—"lemme tell you dis—der ain't no way fer ter make tattlers en tail-b'arers turn out good. No, dey ain't. I bin mixin' up wid fokes now gwine on eighty year, en I ain't seed no tattler come ter no good een'. Dat I ain't. En ef ole man M'thoozlum wuz livin' clean twel yit, he'd up'n tell you de same. Sho ez youer settin' dar. You 'member w'at 'come er de bird w'at went tattlin' 'roun' 'bout Brer Rabbit?"

The little boy didn't remember, but he was very anxious to know, and he also wanted to know what kind of a bird it was that so disgraced itself.

"Hit wuz wunner deze yer uppity little Jack Sparrers, I speck," said the old man; "dey wuz allers bodder'n' longer udder fokes's bizness, en dey keeps at it down ter dis day—peckin' yer, and pickin' dar, en scratchin' out yander. One day, atter he bin fool by ole Brer Tarrypin, Brer Rabbit wuz settin' down in de woods studdyin' how he wuz gwineter git even. He feel mighty lonesome, en he feel mighty mad, Brer Rabbit did. Tain't put down in de tale, but I speck he cusst en r'ar'd 'roun' considerbul. Leas'ways, he wuz settin' out dar by hisse'f, en dar he sot, en study en study, twel bimeby he jump up en holler out:

"'Well, doggone my cats ef I can't gallop 'roun' ole Brer Fox, en I'm gwineter do it. I'll show Miss Meadows en de gals dat I'm de boss er Brer Fox,' sezee.

"Jack Sparrer up in de tree, he hear Brer Rabbit, he did, en he sing out:

"'I'm gwine tell Brer Fox! I'm gwine tell Brer Fox! Chick-a-biddy-win'-a-blowin'-acuns-fallin'! I'm gwine tell Brer Fox!'"

Uncle Remus accompanied the speech of the bird with a peculiar whistling sound in his throat, that was a marvelous imitation of a sparrow's chirp, and the little boy clapped his hands with delight, and insisted on a repetition.

"Dis kinder tarrify Brer Rabbit, en he skasely know w'at he gwine do; but bimeby he study ter hisse'f dat de man w'at see Brer Fox fus wuz boun' ter have de inturn, en den he go hoppin' off to'rds home. He didn't got fur w'en who should he meet but Brer Fox, en den Brer Rabbit, he open up:

" 'W'at dis twix' you en me, Brer Fox?' sez Brer Rabbit, sezee. 'I hear tell you gwine ter sen' me ter 'struckshun, en nab my fambly, en 'stroy my shanty,' sezee.

"Den Brer Fox he git mighty mad.

" 'Who bin tellin' you all dis?' sezee.

"Brer Rabbit make like he didn't want ter tell, but Brer Fox he 'sist en 'sist, twel at las' Brer Rabbit he up en tell Brer Fox dat he hear Jack Sparrer say all dis.

" 'Co'se,' sez Brer Rabbit, sezee, 'w'en Brer Jack Sparrer tell me dat I flew up, I did, en I use some langwidge w'ich I'm mighty glad dey wern't no ladies 'roun' nowhars so dey could hear me go on,' sezee.

"Brer Fox he sorter gap, he did, en say he speck he better be sa'nter'n on. But, bless yo' soul, honey, Brer Fox ain't sa'nter fur, 'fo' Jack Sparrer flipp down on a 'simmon-bush by de side er de road, en holler out:

" 'Brer Fox! Oh, Brer Fox!—Brer Fox!'

"Brer Fox he des sorter canter 'long, he did, en make like he don't hear 'im. Den Jack Sparrer up'n sing out agin:

" 'Brer Fox! Oh, Brer Fox! Hole on, Brer Fox! I got some news fer you. Wait, Brer Fox! Hit'll 'stonish you.'

"Brer Fox he make like he don't see Jack Sparrer, ner needer do he hear 'im, but bimeby he lay down by de road, en sorter stretch hisse'f like he fixin' fer ter nap. De tattlin' Jack Sparrer he flew'd 'long, en keep on callin' Brer Fox, but Brer Fox, he ain't sayin' nuthin'. Den little Jack Sparrer, he hop down on de groun' en flutter

'roun' 'mongst de trash. Dis sorter 'track Brer Fox 'tenshun, en he look at de tattlin' bird, en de bird he keep on callin':

" 'I got sump'n fer ter tell you, Brer Fox.'

" 'Git on my tail, little Jack Sparrer,' sez Brer Fox, sezee, 'kaze I'm de'f in one year, en I can't hear out'n de udder. Git on my tail,' sezee.

"Den de little bird he up'n hop on Brer Fox's tail.

" 'Git on my back, little Jack Sparrer, kaze I'm de'f in one year en I can't hear out'n de udder.'

"Den de little bird hop on his back.

" 'Hop on my head, little Jack Sparrer, kaze I'm de'f in bofe years.'

"Up hop de little bird.

" 'Hop on my toof, little Jack Sparrer, kaze I'm de'f in one year en I can't hear out'n de udder.'

"De tattlin' little bird hop on Brer Fox's toof, en den—"

Here Uncle Remus paused, opened wide his mouth and closed it again in a way that told the whole story.[1]

"Did the Fox eat the bird all—all—up?" asked the little boy.

"Jedge B'ar come 'long nex' day," replied Uncle Remus, "en he fine some fedders, en fum dat word went roun' dat ole man Squinch Owl done kotch nudder watzizname."

---

[1] An Atlanta friend heard this story in Florida, but an alligator was substituted for the fox, and a little boy for the rabbit. There is another version in which the impertinent gosling goes to tell the fox something her mother has said, and is caught; and there may be other versions. I have adhered to the middle Georgia version, which is characteristic enough. It may be well to state that there are different versions of all the stories—the shrewd narrators of the mythology of the old plantation adapting themselves with ready tact to the years, tastes, and expectations of their juvenile audiences.

"One time," said Uncle Remus, whetting his knife slowly and thoughtfully on the palm of his hand, and gazing reflectively in the fire—"one time Brer Wolf——"

"Why, Uncle Remus!" the little boy broke in. "I thought you said the Rabbit scalded the wolf to death a long time ago."

The old man was fairly caught and he knew it; but this made little difference to him. A frown gathered on his usually serene brow as he turned his gaze upon the child—a frown in which both scorn and indignation were visible. Then all at once he seemed to regain control of himself. The frown was chased away by a look of Christian resignation.

"Dar now! W'at I tell you?" he exclaimed as if addressing a witness concealed under the bed. "Ain't I done tole you so? Bless grashus! Ef chilluns ain't gittin' so dey knows mo'n ole fokes, en dey'll spute longer you en spute longer you, ceppin der ma call um, w'ich I speck twon't be long 'fo' she will, en den I'll set yere by de chimbly-cornder en git some peace er mine. W'en ole Miss wuz livin'," continued the old man, still addressing some imaginary person, "hit 'uz mo'n enny her chilluns 'ud dast ter do ter come 'sputin' longer me, en Mars John'll tell you de same enny day you ax 'im."

"Well, Uncle Remus, you know you said the Rabbit poured hot water on the Wolf and killed him," said the little boy.

The old man pretended not to hear. He was engaged in searching among some scraps of leather under his chair, and kept on talking to the imaginary person. Finally, he found and drew forth a nicely plaited whip-thong with a red snapper all waxed and knotted.

"I wuz fixin' up a w'ip fer a little chap," he continued, with a sigh, "but, bless grashus, 'fo' I kin git er done, de little chap done grow'd up twel he know mo'n I duz."

The child's eyes filled with tears and his lips began to quiver, but he said nothing; whereupon Uncle Remus immediately melted.

"I 'clar' to goodness," he said, reaching out and taking the little boy tenderly by the hand, "ef you ain't de ve'y spit en image er ole Miss w'en I brung 'er de las' news er de war. Hit's des like skeerin' up a ghos' w'at you ain't fear'd un."

Then there was a pause, the old man patting the little child's hand caressingly.

"You ain't mad, is you, honey?" Uncle Remus asked finally, "kaze ef you is, I'm gwine out yere en butt my head 'gin de do' jam'."

But the little boy wasn't mad. Uncle Remus had conquered him and he had conquered Uncle Remus in pretty much the same way before. But it was some time before Uncle Remus would go on with the story. He had to be coaxed. At last, however, he settled himself back in the chair and began:

"Co'se, honey, hit mout er bin ole Brer Wolf, er hit mout er bin er n'er Brer Wolf; it mout er bin 'fo' he got kotch up wid, er it mout er bin atterwards. Ez de tale wer gun to me des dat away I gin it unter you. One time Brer Wolf wuz comin' 'long home fum a fishin' frolic. He s'anter 'long de road, he did, wid his string er fish 'cross his shoulder, wen fus news you know ole Miss Pa'tridge, she hop outer de bushes en flutter 'long right at Brer Wolf nose. Brer Wolf he say ter hisse'f dat ole Miss Pa'tridge tryin' fer ter toll 'im 'way fum her nes', en wid dat he lay his fish down en put out inter de bushes whar ole Miss Pa'tridge come fum, en 'bout dat time Brer Rabbit, he happen 'long. Dar wuz de fishes, en dar wuz Brer Rabbit, en w'en dat de case w'at you speck a sorter innerpen'ent man like Brer Rabbit gwine do? I kin tell you dis, dat dem fishes ain't stay whar Brer Wolf put um at, en w'en Brer Wolf come back dey wuz gone.

"Brer Wolf, he sot down en scratch his head, he did, en study en study, en den hit sorter rush inter his mine dat Brer Rabbit bin 'long dar, en den Brer Wolf, he put out fer Brer Rabbit house, en w'en he git dar he hail 'im. Brer Rabbit, he dunno nuthin' tall 'bout no fishes. Brer Wolf he up'n say he bleedzd ter b'leeve Brer Rabbit got dem fishes. Brer Rabbit 'ny it up en down, but Brer Wolf stan' to it dat Brer Rabbit got dem fishes. Brer Rabbit, he say dat if Brer Wolf b'leeve he got de fishes, den he give Brer Wolf lief fer ter kill de bes' cow he got. Brer Wolf, he tuck Brer Rabbit at his word, en go off ter de pastur' en drive up de cattle en kill Brer Rabbit bes' cow.

"Brer Rabbit, he hate mighty bad fer ter lose his cow, but he lay his plans, en he tell his chilluns dat he gwineter have dat beef yit. Brer Wolf, he bin tuck up by de patter-rollers 'fo' now, en he mighty skeerd un um, en fus news you know, yer come Brer Rabbit hollerin' en tellin' Brer Wolf dat de patter-rollers comin'.

"'You run en hide, Brer Wolf,' sez Brer Rabbit, sezee, 'en I'll stay yer en take keer er de cow twel you gits back,' sezee.

"Soon's Brer Wolf hear talk er de patter-rollers, he scramble off inter de underbrush like he bin shot out'n a gun. En he want mo'n gone 'fo' Brer Rabbit, he whirl in en skunt de cow en salt de hide down, en den he tuck'n cut up de kyarkiss en stow it 'way in de smoke-'ouse, en den he tuck'n stick de een' er de cow-tail in de groun'. Atter he gone en done all dis, den Brer Rabbit he squall out fer Brer Wolf:

"'Run yer, Brer Wolf! Run yer! Yo' cow gwine in de groun'! Run yer!'

"W'en ole Brer Wolf got dar, w'ich he come er scootin', dar wuz Brer Rabbit hol'in' on ter de cow-tail, fer ter keep it fum gwine in

de groun'. Brer Wolf, he kotch holt, en dey 'gin a pull er two en up come de tail. Den Brer Rabbit, he wink his off eye en say, sezee:

" 'Dar! De tail done pull out en de cow gone,' sezee.

"But Brer Wolf he wer'n't de man fer ter give it up dat away, en he got 'im a spade, en a pick-axe, en a shovel, en he dig en dig fer dat cow twel diggin' wuz pas' all endu'unce, en ole Brer Rabbit he sot up dar in his front po'ch en smoke his seegyar. Eve'y time ole Brer Wolf stuck de pick-axe in de clay, Brer Rabbit, he giggle ter his chilluns:

" 'He diggy, diggy, diggy, but no meat dar! He diggy, diggy, diggy, but no meat dar!"

"Kaze all de time de cow wuz layin' pile up in his smoke-'ouse, en him en his chilluns wuz eatin' fried beef en inguns eve'y time dey mouf water.

"Now den, honey, you take dis yer w'ip," continued the ole man, twining the leather thong around the little boy's neck, "en scamper up ter de big 'ouse en tell Miss Sally fer ter gin you some un it de nex' time she fine yo' tracks in de sugar-bairl."

MR. RABBIT MEETS HIS MATCH AGAIN

"Dere wuz nudder man dat sorter play it sharp on Brer Rabbit," said Uncle Remus, as, by some mysterious process, he twisted a hog's bristle into the end of a piece of thread—an operation which the little boy watched with great interest. "In dem days," continued the old man, "de beastesses kyar'd on marters same ez fokes. Dey went inter fahmin', en I speck ef de troof wuz ter come out, dey kep' sto', en had der camp-meetin' times en der bobbycues w'en de wedder wuz 'greeble."

Uncle Remus evidently thought that the little boy wouldn't like to hear of any further discomfiture of Brer Rabbit, who had come to be a sort of hero, and he was not mistaken.

"I thought the Terrapin was the only one that fooled the Rabbit," said the little boy, dismally.

"Hit's des like I tell you, honey. Dey ain't no smart man, 'cep' w'at dey's a smarter. Ef ole Brer Rabbit hadn't er got kotch up wid, de nabers 'ud er tuck 'im for a h'ant, en in dem times dey bu'nt witches 'fo' you could squinch yo' eyeballs. Dey did dat."

"Who fooled the Rabbit this time?" the little boy asked.

When Uncle Remus had the bristle "sot" in the thread, he proceeded with the story:

"One time Brer Rabbit en ole Brer Buzzard 'cluded dey'd sorter go snacks, en crop tergedder. Hit wuz a mighty good year, en de truck tu'n out monstus well, but bimeby, w'en de time come fer dividjun, hit come ter light dat ole Brer Buzzard ain't got nuthin'. De crop wuz all gone, en dey want nuthin' dar fer ter show fer it. Brer Rabbit, he make like he in a wuss fix'n Brer Buzzard, en he mope 'roun', he did, like he fear'd dey gwineter sell 'im out.

"Brer Buzzard, he ain't sayin' nuthin', but he keep up a monstus thinkin', en one day he come 'long en holler en tell Brer Rabbit dat he done fine rich gole-mine des 'cross de river.

"'You come en go 'longer me, Brer Rabbit,' sez Brer Tukky Buzzard, sezee. 'I'll scratch en you kin grabble, en 'tween de two un us we'll make short wuk er dat gole-mine,' sezee.

"Brer Rabbit, he wuz high up fer de job, but he study en study, he did, how he gwineter git 'cross de water, kaze ev'y time he git his foot wet all de fambly kotch cole. Den he up'n ax Brer Buzzard how he gwine do, en Brer Buzzard he up'n say dat he kyar Brer Rabbit 'cross, en wid dat ole Brer Buzzard, he squot down, he did, en spread his wings, en Brer Rabbit, he mounted, en up dey riz." There was a pause.

"What did the Buzzard do then?" asked the little boy.

"Dey riz," continued Uncle Remus, "en w'en dey lit, dey lit in de top er de highest sorter pine, en de pine w'at dey lit in wuz growin' on er ilun, en de ilun wuz in de middle er de river, wid de deep water runnin' all 'roun'. Dey ain't mo'n lit 'fo' Brer Rabbit, he know w'ich way de win' 'uz blowin', en by de time ole Brer Buzzard got hisse'f ballunce on a lim', Brer Rabbit, he up'n say, sezee:

"'W'iles we er res'n here, Brer Buzzard, en bein's you bin so good, I got sump'n fer ter tell you,' sezee. 'I got a gole-mine er my own, one w'at I make myse'f, en I speck we better go back ter mine 'fo' we bodder 'longer yone,' sezee.

"Den ole Brer Buzzard, he laff, he did, twel he shake, en Brer Rabbit, he sing out:

"'Hole on, Brer Buzzard! Don't flop yo' wings w'en you laff, kaze den ef you duz, sump'n 'ill drap fum up yer, en my gole-mine won't do you no good, en needer will yone do me no good.'

"But 'fo' dey got down fum dar, Brer Rabbit done tole all 'bout de crop, en he hatter promus fer ter 'vide fa'r en squar. So Brer Buzzard, he kyar 'im back, en Brer Rabbit he walk weak in de knees a mont' atterwuds."

A STORY ABOUT THE LITTLE RABBITS

"Fine um whar you will en w'en you may," remarked Uncle Remus with emphasis, "good chilluns allers gits tuck keer on. Dar wuz Brer Rabbit's chilluns; dey minded der daddy en mammy fum day's een' ter day's een'. W'en ole man Rabbit say 'scoot,' dey scooted, en w'en ole Miss Rabbit say 'scat,' dey scatted. Dey did dat. En dey kep der cloze clean, en dey ain't had no smut on der nose nudder."

Involuntarily the hand of the little boy went up to his face, and he scrubbed the end of his nose with his coatsleeve.

"Dey wuz good chilluns," continued the old man, heartily, "en ef dey hadn't er bin, der wuz one time w'en dey wouldn't er bin no little rabbits—na'er one. Dat's w'at."

"What time was that, Uncle Remus?" the little boy asked.

"De time w'en Brer Fox drapt in at Brer Rabbit house, en didn't foun' nobody dar ceppin' de little Rabbits. Ole Brer Rabbit, he wuz off some'rs raiding on a collard patch, en ole Miss Rabbit she wuz tendin' on a quiltin' in de naberhood, en wiles de little Rabbits wuz playin' hidin'-switch, in drapt Brer Fox. De little Rabbits wuz so fat dat dey fa'rly make his mouf water, but he 'member 'bout Brer Wolf, en he skeered fer ter gobble um up ceppin' he got some skuse. De little Rabbits, dey mighty skittish, en dey sorter huddle deyse'f up tergedder en watch Brer Fox motions. Brer Fox, he sot dar en study w'at sorter skuse he gwineter make up. Bimeby he see a great big stalk er sugar-cane stan'in' up in de cornder, en he cle'r up his th'oat en talk biggity:

" 'Yer! You young Rabs dar, sail 'roun' yer en broke me a piece er dat sweetnin'-tree,' sezee, en den he koff.

"De little Rabbits, dey got out de sugar-cane, dey did, en dey rastle wid it, en sweat over it, but twan't no use. Dey couldn't broke it.

Brer Fox, he make like he ain't watchin', but he keep on holler'n:

"'Hurry up dar, Rabs! I'm a waitin' on you.'

"En de little Rabbits, dey hustle 'roun' en rastle wid it, but dey couldn't broke it. Bimeby dey hear little bird singin' on top er de house, en de song w'at de little bird sing wuz dish yer:

" 'Take yo' toofies en gnyaw it,
Take yo' toofies en saw it,
Saw it en yoke it,
En den you kin broke it.'

"Den de little Rabbits, dey git mighty glad, en dey gnyawed de cane mos' 'fo' ole Brer Fox could git his legs oncrosst, en w'en dey kyard 'im de cane, Brer Fox, he sot dar en study how he gwineter make some mo' skuse fer nabbin' un um, en bimeby he git up en git down de sifter w'at wuz hangin' on de wall, en holler out:

"'Come yer, Rabs! Take dish yer sifter, en run down't de spring en fetch me some fresh water.'

"De little Rabbits, dey run down't de spring, en try ter dip up de water wid de sifter, but co'se hit all run out, en hit keep on runnin' out, twel bimeby de little Rabbits sot down en 'gun ter cry. Den de little bird settin' up in de tree he begin fer ter sing, en dish yer's de song w'at he sing:

" 'Sifter hole water same ez a tray,
Ef you fill it wid moss en dob it wid clay;
De Fox git madder de longer you stay—
Fill it wid moss en dob it wid clay.'

"Up dey jump, de little Rabbits did, en dey fix de sifter so 'twon't leak, en den dey kyar de water ter ole Brer Fox. Den Brer Fox he git mighty mad, en p'int out a great big stick er wood, en tell de little Rabbits fer ter put dat on de fier. De little chaps dey got 'roun' de wood, dey did, en dey lif' at it so hard twel dey could see der own

sins, but de wood ain't budge. Den dey hear de little bird singin', en dish yer's de song w'at he sing:

" 'Spit in yo' han's en tug it en toll it,
    En git behine it, en push it, en pole it;
    Spit in yo' han's en r'ar back en roll it.'

"En des 'bout de time dey got de wood on de fier, der daddy, he come skippin' in, en de little bird, he flew'd away. Brer Fox, he seed his game wuz up, en 'twan't long 'fo' he make his skuse en start fer ter go.

" 'You better stay en take a snack wid me, Brer Fox,' sez Brer Rabbit, sezee. 'Sence Brer Wolf done quit comin' en settin' up wid me, I gittin' so I feels right lonesome dese long nights,' sezee.

"But Brer Fox, he button up his coat-collar tight en des put out fer home. En dat w'at you better do, honey, kaze I see Miss Sally's shadder sailin' backerds en for'ds 'fo' de winder, en de fus' news you know she'll be spectin' un you."

"Dar wuz one season," said Uncle Remus, pulling thoughtfully at his whiskers, "w'en Brer Fox say to hisse'f dat he speck he better whirl in en plant a goober-patch, en in dem days, mon, hit wuz tech en go. De wud wer'n't mo'n out'n his mouf 'fo' de groun' 'uz brok'd up en de goobers 'uz planted. Ole Brer Rabbit, he sot off en watch de motions, he did, en he sorter shet one eye en sing to his chilluns:

" 'Ti-yi! Tungalee!
  I eat um pea, I pick um pea.
  Hit grow in de groun', hit grow so free;
  Ti-yi! Dem goober pea.'

"Sho' 'nuff w'en de goobers 'gun ter ripen up, eve'y time Brer Fox go down ter his patch, he fine whar somebody bin grabblin' 'mongst de vines, en he git mighty mad. He sorter speck who de somebody is, but ole Brer Rabbit he cover his tracks so cute dat Brer Fox dunner how ter ketch 'im. Bimeby, one day Brer Fox take a walk all roun' de groun'-pea patch, en 'twan't long 'fo' he fine a crack in de fence whar de rail done bin rub right smoove, en right dar he sot 'im a trap. He tuck'n ben' down a hick'ry saplin', growin' in de fence-cornder, en tie one een' un a plow-line on de top, en in de udder een' he fix a loop-knot, en dat he fasten wid a trigger right in de crack. Nex' mawnin' w'en ole Brer Rabbit come slippin' 'long en crope thoo de crack, de loop-knot kotch 'im behime de fo' legs, en de saplin' flew'd up, en dar he wuz 'twix' de heavens en de yeth. Dar he swung, en he fear'd he gwineter fall, en he fear'd he wer'n't gwineter fall. W'ile he wuz a fixin' up a tale fer Brer Fox, he hear a lumberin' down de road, en present'y yer cum ole Brer B'ar amblin' 'long fum whar he bin takin' a bee-tree. Brer Rabbit, he hail 'im:

" 'Howdy, Brer B'ar!'

"Brer B'ar, he look 'roun en bimeby he see Brer Rabbit swingin' fum de saplin', en he holler out:

" 'Heyo, Brer Rabbit! How you come on dis mawnin'?'

" 'Much oblije, I'm middlin', Brer B'ar,' sez Brer Rabbit, sezee.

"Den Brer B'ar, he ax Brer Rabbit w'at he doin' up dar in de elements, en Brer Rabbit, he up'n say he makin' dollar minnit. Brer B'ar, he say how. Brer Rabbit say he keepin' crows out'n Brer Fox's groun'-pea patch, en den he ax Brer B'ar, ef he don't wanter make dollar minnit, kaze he got big fambly er chilluns fer ter take keer un, en den he make sech nice skeer-crow. Brer B'ar 'low dat he take

de job, en den Brer Rabbit show 'im how ter ben' down de saplin',
en twan't long 'fo' Brer B'ar wuz swingin' up dar in Brer Rabbit
place. Den Brer Rabbit, he put out fer Brer Fox house, en w'en he
got dar he sing out:

"'Brer Fox! Oh, Brer Fox! Come out yer, Brer Fox, en I'll show
you de man w'at bin stealin' yo' goobers.'

"Brer Fox, he grab up his walkin'-stick, en bofe un um went
runnin' back down ter der goober-patch, en w'en dey got dar, sho
'nuff, dar wuz ole Brer B'ar.

"'Oh, yes! Youer kotch, is you?' sez Brer Fox, en 'fo' Brer B'ar
could 'splain, Brer Rabbit he jump up en down, en holler out:

" 'Hit 'im in de mouf, Brer Fox; hit 'im in de mouf'; en Brer Fox, he draw back wid de walkin'-cane, en blip he tuck 'im, en eve'y time Brer B'ar'd try ter 'splain, Brer Fox'd shower down on him.

"W'iles all dis 'uz gwine on, Brer Rabbit, he slip off en git in a mud-hole en des lef' his eyes stickin' out, kaze he know'd dat Brer B'ar'd be a comin' atter 'im. Sho 'nuff, bimeby here come Brer B'ar down de road, en w'en he git ter de mud-hole, he say:

" 'Howdy, Brer Frog, is you seed Brer Rabbit go by yer?'

" 'He des gone by,' sez Brer Rabbit, en ole man B'ar tuck off down de road like a skeer'd mule, en Brer Rabbit, he come out en dry hisse'f in de sun, en go home ter his fambly same ez enny udder man."

"The Bear didn't catch the Rabbit, then?" inquired the little boy, sleepily.

"Jump up fum dar, honey!" exclaimed Uncle Remus, by way of reply. "I ain't got no time fer ter be settin' yer proppin' yo' eyeleds open."

MR. BEAR CATCHES OLD MR. BULL-FROG

"Well, Uncle Remus," said the little boy, counting to see if he hadn't lost a marble somewhere, "the Bear didn't catch the Rabbit after all, did he?"

"Now you talkin', honey," replied the old man, his earnest face breaking up into little eddies of smiles—"now you talkin' sho. 'Tain't bin proned inter no Brer B'ar fer ter kotch Brer Rabbit. Hit sorter like settin' a mule fer ter trap a hummin'-bird. But Brer B'ar, he tuck'n got hisse'f inter some mo' trubble, w'ich it look like it mighty easy. Ef folks could make der livin' longer gittin' inter trubble," continued the old man, looking curiously at the little boy, "ole Miss Favers wouldn't be bodder'n yo' ma fer ter borry a cup full er sugar eve'y now en den; en it look like ter me dat I knows a nigger dat wouldn't be squattin' 'roun' yer makin' dese yer fish-baskits."

"How did the Bear get into more trouble, Uncle Remus?" asked the little boy.

"Natchul, honey. Brer B'ar, he tuck a notion dat ole Brer Bull-frog wuz de man w'at fool 'im, en he say dat he'd come up wid 'im ef 'twuz a year atterwuds. But 'twan't no year, an 'twan't no mont', en mo'n dat, hit wan't skasely a week, w'en bimeby one day Brer B'ar wuz gwine home fum de takin' un a bee-tree, en lo en beholes, who should he see but ole Brer Bull-frog settin' out on de aidge er de mud-puddle fas' 'sleep! Brer B'ar drap his axe, he did, en crope up, en retch out wid his paw, en scoop ole Brer Bull-frog in des dis away." Here the old man used his hand ladle-fashion, by way of illustration. "He scoop 'im in, en dar he wuz. W'en Brer B'ar got his clampers on 'im good, he sot down en talk at 'im.

" 'Howdy, Brer Bull-frog, howdy! En how yo' fambly? I hope deyer well, Brer Bull-frog, kaze dis day you got some bizness wid me w'at'll las' you a mighty long time.'

"Brer Bull-frog, he dunner w'at ter say. He dunner w'at's up, en he don't say nuthin'. Ole Brer B'ar he keep runnin' on:

" 'Youer de man w'at tuck en fool me 'bout Brer Rabbit t'er day. You had yo' fun, Brer Bull-frog, en now I'll git mine.'

"Den Brer Bull-frog, he gin ter git skeerd, he did, en he up'n say:

" 'W'at I bin doin' Brer B'ar? How I bin foolin' you?'

"Den Brer B'ar laff, en make like he dunno, but he keep on talkin'.

" 'Oh, no, Brer Bull-frog! You ain't de man w'at stick yo' head up out'n de water en tell me Brer Rabbit done gone on by. Oh, no! You ain't de man. I boun' you ain't. 'Bout dat time, you wuz at home wid yo' fambly, whar you allers is. I dunner whar you wuz, but I knows whar you is, Brer Bull-frog, en hit's you en me fer it. Atter de sun goes down dis day you don't fool no mo' folks gwine 'long dis road.'

"Co'se, Brer Bull-frog dunner w'at Brer B'ar drivin' at, but he know sump'n hatter be done, en dat mighty soon, kaze Brer B'ar 'gun to snap his jaws tergedder en foam at de mouf, en Brer Bull-frog holler out:

" 'Oh, pray, Brer B'ar! Lemme off dis time, en I won't never do so no mo'. Oh, pray, Brer B'ar! Do lemme off dis time, en I'll show you de fattes' bee-tree in de woods.'

"Ole Brer B'ar, he chomp his toofies en foam at de mouf. Brer Bull-frog he des up'n squall:

" 'Oh, pray, Brer B'ar! I won't never do so no mo'! Oh, pray, Brer B'ar! Lemme off dis time!'

"But ole Brer B'ar say he gwineter make way wid 'im, en den he sot en study, ole Brer B'ar did, how he gwineter squench Brer Bull-frog. He know he can't drown 'im, en he ain't got no fier fer ter bu'n 'im, en he git mighty pestered. Bimeby ole Brer Bull-frog, he sorter stop his cryin' en his boo-hooin', en he up'n say:

" 'Ef you gwineter kill me, Brer B'ar, kyar me ter dat big flat rock out dar on de aidge er de mill-pon', whar I kin see my fambly, en atter I see um, den you kin take you axe en sqush me.'

"Dis look so fa'r and squar' dat Brer B'ar he 'gree, en he take ole Brer Bull-frog by wunner his behime legs, en sling his axe on his shoulder, en off he put fer de big flat rock. When he git dar he lay Brer Bull-frog down on de rock, en Brer Bull-frog make like he lookin' 'roun' fer his folks. Den Brer B'ar, he draw long breff en pick up his axe. Den he spit in his han's en draw back en come down on de rock—pow!"

"Did he kill the Frog, Uncle Remus?" asked the little boy, as the old man paused to scoop up a thimbleful of glowing embers in his pipe.

"'Deed, en dat he didn't, honey. 'Twix' de time w'en Brer B'ar raise up wid his axe en w'en he come down wid it, ole Brer Bull-frog he lipt up en dove down in de mill-pon', kerblink-kerblunk! En w'en he riz way out in de pon' he riz a singin', en dish yer's de song w'at he sing:

"'Ingle-go-jang, my joy, my joy—
    Ingle-go-jang, my joy!
  I'm right at home, my joy, my joy—
    Ingle-go-jang, my joy!'"

"That's a mighty funny song," said the little boy.

"Funny now, I speck," said the old man, "but 'twern't funny in dem days, en 'twouldn't be funny now ef folks know'd much 'bout de Bull-frog langwidge ez dey useter. Dat's w'at."

"One time," said Uncle Remus, sighing heavily and settling himself back in his seat with an air of melancholy resignation—"one time Brer Rabbit wuz gwine 'long down de road shakin' his big bushy tail, en feelin' des ez scrump-shus ez a bee-martin wid a fresh bug." Here the old man paused and glanced at the little boy, but it was evident that the youngster had become so accustomed to the marvelous developments of Uncle Remus's stories, that the extraordinary statement made no unusual impression upon him. Therefore the old man began again, and this time in a louder and more insinuating tone:

"One time ole man Rabbit, he wuz gwine 'long down de road shakin' his long, bushy tail, en feelin' mighty biggity."

This was effective.

"Great goodness, Uncle Remus!" exclaimed the little boy in open-eyed wonder. "Everybody knows that rabbits haven't got long, bushy tails."

The old man shifted his position in his chair and allowed his venerable head to drop forward until his whole appearance was suggestive of the deepest dejection; and this was intensified by a groan that seemed to be the result of great mental agony. Finally he spoke, but not as addressing himself to the little boy.

"I notices dat dem fokes w'at makes a great 'miration 'bout w'at dey knows is des de fokes w'ich you can't put no 'pennunce in w'en de 'cashun come up. Yer one un um now, en he done come en excuse me er 'lowin' dat rabbits is got long, bushy tails, w'ich goodness knows ef I'd a dremp' it, I'd a whirl in en ondremp it."

"Well, but Uncle Remus, you said rabbits had long, bushy tails," replied the little boy. "Now you know you did."

"Ef I ain't fergit it off'n my mine, I say dat ole Brer Rabbit wuz gwine down de big road shakin' his long, bushy tail. Dat w'at I say, en dat I stan's by."

The little boy looked puzzled, but he didn't say anything. After a while the old man continued:

"Now, den, ef dat's 'greed ter, I'm gwine on, en ef tain't 'greed ter, den I'm gwineter pick up my cane en look atter my own intrust. I got wuk lyin' roun' yer dat's des natally gittin' moldy."

The little boy still remained quiet, and Uncle Remus proceeded:

"One day Brer Rabbit wuz gwine down de road shakin' his long, bushy tail, w'en who should he strike up wid but ole Brer Fox gwine amblin' long wid a big string er fish! W'en dey pass de time er day wid wunner nudder, Brer Rabbit, he open up de confab, he did, en he ax Brer Fox whar he git dat nice string er fish, en Brer Fox, he up'n 'spon' dat he kotch um, en Brer Rabbit, he say whar'bouts, en Brer Fox, he say down at de babtizin' creek, en Brer Rabbit he ax how, kaze in dem days dey wuz monstus fon' er minners, en Brer Fox, he sot down on a log, he did, en he up'n tell Brer Rabbit dat all he gotter do fer ter git er big mess er minners is ter go ter de creek atter sun down, en drap his tail in de water en set dar twel daylight, en den draw up a whole armful er fishes, en dem w'at he don't want, he kin fling back. Right dar's whar Brer Rabbit drap his water-million, kaze he tuck'n sot out dat night en went a fishin'. De wedder wuz sorter cole, en Brer Rabbit, he got 'im a bottle er dram en put out fer de creek, en w'en he git dar he pick out a good place, en he sorter squot down, he did, en let his tail hang in de water. He sot dar, en he sot dar, en he drunk his dram, en he think he gwineter freeze, but bimeby day come, en dar he wuz. He make a pull, en he feel like he comin' in two, en he fetch nudder jerk, en lo en beholes, whar wuz his tail?"

There was a long pause.

"Did it come off, Uncle Remus?" asked the little boy, presently.

"She did dat!" replied the old man with unction. "She did dat, and dat w'at make all deze yer bob-tail rabbits w'at you see hoppin' en skaddlin thoo de woods."

"Are they all that way just because the old Rabbit lost his tail in the creek?" asked the little boy.

"Dat's it, honey," replied the old man. "Dat's w'at dey tells me. Look like dey er bleedzd ter take atter der pa."

MR. TERRAPIN SHOWS HIS STRENGTH

"Brer Tarrypin wuz de out'nes' man," said Uncle Remus, rubbing his hands together contemplatively, and chuckling to himself in a very significant manner. "He wuz de out'nes' man er de whole gang. He wuz dat."

The little boy sat perfectly quiet, betraying no impatience when Uncle Remus paused to hunt, first in one pocket and then in another, for enough crumbs of tobacco to replenish his pipe. Presently the old man proceeded:

"One night Miss Meadows en de gals dey gun a candy-pullin', en so many er de nabers come in 'sponse ter de invite dat dey hatter put de 'lasses in de wash pot en b'il' de fier in de yard. Brer B'ar, he hope[1] Miss Meadows bring de wood, Brer Fox, he men' de fier, Brer Wolf, he kep' de dogs off, Brer Rabbit, he grease de bottom er de plates fer ter keep de candy fum stickin', en Brer Tarrypin, he klum up in a cheer, en say he'd watch en see dat de 'lasses didn't bile over. Dey wuz all dere, en dey wer'n't cuttin' up no didos, nudder, kase Miss Meadows, she done put her foot down, she did, en say dat w'en dey come ter her place dey hatter hang up a flag er truce at de front gate en 'bide by it.

"Well, den, w'iles dey wuz all a settin' dar en de 'lasses wuz a bilin' en a blubberin', dey got ter runnin' on talkin' mighty biggity. Brer Rabbit, he say he de swiffes'; but Brer Tarrypin, he rock 'long in de cheer en watch de 'lasses. Brer Fox, he say he de sharpes', but Brer Tarrypin he rock 'long. Brer Wolf he say he de mos' suvvigus, but Brer Tarrypin, he rock en he rock 'long. Brer B'ar, he say he de mos' stronges', but Brer Tarrypin he rock, en he keep on rockin'. Bimeby he sorter shet one eye, en say, sezee:

"'Hit look like 'periently dat de ole hardshell ain't nowhars 'long-

[1] Holp; helped.

side er dis crowd, yit yer I is, en I'm de same man w'at show Brer Rabbit dat he ain't de swiffes'; en I'm de same man w'at kin show Brer B'ar dat he ain't de stronges',' sezee.

"Den dey all laff en holler, kaze it look like Brer B'ar mo' stronger dan a steer. Bimeby, Miss Meadows, she up'n ax, she did, how he gwine do it.

" 'Gimme a good strong rope,' sez Brer Tarrypin, sezee, 'en lemme git in er puddle er water, en den let Brer B'ar see ef he kin pull me out,' sezee.

"Den dey all laff g'in, en Brer B'ar, he ups en sez, sezee: 'We ain't got no rope,' sezee.

" 'No,' sez Brer Tarrypin, sezee, 'en needer is you got de strenk,' sezee, en den Brer Tarrypin, he rock en rock 'long, en watch de 'lasses a bilin' en a blubberin'.

"Atter w'ile Miss Meadows, she up en say, she did, dat she'd take'n loan de young men her bed-cord, en w'iles de candy wuz a coolin' in de plates, dey could all go ter de branch en see Brer Tarrypin kyar out his projick. Brer Tarrypin," continued Uncle Remus, in a tone at once confidential and argumentative, "wer'n't much bigger'n de pa'm er my han', en it look mighty funny fer ter year 'im braggin' 'bout how he kin outpull Brer B'ar. But dey got de bed-cord atter w'ile, en den dey all put out ter de branch. W'en Brer Tarrypin fine de place he wanter, he tuck one een' er de bed-cord, en gun de yuther een' to Brer B'ar.

" 'Now den, ladies en gents,' sez Brer Tarrypin, sezee, 'you all go wid Brer B'ar up dar in de woods en I'll stay yer, en w'en you year me holler, den's de time fer Brer B'ar fer ter see ef he kin haul in de slack er de rope. You all take keer er dat ar een',' sezee, 'en I'll take keer er dish yer een',' sezee.

"Den dey all put out en lef' Brer Tarrypin at de branch, en we'n dey got good en gone, he dove down inter de water, he did, en tie de bed-cord hard en fas' ter wunner deze yer big clay-roots, en den he riz up en gin a whoop.

"Brer B'ar he wrop de bed-cord roun' his han', en wink at de gals, en wid dat he gin a big juk, but Brer Tarrypin ain't budge. Den he take bofe han's en gin a big pull, but, all de same, Brer Tarrypin ain't budge. Den he tu'n 'roun,' he did, en put de rope cross his shoulders en try ter walk off wid Brer Tarrypin, but Brer Tarrypin look like he don't feel like walkin'. Den Brer Wolf, he put in en hope Brer B'ar pull, but dez like he didn't, en den dey all hope 'im, en, bless grashus! w'iles dey wuz all a pullin', Brer Tarrypin, he holler, en ax um w'y dey don't take up de slack. Den w'en Brer Tarrypin feel um quit pullin', he dove down, he did, en ontie de rope, en by de time dey got ter de branch, Brer Tarrypin, he wuz settin' in de aidge er de water des ez natchul ez de nex' un, en he up'n say, sezee:

"'Dat las' pull er yone wuz a mighty stiff un, en a leetle mo'n you'd er had me,' sezee. 'Youer monstus stout, Brer B'ar,' sezee, 'en you pulls like a yoke er steers, but I sorter had de purchis on you,' sezee.

"Den Brer B'ar, bein's his mouf 'gun ter water atter de sweetnin', he up'n say he speck de candy's ripe, en off dey put atter it!"

"It's a wonder," said the little boy, after a while, "that the rope didn't break."

"Break who?" exclaimed Uncle Remus, with a touch of indignation in his tone. "Break who? In dem days, Miss Meadows's bed-cord would a hilt a mule."

This put an end to whatever doubts the child might have entertained.

"Hit look like ter me," said Uncle Remus, frowning, as the little boy came hopping and skipping into the old man's cabin, "dat I see a young un 'bout yo' size playin' en makin' free wid dem ar chilluns er ole Miss Favers's yistiddy, en w'en I seed dat, I drap my axe, en I come in yer en sot flat down right whar youer settin' now, en I say ter myse'f dat it's 'bout time fer ole Remus fer ter hang up en quit. Dat's des zackly w'at I say."

"Well, Uncle Remus, they called me," said the little boy, in a penitent tone. "They come and called me, and said they had a pistol and some powder over there."

"Dar now!" exclaimed the old man, indignantly. "Dar now! W'at I bin sayin'? Hit's des a born blessin' dat you wa'n't brung home on a litter wid bofe eyeballs hangin' out en one year clean gone; dat's w'at 'tis! Hit's des a born blessin'. Hit hope me up might'ly de udder day w'en I hear Miss Sally layin' down de law 'bout you en dem Favers chillun, yit, lo en beholes, de fus news I knows yer you is han'-in-glove wid um. Hit's nuff fer ter fetch ole Miss right tone at once confidential and argumentative, "wern't much bigger'n up out'n dat berryin'-groun' fum down dar in Putmon County, en w'at yo' gran'ma wouldn't er stood me en yo' ma ain't gwineter stan' nudder, en de nex' time I hear 'bout sech a come off as dis, right den en dar I'm boun' ter lay de case 'fo' Miss Sally. Dem Favers's wa'n't no 'count 'fo' de war, en dey wa'n't no 'count endurin' er de war, en dey ain't no 'count atterwards, en w'iles my head's hot you ain't gwineter go mixin' up yo'se'f wid de riff-raff er creashun."

The little boy made no further attempt to justify his conduct. He was a very wise little boy, and he knew that, in Uncle Remus's eyes, he had been guilty of a flagrant violation of the family code. Therefore, instead of attempting to justify himself, he pleaded guilty, and promised that he would never do so any more. After this there was a long period of silence, broken only by the vigorous style in which Uncle Remus puffed away at his pipe. This was the invariable result. Whenever the old man had occasion to reprimand the little boy—and the occasions were frequent—he would relapse into a dignified but stubborn silence. Presently the youngster drew forth from his pocket a long piece of candle. The sharp eyes of the old man saw it at once.

"Don't you come a tellin' me dat Miss Sally gun you dat," he exclaimed, "kaze she didn't. En I lay you hatter be monstus sly 'fo' you gotter chance fer ter snatch up dat piece er cannle."

"Well, Uncle Remus," the little boy explained, "it was lying there all by itself, and I just thought I'd fetch it out to you."

"Dat's so, honey," said Uncle Remus, greatly mollified; "dat's so, kaze by now some er dem yuther niggers 'ud er done had her light up. Dey er mighty biggity, dem house niggers is, but I notices dat dey don't let nuthin' pass. Dey goes 'long wid der han's en der mouf open, en w'at one don't ketch de tother one do."

There was another pause, and finally the little boy said:

"Uncle Remus, you know you promised to-day to tell me why the 'Possum has no hair on his tail."

"Law, honey! Ain't you done gone en fergot dat off'n yo' mine yit? Hit look like ter me," continued the old man, leisurely refilling his pipe, "dat she sorter run like dis: One time ole Brer Possum, he git so hongry, he did, dat he bleedzd fer ter have a mess er 'simmons. He monstus lazy man, ole Brer Possum wuz, but bimeby his stummuck 'gun ter growl en holler at 'im so dat he des hatter rack 'roun' en hunt up sump'n; en w'iles he wuz rackin' 'roun', who sh'd he run up wid but Brer Rabbit, en dey wuz hail-fellers, kaze Brer

Possum, he ain't bin bodder'n Brer Rabbit like dem yuther beas's. Dey sot down by de side er de big road, en dar dey jabber en confab 'mong wunner nudder, twel bimeby old Brer Possum, he take 'n tell Brer Rabbit dat he mos' pe'sh out, en Brer Rabbit, he lip up in de a'r, he did, en smack his han's tergedder, en say dat he know right whar Brer Possum kin git a bait er 'simmons. Den Brer Possum, he say whar, en Brer Rabbit, he say w'ich 'twuz over at Brer B'ar's 'simmon orchard."

"Did the Bear have a 'simmon orchard, Uncle Remus?" the little boy asked.

"Co'se, honey, kase in dem days Brer B'ar wuz a bee-hunter. He make his livin' findin' bee trees, en de way he fine um he plant 'im some 'simmon-trees, w'ich de bees dey'd come ter suck de 'simmons en den ole Brer B'ar he'd watch um whar dey'd go, en den he'd be mighty ap' fer ter come up wid um. No matter 'bout dat, de 'simmon patch 'uz dar des like I tell you, en ole Brer Possum mouf 'gun ter water soon's he year talk un um, en mos' 'fo' Brer Rabbit done tellin' 'im de news, Brer Possum, he put out, he did, en 'twa'n't long 'fo' he wuz perch up in de highes' tree in Brer B'ar 'simmon patch. But Brer Rabbit, he done 'termin' fer ter see some fun, en w'iles all dis 'uz gwine on, he run 'roun' ter Brer B'ar house, en

holler en tell 'im w'ich dey wuz somebody 'stroyin' un his 'simmons, en Brer B'ar, he hustle off fer ter ketch 'im.

"'I'll des git one mo' 'simmon en den I'll go; one 'simmon mo' en den I'll go.'

"Las' he year Brer B'ar comin' sho nuff, but 'twuz de same ole chune—'One 'simmon mo' en den I'll go'—en des 'bout dat time Brer B'ar busted inter de patch, en gin de tree a shake, en Brer Possum, he drapt out longer de yuther ripe 'simmons, but time he totch de groun' he got his foots tergedder, en he lit out fer de fence same ez a race-hoss, en 'cross dat patch him en Brer B'ar had it, en Brer B'ar gain' eve'y jump, twel time Brer Possum make de fence Brer B'ar grab 'im by de tail, en Brer Possum, he went out 'tween de rails en gin a powerful juk en pull his tail out 'twix Brer B'ar tushes; en, lo en beholes, Brer B'ar hole so tight en Brer Possum pull so hard dat all de ha'r come off in Brer B'ar's mouf, w'ich, ef Brer Rabbit hadn't er happen up wid a go'd er water. Brer B'ar'd er got strankle.

"Fum dat day ter dis," said Uncle Remus, knocking the ashes carefully out of his pipe, "Brer Possum ain't had no ha'r on his tail, en needer do his chilluns."

The next time the little boy sought Uncle Remus out, he found the old man unusually cheerful and good-humored. His rheumatism had ceased to trouble him, and he was even disposed to be boisterous. He was singing when the little boy got near the cabin, and the child paused on the outside to listen to the vigorous but mellow voice of the old man, as it rose and fell with the burden of the curiously plaintive song—a senseless affair so far as the words were concerned, but sung to a melody almost thrilling in its sweetness:

"Han' me down my walkin'-cane
    (Hey my Lily! Go down de road!),
  Yo' true lover gone down de lane
    (Hey my Lily! Go down de road!)."

The quick ear of Uncle Remus, however, had detected the presence of the little boy, and he allowed his song to run into a recitation of nonsense, of which the following, if it be rapidly spoken, will give a faint idea:

"Ole M'er Jackson, fines' confraction, fell down sta'rs fer to git satisfaction; big Bill Fray, he rule de day, eve'ything he call fer come one, two by three. Gwine 'long one day, met Johnny Huby, ax him grine nine yards er steel fer me, tole me w'ich he couldn't; den I hist 'im over Hickerson Dickerson's barn-doors; knock 'im ninety-nine miles under water, w'en he rise, he rise in Pike straddle un a hanspike, en I lef' 'im dar smokin' er de hornpipe, Juba reda seda breda. Aunt Kate at de gate; I want to eat, she fry de meat en gimme skin, w'ich I fling it back agin. Juba!"

All this, rattled off at a rapid rate and with apparent seriousness, was calculated to puzzle the little boy, and he slipped into his accustomed seat with an expression of awed bewilderment upon his face.

"Hit's all des dat away, honey," continued the old man, with the air of one who had just given an important piece of information. "En w'en you bin cas'n shadders long ez de ole nigger, den you'll fine out who's w'ich, en w'ich's who."

The little boy made no response. He was in thorough sympathy with all the whims and humors of the old man, and his capacity for enjoying them was large enough to include even those he could not understand. Uncle Remus was finishing an axe-handle, and upon these occasions it was his custom to allow the child to hold one end while he applied sand-paper to the other. These relations were pretty soon established, to the mutual satisfaction of the parties most interested, and the old man continued his remarks, but this time not at random:

"W'en I see deze yer swell-head folks like dat 'oman w'at come en tell yo' ma 'bout you chunkin' at her chilluns, w'ich yo' ma make Mars John strop you, hit make my mine run back to ole Brer B'ar. Ole Brer B'ar, he got de swell-headedness hisse'f, en ef der wuz enny swinkin', hit swunk too late fer ter he'p ole Brer B'ar. Leas'ways dat's w'at dey tells me, en I ain't never yearn it 'sputed."

"Was the bear's head sure enough swelled, Uncle Remus?"

"Now you talkin', honey!" exclaimed the old man.

"Goodness! What made it swell?"

This was Uncle Remus's cue. Applying the sand-paper to the axe-helve with gentle vigor, he began:

"One time when Brer Rabbit wuz gwine lopin' home fum a frolic w'at dey bin havin' up at Miss Meadows's, who should he happin up wid but ole Brer B'ar. Co'se, atter w'at done pass 'twix um dey wa'n't no good feelin's 'tween Brer Rabbit en ole Brer B'ar, but Brer Rabbit, he wanter save his manners, en so he holler out:

" 'Heyo, Brer B'ar! How you come on? I ain't seed you in a coon's age. How all down at yo' house? How Miss Brune en Miss Brindle?' "

"Who was that, Uncle Remus?" the little boy interrupted.

"Miss Brune en Miss Brindle? Miss Brune wuz Brer B'ar's ole 'oman, en Miss Brindle wuz his gal. Dat w'at dey call um in dem days. So den Brer Rabbit, he ax him howdy, he did, en Brer B'ar, he 'spon' dat he wuz mighty po'ly, en dey amble 'long, dey did, sorter familious like, but Brer Rabbit, he keep one eye on Brer B'ar, en Brer B'ar, he study how he gwine nab Brer Rabbit. Las' Brer Rabbit, he up'n say, sezee:

" 'Brer B'ar, I speck I got some bizness cut out fer you,' sezee.

" 'Wat dat, Brer Rabbit?' sez Brer B'ar, sezee.

" 'W'iles I wuz cleanin' up my new-groun' day 'fo' yistiddy,' sez Brer Rabbit, sezee, 'I come 'cross wunner deze yer ole time bee-trees. Hit start holler at de bottom, en stay holler plum ter de top, en de honey's des natally oozin' out, en ef you'll drap yo' 'gagements en go 'longer me,' sez Brer Rabbit, sezee, 'you'll git a bait dat'll las' you en yo' fambly twel de middle er nex' mont',' sezee.

"Brer B'ar say he much oblije en he b'leeve he'll go 'long, en wid dat dey put out fer Brer Rabbit's new-groun', w'ich twa'n't so mighty fur. Leas'ways, dey got dar atter w'ile. Ole Brer B'ar, he 'low dat he kin smell de honey. Brer Rabbit, he 'low dat he kin see de honey-koam. Brer B'ar, he 'low dat he kin hear de bees a zoonin'. Dey stan' 'roun' en talk biggity, dey did, twel bimeby Brer Rabbit, he up'n say, sezee:

" 'You do de clim'in', Brer B'ar, en I'll do de rushin' 'roun'; you clime up ter de hole, en I'll take dis yer pine pole en shove de honey up whar you kin git 'er,' sezee.

"Ole Brer B'ar, he spit on his han's en skint up de tree, en jam his head in de hole, en sho nuff, Brer Rabbit, he grab de pine pole, en de way he stir up dem bees wuz sinful—dat's w'at it wuz. Hit wuz sinful. En de bees dey swawm'd on Brer B'ar's head, twel 'fo' he could take it out'n de hole hit wuz done swell up bigger dan dat dinner-pot, en dar he swung, en ole Brer Rabbit, he dance 'roun' en sing:

" 'Tree stan' high, but honey mighty sweet—
    Watch dem bees wid stingers on der feet.'

"But dar ole Brer B'ar hung, en ef his head ain't swunk, I speck he hangin' dar yit—dat w'at I speck."

"Hit turn out one time," said Uncle Remus, grinding some crumbs of tobacco between the palms of his hands, preparatory to enjoying his usual smoke after supper—"hit turn out one time dat Brer Rabbit make so free wid de man's collard-patch dat de man he tuck'n sot a trap fer ole Brer Rabbit."

"Which man was that, Uncle Remus?" asked the little boy.

"Des a man, honey. Dat's all. Dat's all I knows—des wunner dese yer mans w'at you see trollopin 'roun' eve'y day. Nobody ain't never year w'at his name is, en ef dey did dey kep' de news mighty close fum me. Ef dish yer man is bleedzd fer ter have a name, den I'm done, kaze you'll hatter go fudder dan me. Ef you bleedzd ter know mo' dan w'at I duz, den you'll hatter hunt up some er deze yer niggers w'at's sprung up sence I commence fer ter shed my ha'r."

"Well, I just thought, Uncle Remus," said the little boy, in a tone remarkable for self-depreciation, "that the man had a name."

"Tooby sho," replied the old man, with unction, puffing away at his pipe. "Co'se. Dat w'at make I say w'at I duz. Dish yer man mout a had a name, en den ag'in he moutn't. He mout er bin name Slip-shot Sam, en he mouter bin name ole One-eye Riley, w'ich ef 'twuz hit ain't bin handed roun' ter me. But dis yer man, he in de tale, en w'at we gwine do wid 'im? Dat's de p'int, kase w'en I git ter huntin' 'roun' 'mong my 'membunce atter dish yer Mister W'atyoumay-collum's name, she ain't dar. Now den, less des call 'im Mr. Man en let 'im go at dat."

The silence of the little boy gave consent.

"One time," said Uncle Remus, carefully taking up the thread of the story where it had been dropped, "hit turn out dat Brer Rabbit bin makin' so free wid Mr. Man's greens en truck dat Mr. Man, he tuck'n sot a trap fer Brer Rabbit, en Brer Rabbit he so greedy dat he tuck'n walk right spang in it 'fo' he know hisse'f. Well, 'twa'n't long 'fo' yer come Mr. Man, broozin' 'roun', en he ain't no sooner see ole Brer Rabbit dan he smack his han's tergedder en holler out:

" 'Youer nice feller, you is! Yer you bin gobblin' up my green truck, en now you tryin' ter tote off my trap. Youer mighty nice chap—dat's w'at you is! But now dat I got you, I'll des 'bout settle wid you fer de ole en de new.'

"En wid dat, Mr. Man, he go off, he did, down in de bushes atter han'ful er switches. Ole Brer Rabbit he ain't sayin' nuthin', but he feelin' mighty lonesome, en he sot dar lookin' like eve'y minnit wuz gwineter be de nex'. En w'iles Mr. Man wuz off prepa'r'n his bresh-broom, who should come p'radin' 'long but Brer Fox? Brer Fox make a great 'miration, he did, 'bout de fix w'at he fine Brer Rabbit in, but Brer Rabbit he make like he fit ter kill hisse'f laffin', en he up'n tell Brer Fox, he did, dat Miss Meadows's fokes want 'im ter go down ter der house in 'tennunce on a weddin', en he 'low w'ich he couldn't, en dey 'low how he could, en den bimeby dey take'n tie 'im dar w'iles dey go atter de preacher, so he be dar w'en dey come back. En mo'n dat, Brer Rabbit up'n tell Brer Fox dat his chillun's mighty low wid de fever, en he bleedzd ter go atter some pills fer'm, en he ax Brer Fox fer ter take his place en go down ter Miss Meadows's en have nice time wid de gals. Brer Fox, he in fer dem kinder pranks, en 'twa'n't no time 'fo' Brer Rabbit had ole Brer Fox harness up dar in his place, en den he make like he got ter make 'as'e en git de pills fer dem sick chilluns. Brer Rabbit wa'n't mo'n out er sight 'fo' yer come Mr. Man wid a han'ful er hick'ries, but w'en he see Brer Fox tied up dar, he look like he 'stonished.

" 'Heyo!' sez Mr. Man, sezee. 'You done change color, en you done got bigger, en yo' tail done grow out. W'at kin'er w'atzyname is you, ennyhow?' sezee.

"Brer Fox, he stay still, en Mr. Man, he talk on:

"'Hit's mighty big luck,' sezee, 'ef w'en I ketch de chap w'at nibble my greens, likewise I ketch de feller w'at gnyaw my goose,' sezee, en wid dat he let inter Brer Fox wid de hick'ries, en de way he play rap-jacket wuz a caution ter de naberhood. Brer Fox, he juk en he jump, en he squeal en he squall, but Mr. Man, he shower down on 'im, he did, like fightin' a red was'-nes'."

The little boy laughed, and Uncle Remus supplemented this endorsement of his descriptive powers with a most infectious chuckle.

"Bimeby," continued the old man, "de switches, dey got frazzle out, en Mr. Man, he put out atter mo', en w'en he done got fa'rly outer yearin', Brer Rabbit, he show'd up, he did, kaze he des bin hidin' out in de bushes lis'nin' at de racket, en he 'low hit mighty funny dat Miss Meadows ain't come 'long, kaze he done bin down ter de doctor house, en dat's fudder dan de preacher, yit. Brer Rabbit make like he hurr'in' on home, but Brer Fox, he open up, he did, en he say:

"'I thank you fer ter tu'n me loose, Brer Rabbit, en I'll be 'blije,' sezee, 'kaze you done tie me up so tight dat it make my head swim, en I don't speck I'd las' fer ter git ter Miss Meadows's,' sezee.

"Brer Rabbit, he sot down sorter keerless like, en begin fer ter scratch one year like a man studyin' 'bout sump'n.

"'Dat's so, Brer Fox,' sezee, 'you duz look sorter stove up. Look like sump'n bin onkoamin' yo' ha'rs,' sezee.

"Brer Fox ain't sayin' nothin', but Brer Rabbit, he keep on talkin':

"'Dey ain't no bad feelin's 'twix' us, is dey, Brer Fox? Kaze ef dey is, I ain't got no time fer ter be tarryin' 'roun' yer.'

"Brer Fox say w'ich he don't have no onfrennelness, en with dat Brer Rabbit cut Brer Fox loose des in time fer ter hear Mr. Man w'isserlin up his dogs, en one went one way en de udder went nudder."

HOW MR. RABBIT
SUCCEEDED IN RAISING A DUST

"In dem times," said Uncle
Remus, gazing admiringly at himself in a fragment of looking-glass,
"Brer Rabbit, en Brer Fox, en Brer Coon, en dem yuther beas's
go co'tin' en sparklin' 'roun' de naberhood mo' samer dan folks.
'Twan't no 'Lemme a hoss,' ner 'Fetch me my buggy,' but dey
des up'n lit out en tote deyse'f. Dar's ole Brer Fox, he des wheel
'roun' en fetch his flank one swipe wid 'is tongue en he'd
be koam up; en Brer Rabbit, he des spit on his han' en twis' it
'roun' 'mongst de roots un his years en his ha'r'd be roach. Dey wuz
dat flirtashus," continued the old man, closing one eye at his image
in the glass, "dat Miss Meadows en de gals don't see no peace fum
one week een' ter de udder. Chuseday wuz same as Sunday, en Fri-
day wuz same as Chuseday, en hit come down ter dat pass dat w'en
Miss Meadows 'ud have chicken-fixins fer dinner, in 'ud drap Brer
Fox en Brer Possum, en w'en she'd have fried greens in 'ud pop ole
Brer Rabbit, twel 'las' Miss Meadows, she tuck'n tell de gals dat she
be dad-blame ef she gwineter keep no tavvun. So dey fix it up 'mong
deyse'f, Miss Meadows en de gals did, dat de nex' time de gents call
dey'd gin um a game. De gents, dey wuz a co'tin, but Miss Meadows,
she don't wanter marry none un um, en needer duz de gals, en likewise dey don't wanter have um pester'n 'roun'. Las', one Chuseday,
Miss Meadows, she tole um dat ef dey come down ter her house de
nex Sat'day evenin', de whole caboodle un um 'ud go down de road
a piece, whar der wuz a big flint rock, en de man w'at could take a
sludge-hammer en knock de dus' out'n dat rock, he wuz de man w'at
'ud git de pick er de gals. Dey all say dey gwine do it, but ole Brer
Rabbit, he crope off whar der wuz a cool place under some jimson
weeds, en dar he sot wukkin his mind how he gwineter git dus' out'n

dat rock. Bimeby, w'ile he wuz a settin' dar, up he jump en crack his heels tergedder en sing out:

" 'Make a bow ter de Buzzard en den ter de Crow,
  Takes a limber-toe gemmun fer ter jump Jim Crow,'

en wid dat he put out for Brer Coon house en borrer his slippers. W'en Sat'day evenin' come, dey wuz all dere. Miss Meadows en de gals, dey wuz dere; en Brer Coon, en Brer Fox, en Brer Possum, en Brer Tarrypin, dey wuz dere."

"Where was the Rabbit?" the little boy asked.

"Youk'n put yo' 'pennunce in ole Brer Rabbit," the old man replied, with a chuckle. "He wuz dere, but he shuffle up kinder late, kaze w'en Miss Meadows en de ballunce un um done gone down ter de place, Brer Rabbit, he crope 'roun' ter de ash-hopper, en fill Brer Coon slippers full er ashes, en den he tuck'n put um on en march off. He got dar atter 'w'ile, en soon's Miss Meadows en de gals seed 'im, dey up'n giggle, en make a great 'miration kaze Brer Rabbit got on slippers. Brer Fox, he so smart, he holler out, he did, en say he lay Brer Rabbit got de groun'-eatch, but Brer Rabbit, he sorter shet one eye, he did, en say, sezee:

" 'I bin so useter ridin' hoss-back, ez deze ladies knows, dat I'm gittin' sorter tender-footed;' en dey don't hear much mo' fum Brer Fox dat day, kaze he 'member how Brer Rabbit done bin en rid him; en hit 'uz des 'bout much ez Miss Meadows en de gals could do fer ter keep der snickers fum gittin' up a 'sturbance 'mong de conger-gashun. But, never mine dat, old Brer Rabbit, he wuz dar, en he so brash dat leetle mo' en he'd er grab up de sludge-hammer en er open up de racket 'fo' ennybody gun de word; but Brer Fox, he shove Brer Rabbit out'n de way en pick up de sludge hisse'f. Now den," continued the old man, with pretty much the air of one who had been the master of similar ceremonies, "de progance wuz dish yer. Eve'y

gent wer ter have th'ee licks at de rock, en de gent w'at fetch de dus' he wer de one w'at gwineter take de pick er de gals. Ole Brer Fox, he grab de sludge-hammer, he did, en he come down on de rock—*blim!* No dus' ain't come. Den he draw back en down he come ag'in—*blam!* No dus' ain't come. Den he spit in his han's, en give 'er a big swing en down she come—*ker-blap!* En yit no dus' ain't flew'd. Den Brer Possum he make triul, en Brer Coon, en all de ballunce un um 'cep' Brer Tarrypin, en he 'low dat he got a crick in his neck. Den Brer Rabbit, he grab holt er de sludge, en he lipt up in de a'r en come down on de rock all at de same time—*pow!*—en de ashes, dey flew'd up so, dey did, dat Brer Fox, he tuck'n had a sneezin' spell, en Miss Meadows en de gals dey up'n koff. Th'ee times Brer Rabbit jump up en crack his heels tergedder en come down wid de sludge-hammer—*ker-blam!*—en eve'y time he jump up, he holler out:

"'Stan' fudder, ladies! Yer come de dus' l' en sho nuff, de dus' come.

"Leas'ways," continued Uncle Remus, "Brer Rabbit got one er de gals, en dey had a weddin' en a big infa'r."

"Which of the girls did the Rabbit marry?" asked the little boy, dubiously.

"I did year tell un 'er name," replied the old man, with a great affectation of interest, "but look like I done gone en fergit it off'n my mine. Ef I don't disremember," he continued, "hit wuz Miss Molly Cottontail, en I speck we better let it go at dat."

The next time the little boy got permission to call upon Uncle Remus, the old man was sitting in his door, with his elbows on his knees and his face buried in his hands, and he appeared to be in great trouble.

"What's the matter, Uncle Remus?" the youngster asked.

"Nuff de matter, honey—mo' dan dey's enny kyo fer. Ef dey ain't some quare gwines on 'roun' dis place I ain't name Remus."

The serious tone of the old man caused the little boy to open his eyes. The moon, just at its full, cast long, vague, wavering shadows in front of the cabin. A colony of tree-frogs somewhere in the distance were treating their neighbors to a serenade, but to the little boy it sounded like a chorus of lost and long-forgotten whistlers. The sound was wherever the imagination chose to locate it—to the right, to the left, in the air, on the ground, far away or near at hand, but always dim and always indistinct. Something in Uncle Remus's tone exactly fitted all these surroundings, and the child nestled closer to the old man.

"Yasser," continued Uncle Remus, with an ominous sigh and a mysterious shake of the head, "ef dey ain't some quare gwines on in dish yer naberhood, den I'm de ballheadest creetur 'twix' dis en nex' Jinawerry wus a year 'go, w'ich I knows I ain't. Dat's what."

"What is it, Uncle Remus?"

"I know Mars John bin drivin' Cholly sorter hard terday, en I say ter myse'f dat I'd drap 'roun' 'bout dus' en fling nudder year er corn in de troff en kinder gin 'im a techin' up wid de kurrier-koam; en bless grashus! I ain't bin in de lot mo'n a minnit 'fo' I seed sump'n wuz wrong wid de hoss, and sho' nuff dar wuz his mane full er witch-stirrups."

"Full of what, Uncle Remus?"

"Full er witch-stirrups, honey. Ain't you seed no witch-stirrups? Well, w'en you see two stran' er ha'r tied tergedder in a hoss' mane, dar you see a witch-stirrup, en, mo'n dat, dat hoss done bin rid by um."

"Do you reckon they have been riding Charley?" inquired the little boy.

"Co'se, honey. Tooby sho dey is. W'at else dey bin doin'?"

"Did you ever see a witch, Uncle Remus?"

"Dat ain't needer yer ner dar. W'en I see coon track in de branch, I know de coon bin 'long dar."

The argument seemed unanswerable, and the little boy asked, in a confidential tone:

"Uncle Remus, what are witches like?"

"Dey comes diffunt," responded the cautious old darkey. "Dey comes en dey cunjus fokes. Squinch-owl holler eve'y time he see a witch, en w'en you hear de dog howlin' in de middle er de night, one un um's mighty ap' ter be prowlin' 'roun'. Cunjun fokes kin tell a witch de minnit dey lays der eyes on it, but dem w'at ain't cunjun, hit's mighty hard ter tell w'en dey see one, kase dey might come in de 'pearunce un a cow en all kinder beas's. I ain't bin useter no cunjun myse'f, but I bin livin' long nuff fer ter know w'en you meets up wid a big black cat in de middle er de road, wid yaller eyeballs, dars yo' witch fresh fum de Ole Boy. En, fuddermo', I know dat 'tain't proned inter no dogs fer ter ketch de rabbit w'at use in a berryin'-groun'. Dey er de mos' ongodlies' creeturs w'at you ever laid eyes on," continued Uncle Remus, with unction. "Down dar in Putmon County yo' Unk Jeems, he make like he gwineter ketch wunner dem dar graveyard rabbits. Sho nuff, out he goes, en de dogs ain't no mo'n got ter de place fo' up jump de ole rabbit right 'mong um, en atter runnin' 'roun' a time or two, she skip right up ter Mars Jeems, en Mars Jeems, he des put de gun-bairl right on 'er en lammed aloose. Hit tored up de groun' all 'roun', en de dogs, dey rush up, but dey wan't no rabbit dar; but bimeby Mars Jeems, he seed de dogs tuckin' der tails 'tween der legs, en he look up, en dar wuz de rabbit caperin' 'roun' on a toomstone, en wid dat Mars Jeems say he sorter feel like de time done come w'en yo' gran'ma was 'specktin' un him home, en he call off de dogs en put out. But dem wuz ha'nts. Witches is deze yer kinder fokes w'at kin drap der body en change inter a cat en a wolf en all kinder creeturs."

"Papa says there ain't any witches," the little boy interrupted.

"Mars John ain't live long ez I is," said Uncle Remus, by way of comment. "He ain't bin broozin' 'roun' all hours er de night en day. I know'd a nigger w'ich his brer wuz a witch, kaze he up'n tole me how he tuck'n kyo'd 'im; en he kyo'd 'im good, mon."

"How was that?" inquired the little boy.

"Hit seem like," continued Uncle Remus, "dat witch fokes is got a slit in de back er de neck, en w'en dey wanter change derse'f, dey des pull de hide over der head same ez if 'twuz a shut, en dar dey is."

"Do they get out of their skins?" asked the little boy, in an awed tone.

"Tooby sho, honey. You see yo' pa pull his shut off? Well, dat des 'zackly de way dey duz. But dish yere nigger w'at I'm tellin' you 'bout, he kyo'd his brer de ve'y fus pass he made at him. Hit got so dat fokes in de settlement didn't have no peace. De chilluns 'ud wake up in de mawnins wid der ha'r tangle up, en wid scratches on um like dey bin thoo a brier-patch, twel bimeby one day de nigger he 'low dat he'd set up dat night en keep one eye on his brer; en sho' nuff dat night, des ez de chickens wuz crowin' fer twelve, up jump de brer an pull off his skin en sail out'n de house in de shape un a bat, en w'at duz de nigger do but grab up de hide, en turn it wrongsud-out'ards en sprinkle it wid salt. Den he lay down en watch fer ter see w'at de news wuz gwineter be. Des 'fo' day yer come a big black cat in de do', en de nigger git up, he did, en druv her away. Bimeby, yer come a big black dog snuffin' roun', en de nigger up wid a chunk en lammed 'im side er de head. Den a squinch-owl lit on de koam er de house, en de nigger jam de shovel in de fier en make 'im flew away. Las', yer come a great big black wolf wid his eyes shinin' like fier coals, en he grab de hide and rush out. 'Twa'n't long 'fo' de nigger year his brer holler'n en squallin', en he tuck a light, he did, en went out, en dar wuz his brer des a waller'n on de groun' en squirmin' 'roun', kaze de salt on de skin wuz stingin' wuss'n ef he had his britches lineded wid yaller-jackets. By nex' mawnin' he got so he could sorter shuffle 'long, but he gun up cunjun, en ef dere wuz enny mo' witches in dat settlement dey kep' mighty close, en dat nigger he ain't skunt hisse'f no mo' not endurin' er my 'membunce."

The result of this was that Uncle Remus had to take the little boy by the hand and go with him to the "big house," which the old man was not loath to do; and, when the child went to bed, he lay awake a long time expecting an unseemly visitation from some mysterious source. It soothed him, however, to hear the strong, musical voice of his sable patron, not very far away, tenderly contending with a lusty tune; and to this accompaniment the little boy dropped asleep:

"Hit's eighteen hunder'd, forty-en-eight,
  Christ done made dat crooked way straight—
    En I don't wanter stay here no longer;
  Hit's eighteen hunder'd, forty-en-nine,
  Christ done turn dat water inter wine—
    En I don't wanter stay here no longer;

"JACKY-MY-LANTERN" [1]

Upon his next visit to Uncle Remus, the little boy was exceedingly anxious to know more about witches, but the old man prudently refrained from exciting the youngster's imagination any further in that direction. Uncle Remus had a board across his lap, and, armed with a mallet and a shoe-knife, was engaged in making shoe-pegs.

"W'iles I wuz crossin' de branch des now," he said, endeavoring to change the subject. "I come up wid a Jacky-my-lantern, en she wuz bu'nin' wuss'n a bunch er lightnin'-bugs, mon. I know'd she wuz a fixin' fer ter lead me inter dat quogmire down in de swamp, en I steer'd cle'r un 'er. Yasser. I did dat. You ain't never seed no Jacky-my-lantuns, is you, honey?"

The little boy never had, but he had heard of them, and he wanted to know what they were, and thereupon Uncle Remus proceeded to tell him.

"One time," said the old darkey, transferring his spectacles from his nose to the top of his head and leaning his elbows upon his peg-board, "dere wuz a blacksmif man, en dish yer blacksmif man, he tuck'n stuck closer by his dram dan he did by his bellus. Monday mawnin' he'd git on a spree, en all dat week he'd be on a spree, en de nex' Monday mawnin' he'd take a fresh start. Bimeby, one day, atter de blacksmif bin spreein' 'roun' en cussin' might'ly, he hear a sorter rustlin' fuss at de do', en in walk de Bad Man."

"Who, Uncle Remus?" the little boy asked.

[1] This story is popular on the coast and among the rice-plantations, and, since the publication of some of the animal-myths in the newspapers, I have received a version of it from a planter in southwest Georgia; but it seems to me to be an intruder among the genuine myth-stories of the Negroes. It is a trifle too elaborate. Nevertheless, it is told upon the plantations with great gusto, and there are several versions in circulation.

"De Bad Man, honey; de Ole Boy hisse'f right fresh from de ridjun w'at you year Miss Sally readin' 'bout. He done hide his hawns, en his tail en his hoof, en he come dress up like w'ite fokes. He tuck off his hat en he bow, en den he tell de blacksmif who he is, en dat he done come atter 'im. Den de blacksmif, he gun ter cry en beg, en he beg so hard en he cry so loud dat de Bad Man say he make a trade wid 'im. At de een' er one year de sperit er de blacksmif wuz to be his'n, en endurin' er dat time de blacksmif mus' put in his hottes' licks in de intruss er de Bad Man, en den he put a spell on de cheer de blacksmif was settin' in, en on his sludge-hammer. De man w'at sot in de cheer couldn't git up less'n de blacksmif let 'im, en de man w'at pick up de sludge 'ud hatter keep on knockin' wid it twel de blacksmif say quit; en den he gun 'im money plenty, en off he put.

"De blacksmif, he sail in fer ter have his fun, en he have so much dat he done clean forgot 'bout his contrack, but bimeby, one day he look down de road, en dar he see de Bad Man comin', en den he know'd de year wuz out. W'en de Bad Man got in de do', de blacksmif wuz poundin' 'way at a hoss-shoe, but he wa'n't so bizzy dat he didn't ax 'im in. De Bad Man sorter do like he ain't got no time fer ter tarry, but de blacksmif say he got some little jobs dat he bleedzd ter finish up, en den he ax de Bad Man fer ter set down a minnit; en de Bad Man, he tuck'n sot down, en he sot in dat cheer w'at he done conju'd, en, co'se, dar he wuz. Den de blacksmif, he 'gun ter poke fun at de Bad Man, en he ax him don't he want a dram, en won't he hitch his cheer up little nigher de fier, en de Bad Man he beg en he beg, but 'twan't doin' no good, kase de blacksmif 'low dat he gwineter keep 'im dar twel he promus dat he let 'im off one year mo', en, sho nuff, de Bad Man promus dat ef de blacksmif let 'im up he give 'im a n'er showin'. So den de blacksmif gun de wud, en de Bad Man sa'nter off down de big road, settin' traps en layin' his progance fer ter ketch mo' sinners.

"De nex' year hit pass same like t'er one. At de 'p'inted time yer come de Ole Boy atter de blacksmif, but still de blacksmif had some jobs dat he bleedzd ter finish up, en he ax de Bad Man fer ter take holt er de sludge en he'p 'im out; en de Bad Man, he 'low dat r'er'n be disperlite, he don't keer ef he do hit 'er a biff er two; en wid dat he grab up de sludge, en dar he wuz 'gin, kase he done conju'd de sludge so dat whosomedever tuck 'er up can't put 'er down less'n de blacksmif say de wud. Dey perlaver'd dar, dey did, twel bimeby de Bad Man he up'n let 'im off n'er year.

"Well, den, dat year pass same ez t'er one. Mont' in en mont' out dat man wuz rollin' in dram, en bimeby yer come de Bad Man. De blacksmif cry en he holler, en he rip 'roun' en t'ar his ha'r, but hit des like he didn't, kase de Bad Man grab 'im up en cram 'im in a bag en tote 'im off. W'iles dey wuz gwine 'long dey come up wid a passel er fokes w'at wuz havin' wunner deze yer fote er July bobby-cues, en de Ole Boy, he 'low dat maybe he kin git some mo' game, en w'at do he do but jine in wid um. He jines in en he talk politics same like t'er fokes, twel bimeby dinnertime come 'roun', en dey ax 'im up, w'ich 'greed wid his stummuck, en he pozzit his bag underneed de table 'longside de udder bags w'at de hongry fokes'd brung.

"No sooner did de blacksmif git back on de groun' dan he 'gun ter wuk his way outer de bag. He crope out, he did, en den he tuck'n change de bag. He tuck'n tuck a n'er bag en lay it down whar dish yer bag wuz, en den he crope outer de crowd en lay low in de under-bresh.

"Las', w'en de time come fer ter go, de Ole Boy up wid his bag en slung her on his shoulder, en off he put fer de Bad Place. W'en he got dar he tuck'n drap de bag off'n his back an call up de imps, en dey des come a squallin' en a caperin', w'ich I speck dey mus' a bin hongry. Leas'ways dey des swawm'd 'roun', hollerin out:

" 'Daddy, w'at you brung—daddy, w'at you brung?'

"So den dey open de bag, en lo en beholes, out jump a big bull-dog, en de way he shuck dem little imps wuz a caution, en he kep' on gnyawin' un um twel de Ole Boy open de gate en tu'n 'im out."

"And what became of the blacksmith?" the little boy asked, as Uncle Remus paused to snuff the candle with his fingers.

"I'm drivin' on 'roun', honey. Atter 'long time, de blacksmif he tuck'n die, en w'en he go ter de Good Place de man at de gate dunner who he is, en he can't squeeze in. Den he go down ter de Bad Place, en knock. De Ole Boy, he look out, he did, en he know'd de black-smif de minnit he laid eyes on 'im; but he shake his head en say, sezee:

" 'You'll hatter skuze me, Brer Blacksmif, kase I dun had 'speunce 'longer you. You'll hatter go some'rs else ef you wanter raise enny racket,' sezee, en wid dat he shet de do'.

"En dey do say," continued Uncle Remus, with unction, "dat sence dat day de blacksmif bin sorter huv'rin' 'roun' 'twix' de heavens en de ye'th, en dark nights he shine out so fokes call 'im Jacky-my-lantun. Dat's w'at dey tells me. Hit may be wrong er't may be right, but dat's w'at I years."

One night, while the little boy was watching Uncle Remus twisting and waxing some shoe-thread, he made what appeared to him to be a very curious discovery. He discovered that the palms of the old man's hands were as white as his own, and the fact was such a source of wonder that he at last made it the subject of remark. The response of Uncle Remus led to the earnest recital of a piece of unwritten history that must prove interesting to ethnologists.

"Tooby sho de pa'm er my han's w'ite, honey," he quietly remarked; "en, w'en it come ter dat, dey wuz a time w'en all de w'ite fokes 'uz black—blacker dan me, kaze I done bin yer so long dat I bin sorter bleach out."

The little boy laughed. He thought Uncle Remus was making him the victim of one of his jokes; but the youngster was never more mistaken. The old man was serious. Nevertheless, he failed to rebuke the ill-timed mirth of the child, appearing to be altogether engrossed in his work. After a while he resumed:

"Yasser. Fokes dunner w'at bin yit, let 'lone w'at gwinter be. Niggers is niggers now, but de time wuz w'en we 'uz all niggers tergedder."

"When was that, Uncle Remus?"

"Way back yander. In dem times we 'uz all un us black; we 'uz all niggers tergedder, en 'cordin' ter all de 'counts w'at I years fokes 'uz gittin 'long 'bout ez well in dem days ez dey is now. But atter 'w'ile de news come dat dere wuz a pon' er water some'rs in de naberhood, w'ich ef dey'd git inter dey'd be wash off nice en w'ite, en den one un um, he fine de place en make er splunge inter de pon', en come out w'ite ez a town gal. En den, bless grashus! w'en de fokes seed it, dey make a break fer de pon', en dem w'at wuz de

135

soopless, dey got in fus' en dey come out w'ite; en dem w'at wuz de nex' soopless, dey got in nex', en dey come out merlatters; en dey wuz sech a crowd un um dat dey mighty nigh use de water up, w'ich w'en dem yuthers come 'long, de morest dey could do wuz ter paddle about wid der foots en dabble in it wid der han's. Dem wuz de niggers, en down ter dis day dey ain't no w'ite 'bout a nigger 'ceppin de pa'ms er der han's en de soles er der foot."

The little boy seemed to be very much interested in this new account of the origin of races, and he made some further inquiries, which elicited from Uncle Remus the following additional particulars:

"De Injun en de Chinee got ter be 'counted 'long er de merlatter. I ain't seed no Chinee dat I knows un, but dey tells me dey er sorter 'twix' a brown en a brindle. Dey er all merlatters."

"But mamma says the Chinese have straight hair," the little boy suggested.

"Co'se, honey," the old man unhesitatingly responded, "dem w'at git ter de pon' time nuff fer ter git der head in de water, de water hit onkink der ha'r. Hit bleedzd ter be dat away."

MR. FOX AND MISS GOOSE

It had been raining all day so that Uncle Remus found it impossible to go out. The storm had begun, the old man declared, just as the chickens were crowing for day, and it had continued almost without intermission. The dark gray clouds had blotted out the sun, and the leafless limbs of the tall oaks surrendered themselves drearily to the fantastic gusts that drove the drizzle fitfully before them. The lady to whom Uncle Remus belonged had been thoughtful of the old man, and 'Tildy, the housegirl, had been commissioned to carry him his meals. This arrangement came to the knowledge of the little boy at supper time, and he lost no time in obtaining permission to accompany 'Tildy.

Uncle Remus made a great demonstration over the thoughtful kindness of his "Miss Sally."

"Ef she aint one blessid w'ite 'oman," he said, in his simple, fervent way, "den dey aint none un um 'roun' in deze parts."

With that he addressed himself to the supper, while the little boy sat by and eyed him with that familiar curiosity common to children. Finally the youngster disturbed the old man with an inquiry:

"Uncle Remus, do geese stand on one leg all night, or do they sit down to sleep?"

"Tooby sho' dey does, honey; dey sets down same ez you does. Co'se, dey don't cross der legs," he added, cautiously, "kase dey sets down right flat-footed."

"Well, I saw one the other day, and he was standing on one foot, and I watched him and watched him, and he kept on standing there."

"Ez ter dat," responded Uncle Remus, "dey mought stan' on one foot an' drap off ter sleep en fergit deyse'f. Deze yer gooses," he continued, wiping the crumbs from his beard with his coat-tail, "is

mighty kuse fowls; deyer mighty kuse. In ole times dey wuz 'mongs
de big-bugs, en in dem days, w'en ole Miss Goose gun a-dinin', all de
quality wuz dere. Likewise, en needer wuz dey stuck-up, kase wid
all der kyar'n's on, Miss Goose wer'n't too proud fer ter take in
washin' fer de neighborhoods, en she make money, en get slick en
fat lak Sis Tempy.

"Dis de way marters stan' w'en one day Brer Fox en Brer Rabbit,
dey wuz settin' up at de cotton-patch, one on one side de fence, en
t'er one on t'er side, gwine on wid one er n'er, w'en fus' news dey
know, dey year sump'n—*blim, blim, blim!*

"Brer Fox, he ax w'at dat fuss is, en Brer Rabbit, he up'n 'spon'
dat it's ole Miss Goose down at de spring. Den Brer Fox, he up'n ax
w'at she doin', en Brer Rabbit, he say, sezee, dat she battlin' cloze."

"Battling clothes, Uncle Remus?" said the little boy.

"Dat w'at dey call it dem days, honey. Deze times, dey rubs cloze
on deze yer bodes w'at got furrers in um, but dem days dey des tuck'n
tuck de cloze en lay um out on a bench, en ketch holt er de battlin'-
stick en natally paddle de fillin' outen um.

"W'en Brer Fox year dat ole Miss Goose wuz down dar dabblin' in
soapsuds en washin' cloze, he sorter lick he chops, en 'low dat some
er dese odd-come-shorts he gwine ter call en pay he 'specks. De
minnit he say dat, Brer Rabbit, he know sump'n' 'uz up, en he 'low
ter hisse'f dat he 'speck he better whirl in en have some fun w'iles it
gwine on. Bimeby Brer Fox up'n say ter Brer Rabbit dat he bleedzd
ter be movin' 'long todes home, en wid dat dey bofe say good-bye.

"Brer Fox, he put out ter whar his fambly wuz, but Brer Rabbit,
he slip 'roun', he did, en call on ole Miss Goose. Ole Miss Goose
she wuz down at de spring, washin', en b'ilin', en battlin' cloze; but
Brer Rabbit he march up en ax her howdy, en den she tuck'n ax
Brer Rabbit howdy.

"'I'd shake han's 'long wid you, Brer Rabbit,' sez she, 'but dey er all full er suds,' sez she.

"'No marter 'bout dat, Miss Goose,' sez Brer Rabbit, sezee, 'so long ez yo' will's good,' sezee."

"A goose with hands, Uncle Remus!" the little boy exclaimed.

"How you know goose aint got han's?" Uncle Remus inquired, with a frown. "Is you been sleepin' longer ole man Know-All? Little mo' en you'll up'n stan' me down dat snakes aint got no foots, and yit you take en lay a snake down yer 'fo' de fier, en his foots 'll come out right 'fo' yo' eyes."

Uncle Remus paused here, but presently continued:

"Atter ole Miss Goose en Brer Rabbit done pass de time er day wid one er ne'r, Brer Rabbit, he ax 'er, he did, how she come on deze days, en Miss Goose say, mighty po'ly.

"'I'm gittin' stiff en I'm gittin' clumpsy,' sez she, 'en mo'n dat I'm gittin' bline,' sez she. 'Des 'fo' you happen 'long, Brer Rabbit, I drap my specks in de tub yer, en ef you'd 'a' come 'long 'bout dat time,' sez ole Miss Goose, sez she, 'I lay I'd er tuck you for dat nasty, owdashus Brer Fox, en it ud er bin a born blessin' ef I had n't er scald you wid er pan er b'ilin' suds,' sez she. 'I'm dat glad I foun' my specks I dunner w'at ter do,' sez ole Miss Goose, sez she.

"Den Brer Rabbit, he up'n say dat bein's how Sis Goose done fotch up Brer Fox name, he got sump'n' fer ter tell 'er, en den he let out 'bout Brer Fox gwine ter call on 'er.

"'He comin',' sez Brer Rabbit, sezee; 'he comin' sho', en w'en he come hit'll be des 'fo' day,' sezee.

"Wid dat, ole Miss Goose wipe 'er han's on 'er apun, en put 'er specks up on 'er forrerd, en look lak she done got trouble in 'er mine.

"'Laws-a-massy!' sez she. 'Spozen he come, Brer Rabbit! W'at I gwine do? En dey aint a man 'bout de house, n'er,' sez she.

"Den Brer Rabbit, he shot one eye, en he say, sezee:

"'Sis Goose, de time done come w'en you bleedzd ter roos' high. You look lak you got de dropsy,' sezee, 'but don't mine dat, kase ef you don't roos' high, youer goner,' sezee.

"Den ole Miss Goose ax Brer Rabbit w'at she gwine do, en Brer Rabbit he up en tell Miss Goose dat she mus' go home en tie up a bundle er de w'ite fokes' cloze, en put um on de bed, en den she mus' fly up on a rafter, en let Brer Fox grab de cloze en run off wid um.

"Ole Miss Goose say she much 'blige, en she tuck'n tuck her things en waddle off home, en dat night she do lak Brer Rabbit say wid de bundle er cloze, en den she sont wud ter Mr. Dog, en Mr. Dog he come down, en say he'd sorter set up wid 'er.

"Des 'fo' day, yer come Brer Fox creepin' up, en he went en push on de do' easy, en de do' open, en he see sump'n' w'ite on de bed w'ich he took fer Miss Goose, en he grab it en run. 'Bout dat time Mr. Dog sail out fum und' de house, he did, en ef Brer Fox had n't er drapt de cloze, he'd er got kotch. Fum dat, wud went 'roun' dat Brer Fox bin tryin' ter steal Miss Goose cloze, en he come mighty nigh losin' his stannin' at Miss Meadows. Down ter dis day," Uncle Remus continued, preparing to fill his pipe, "Brer Fox b'leeve dat Brer Rabbit wuz de 'casion er Mr. Dog bein' in de neighborhoods at dat time er night, en Brer Rabbit aint 'spute it. De bad feelin' 'twix' Brer Fox en Mr. Dog start right dar, en hits bin agwine on twel now dey aint git in smellin' distuns er one er n'er widout dey's a row."

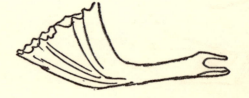

There was a pause after the story of old Miss Goose. The culmination was hardly sensational enough to win the hearty applause of the little boy, and this fact appeared to have a depressing influence upon Uncle Remus. As he leaned slightly forward, gazing into the depths of the great fireplace, his attitude was one of pensiveness.

"I 'speck I done wo' out my welcome up at de big house," he said, after a while. "I mos' knows I is," he continued, setting himself resignedly in his deep-bottomed chair. "Kase de las' time I uz up dar, I had my eye on Miss Sally mighty nigh de whole blessid time, en w'en you see Miss Sally rustlin' 'roun' makin' lak she fixin' things up dar on de mantle-shelf, en bouncin' de cheers 'roun', en breshin' dus' whar dey aint no dus', en flyin' 'roun' singin' sorter louder dan common, den I des knows sump'n' done gone en rile 'er."

"Why, Uncle Remus!" exclaimed the little boy. "Mamma was just glad because I was feeling so good."

"Mought er bin," the old man remarked, in a tone that was far from implying conviction. "Ef 't wa'n't dat, den she wuz gittin' tired er seein' me lounjun' 'roun' up dar night atter night, en ef 't wa'n't dat, den she wuz watchin' a chance fer ter preach ter yo' pa. Oh, I done bin know Miss Sally long fo' yo' pa is!" exclaimed Uncle Remus, in response to the astonishment depicted upon the child's face. "I bin knowin' 'er sence she wuz so high, en endurin' er all dat time I aint seed no mo' up'n spoken w'ite 'oman dan w'at Miss Sally is.

"But dat aint needer yer ner dar. You done got so youk'n rush down yer des like you useter, en we kin set yer en smoke, en tell tales, en study up 'musements same like we wuz gwine on 'fo' you got dat splinter in yo' foot.

"I mines me er one time"—with an infectious laugh—"w'en ole Brer Rabbit got Brer Fox in de wuss trubble w'at a man wuz mos' ever got in yit, en dat 'uz w'en he fool 'im 'bout de hoss. Aint I never tell you 'bout dat? But no marter ef I is. Hoe-cake aint cook done good twel hit's turnt over a couple er times.

"Well, atter Brer Fox done git rested fum keepin' out er de way er Mr. Dog, en sorter ketch up wid his rations, he say ter hisse'f dat he be dog his cats ef he don't slorate ole Brer Rabbit ef it take 'im a mont'; en dat, too, on top er all de 'spe'unce w'at he done bin had wid um. Brer Rabbit he sorter git win' er dis, en one day, w'iles he gwine 'long de road studyin' how he gwineter hol' he hand wid Brer Fox, he see a great big Hoss layin' stretch out flat on he side in de pastur'; en he tuck'n crope up, he did, fer ter see ef dish yer Hoss done gone en die. He crope up en he crope 'roun', en bimeby he see de Hoss switch he tail, en den Brer Rabbit know he aint dead. Wid dat, Brer Rabbit lope back ter de big road, en mos' de fus' man w'at he see gwine on by wuz Brer Fox, en Brer Rabbit he tuck atter 'im, en holler:

" 'Brer Fox! O Brer Fox! Come back! I got some good news fer you. Come back, Brer Fox,' sezee.

"Brer Fox, he tu'n 'roun', he did, en w'en he see who callin' 'im, he come gallopin' back, kaze it seem like dat des ez gooder time ez any fer ter nab Brer Rabbit; but 'fo' he git in nabbin' distance, Brer Rabbit he up'n say, sezee:

" 'Come on, Brer Fox! I done fine de place whar you kin lay in fresh meat 'nuff ter las' you plum twel de middle er nex' year,' sezee.

"Brer Fox, he ax wharbouts, en Brer Rabbit, he say, right over dar in de pastur', en Brer Fox ax w'at is it, en Brer Rabbit, he say w'ich 'twuz a whole Hoss layin' down on de groun' whar dey kin ketch 'im en tie 'im. Wid dat, Brer Fox, he say come on, en off dey put.

"W'en dey got dar, sho' nuff, dar lay de Hoss all stretch out in de sun, fas' 'sleep, en den Brer Fox en Brer Rabbit, dey had a 'spute 'bout how dey gwine ter fix de Hoss so he can't git loose. One say one way en de yuther say n'er way, en dar dey had it, twel atter w'ile Brer Rabbit, he say, sezee:

" 'De onliest plan w'at I knows un, Brer Fox,' sezee, 'is fer you ter git down dar en lemme tie you ter de Hoss tail, en den, w'en he try ter git up, you kin hol' 'im down,' sezee. 'Ef I wuz big man like w'at you is,' sez Brer Rabbit, sezee, 'you mought tie me ter dat Hoss' tail, en ef I aint hol' 'im down, den Joe's dead en Sal's a widder. I des knows you kin hol' 'im down," sez Brer Rabbit, sezee, 'but yit, ef you 'feared, we des better drap dat idee en study out some yuther plan,' sezee.

"Brer Fox sorter jubus 'bout dis, but he bleedzd ter play biggity 'fo' Brer Rabbit, en he tuck'n 'gree ter de progrance, en den Brer Rabbit, he tuck'n tie Brer Fox ter de Hoss' tail, en atter he git 'im tie dar hard en fas', he sorter step back, he did, en put he han's 'kimbo, en grin, en den he say, sezee:

" 'Ef ever dey wuz a Hoss kotch, den we done kotch dis un. Look sorter lak we done put de bridle on de wrong een',' sezee, 'but I lay Brer Fox is got de strenk fer ter hol' 'im,' sezee.

"Wid dat, Brer Rabbit cut 'im a long switch en trim it up, en w'en he get it fix, up he step en hit de Hoss a rap—*pow!* De Hoss 'uz dat s'prise at dat kinder doin's dat he make one jump, en lan' on he foots. W'en he do dat, dar wuz Brer Fox danglin' in de a'r, en Brer Rabbit, he dart out de way en holler:

" 'Hol' 'im down, Brer Fox! Hol' 'im down! I'll stan' out yer en see fa'r play. Hol' 'im down, Brer Fox! Hol' 'im down!'

"Co'se, w'en de Hoss feel Brer Fox hangin' dar onter he tail, he thunk sump'n' kuse de marter, en dis make 'im jump en r'ar wusser en wusser, en he shake up Brer Fox same like he wuz a rag in de win', en Brer Rabbit, he jump en holler:

"'Hol' 'im down, Brer Fox! Hol' 'im down! You got 'im now, sho'! Hol' yo' grip, en hol' 'im down,' sezee.

"De Hoss, he jump en he hump, en he rip en he r'ar, en he snort en he t'ar. But yit Brer Fox hang on, en still Brer Rabbit skip 'roun' en holler:

"'Hol' 'im down, Brer Fox! You got 'im whar he can't needer back ner squall. Hol' 'im down, Brer Fox!' sezee.

"Bimeby, w'en Brer Fox git chance, he holler back, he did:

"'How in de name er goodness I gwine ter hol' de Hoss down 'less I git my claw in de groun'?'

"Den Brer Rabbit, he stan' back little furder en holler little louder:

"'Hol' 'im down, Brer Fox! Hol' 'im down! You got 'im now, sho'! Hol' 'im down!'

"Bimeby de Hoss 'gun ter kick wid he behime legs, en de fus' news you know, he fetch Brer Fox a lick in de stomach dat fa'rly make 'im squall, en den he kick 'im ag'in, en dis time he break Brer Fox loose, en sont 'im a-whirlin'; en Brer Rabbit, he keep on a-jumpin' 'roun' en hollerin':

"'Hol' 'im down, Brer Fox!'"

"Did the fox get killed, Uncle Remus?" asked the little boy.

"He wa'n't 'zackly kilt, honey," replied the old man, "but he wuz de nex' do' ter 't. He 'uz all broke up, en w'iles he 'uz gittin' well, hit sorter come 'cross he min' dat Brer Rabbit done play n'er game on 'im."

"What did Brother Rabbit do after that?" the little boy asked presently.

"Now, den, you don't wanter push ole Brer Rabbit too close," replied Uncle Remus significantly. "He mighty tender-footed creetur, en de mo' w'at you push 'im, de furder he lef' you."

There was prolonged silence in the old man's cabin, until, seeing that the little boy was growing restless enough to cast several curious glances in the direction of the toolchest in the corner, Uncle Remus lifted one leg over the other, scratched his head reflectively, and began:

"One time, atter Brer Rabbit done bin trompin' 'roun' huntin' up some sallid fer ter make out he dinner wid, he fine hisse'f in de neighborhoods er Mr. Man house, en he pass 'long twel he come ter de gyardin-gate, en nigh de gyardin-gate he see Little Gal playin' 'roun' in de san'. W'en Brer Rabbit look 'twix' de gyardin-palin's en see de colluds, en de sparrer-grass, en de yuther gyardin truck growin' dar, hit make he mouf water. Den he take en walk up ter de Little Gal, Brer Rabbit did, en pull he roach,[1] en bow, en scrape he foot, en talk mighty nice en slick.

" 'Howdy, Little Gal,' sez Brer Rabbit, sezee; 'how you come on?' sezee.

"Den de Little Gal, she 'spon' howdy, she did, en she ax Brer Rabbit how he come on, en Brer Rabbit, he 'low he mighty po'ly, en den he ax ef dis de Little Gal w'at 'er pa live up dar in de big w'ite house, w'ich de Little Gal, she up'n say 'twer'. Brer Rabbit, he say he mighty glad, kaze he des bin up dar fer to see 'er pa, en he say dat 'er pa, he sont 'im out dar fer ter tell de Little Gal dat she mus' open de gyardin-gate so Brer Rabbit kin go in en git some truck. Den de

[1] Topknot, foretop.

Little Gal, she jump 'roun', she did, en she open de gate, en wid dat, Brer Rabbit, he hop in, he did, en got 'im a mess er greens, en hop out ag'in, en w'en he gwine off he make a bow, he did, en tell de Little Gal dat he much 'blije', en den atter dat he put out fer home.

"Nex' day, Brer Rabbit, he hide out, he did, twel he see de Little Gal come out ter play, en den he put up de same tale, en walk off wid a n'er mess er truck, en hit keep on dis a-way, twel bimeby Mr. Man, he 'gun ter miss his greens, en he keep on a-missin' un um, twel he got ter excusin' eve'ybody on de place er 'stroyin' un um, en w'en dat come ter pass, de Little Gal, she up'n say:

"'My goodness, pa!' sez she. 'You done tole Mr. Rabbit fer ter come and make me let 'im in de gyardin atter some greens, en aint he done come en ax me, en aint I done gone en let 'im in?' sez she.

"Mr. Man aint hatter study long 'fo' he see how de lan' lay, en den he laff, en tell de Little Gal dat he done gone en disremember all 'bout Mr. Rabbit, en den he up'n say, sezee:

"'Nex' time Mr. Rabbit come, you tak'n tu'n 'im in, en den you run des ez fas' ez you kin en come en tell me, kase I got some bizness wid dat young chap dat's bleedze ter be 'ten' ter,' sezee.

"Sho' nuff, nex' mawnin' dar wuz de Little Gal playin' 'roun', en yer come Brer Rabbit atter he 'lowance er greens. He wuz ready wid de same tale, en den de Little Gal, she tu'n 'im in, she did, en den she run up ter de house en holler:

"'O pa! Pa! O pa! Yer Brer Rabbit in de gyardin now! Yer he is, pa!'

"Den Mr. Man, he rush out, en grab up a fishin'-line w'at bin hangin' in de back po'ch, en mak fer de gyardin, en w'en he git dar, dar wuz Brer Rabbit tromplin' 'roun' on de strawbe'y-bed en mashin' down de termartusses. W'en Brer Rabbit see Mr. Man, he squot behime a collud leaf, but 't wa'n't no use. Mr. Man done seed him, en 'fo' you kin count 'lev'm, he done got ole Brer Rabbit tie hard en

fas' wid de fishin'-line. Atter he got him tie good, Mr. Man step back, he did, en say, sezee:

"'You done bin fool me lots er time, but dis time you er mine. I'm gwine ter take you en gin you a larrupin',' sezee, 'en den I'm gwine ter skin you en nail yo' hide on de stable do',' sezee; 'en den ter make sho dat you git de right kinder larrupin', I'll des step up ter de house,' sezee, 'en fetch de little red cowhide, en den I'll take en gin you brinjer,' sezee.

"Den Mr. Man call to der Little Gal ter watch Brer Rabbit w'iles he gone.

"Brer Rabbit aint sayin' nothin', but Mr. Man aint mo'n out de gate 'fo' he 'gun ter sing; en in dem days Brer Rabbit wuz a singer, mon," continued Uncle Remus, with unusual emphasis, "en w'en he chuned up fer ter sing he make dem yuther creeturs hol' der bref."

"What did he sing, Uncle Remus?" asked the little boy.

"Ef I aint fergit dat song off'n my min'," said Uncle Remus, looking over his spectacles at the fire, with a curious air of attempting to remember something, "hit run sorter dish yer way:

"'De jay-bird hunt de sparrer-nes',
　De bee-martin sail all 'roun';
　De squer'l, he holler from de top er de tree,
　Mr. Mole, he stay in de groun';
　He hide en he stay twel de dark drap down—
　Mr. Mole, he hide in de groun'.'

"W'en de Little Gal year dat, she laugh, she did, and she up'n ax Brer Rabbit fer ter sing some mo', but Brer Rabbit, he sorter cough, he did, en 'low dat he got a mighty bad ho'seness down inter he win'pipe some'rs. De Little Gal, she swade,[2] en swade, en bimeby

[2] Persuaded.

150

Brer Rabbit, he up'n 'low dat he kin dance mo' samer dan w'at he kin sing. Den de Little Gal, she ax 'im won't he dance, en Brer Rabbit, he 'spon' how in de name er goodness kin a man dance w'iles he all tie up dis a-way, en den de Little Gal, she say she kin ontie 'im, en Brer Rabbit, he say he aint keerin' ef she do. Wid dat de Little Gal, she retch down en onloose de fish-line, en Brer Rabbit, he sorter stretch hisse'f en look 'roun'."

Here Uncle Remus paused and sighed, as though he had relieved his mind of a great burden. The little boy waited a few minutes for the old man to resume, and finally he asked:

"Did the Rabbit dance, Uncle Remus?"

"Who? Him?" exclaimed the old man, with a queer affectation of elation. "Bless yo' soul, honey! Brer Rabbit gedder up his foots und' 'im, en he dance outer dat gyardin, en he dance home. He did dat! Sho'ly you don't 'speck dat a ole-timer w'at done had 'spe'unce like Brer Rabbit gwine ter stay dar en let dat ar Mr. Man sackyfice 'im? *Shoo!* Brer Rabbit dance, but he dance home. You year me!"

HOW MR. FOX WAS TOO SMART

Uncle Remus chuckled a moment over the escape of Brother Rabbit, and then turned his gaze upward toward the cobwebbed gloom that seemed to lie just beyond the rafters. He sat thus silent and serious a little while, but finally squared himself around in his chair and looked the little boy full in the face. The old man's countenance expressed a curious mixture of sorrow and bewilderment. Catching the child by the coatsleeve, Uncle Remus pulled him gently to attract his attention.

"Hit look like ter me," he said presently, in the tone of one approaching an unpleasant subject, "dat no longer'n yistiddy I see one er dem ar Favers chillun clim'in' dat ar big red-oak out yan', en den it seem like dat a little chap 'bout yo' size, he tuck'n start up ter see ef he can't play smarty like de Favers's yearlin's. I dunner w'at in de name er goodness you wanter be a-copyin' atter dem ar Faverses fer. Ef you er gwine ter copy atter yuther folks, copy atter dem w'at's some 'count. Yo' pa, he got de idee dat some folks is good ez yuther folks; but Miss Sally, she know better. She know dat dey aint no Favers 'pon de top side er de yeth w'at kin hol' der han' wid de Abercrombies in p'int er breedin' en raisin.' Dat w'at Miss Sally know. I bin keepin' track er dem Faverses sence way back yan' long 'fo' Miss Sally wuz born'd. Ole Cajy Favers, he went ter de po'house, en ez ter dat Jim Favers, I boun' you he know de inside er all de jails in dish yer State er Jawjy. Dey allers did hate niggers kase dey aint had none, en dey hates um down ter dis day.

"Year 'fo' las'," Uncle Remus continued, "I year yo' Unk' Jeems Abercrombie tell dat same Jim Favers dat ef he lay de weight er he han' on one er his niggers, he'd slap a load er buck shot in 'im; en, bless yo' soul, honey, yo' Unk' Jeems wuz des de man ter do it. But dey er monst'us perlite unter me, dem Faverses is," pursued the old man, allowing his indignation, which had risen to a white heat, to cool off, "en dey better be," he added spitefully, "kase I knows der pedigree fum de fus' ter de las', en w'en I gits my Affikin up, dey aint nobody, 'less it's Miss Sally 'erse'f, w'at kin keep me down."

"But dat aint needer yer ner dar," said Uncle Remus, renewing his attack upon the little boy. "W'at you wanter go copyin' atter dem Favers chillun fer? Youer settin' back dar, right dis minnit, bettin' longer yo'se'f dat I aint gwine ter tell Miss Sally, en dar whar youer lettin' yo' foot slip, kaze I'm gwine ter let it pass dis time, but de ve'y nex' time w'at I ketches you in hollerin' distuns er dem Faverses, right den en dar I'm gwine ter take my foot in my han' en go en tell Miss Sally, en ef she don't natally skin you 'live, den she aint de same 'oman w'at she useter be.

"All dish yer copyin' atter deze yer Faverses put me in min' er de time w'en Brer Fox got ter copyin' atter Brer Rabbit. I done tole you 'bout de time w'en Brer Rabbit git de game fum Brer Fox by makin' like he dead?"

The little boy remembered it very distinctly, and said as much.

"Well, den, ole Brer Fox, w'en he see how slick de trick wuk wid Brer Rabbit, he say ter hisse'f dat he b'leeve he'll up'n try de same kinder game on some yuther man, en he keep on watchin' fer he chance, twel bimeby, one day, he year Mr. Man comin' down de big road in a one-hoss waggin, kyar'n some chickens, en some eggs, en some butter, ter town. Brer Fox year 'im comin', he did, en w'at do he do but go en lay down in de road front er de waggin. Mr. Man, he druv 'long, he did, cluckin' ter de hoss en hummin' ter hisse'f, en w'en dey git mos' up ter Brer Fox, de hoss, he shy, he did, en Mr. Man, he tuck'n holler Wo! en de hoss, he tuck'n wo'd. Den Mr. Man, he look down, en he see Brer Fox layin' out dar on de groun' des like he cole en stiff, en w'en Mr. Man see dis, he holler out:

" 'Heyo! Dar de chap w'at been nabbin' up my chickens, en somebody done gone en shot off a gun at 'im, w'ich I wish she'd er bin two guns—dat I does!"

"Wid dat, Mr. Man, he druv on en lef' Brer Fox layin' dar. Den Brer Fox, he git up en run 'roun' thoo de woods en lay down front er Mr. Man ag'in, en Mr. Man come drivin' 'long, en he see Brer Fox, en he say, sezee:

" 'Heyo! Yer de ve'y chap what been 'stroyin' my pigs. Somebody done gone en kilt 'im, en I wish dey'd er kilt 'im long time ago.'

"Den Mr. Man, he druv on, en de waggin-w'eel come mighty nigh mashin' Brer Fox nose; yit, all de same, Brer Fox lipt up en run 'roun' 'head er Mr. Man, en lay down in de road, en w'en Mr. Man come 'long, dar he wuz all stretch out like he big 'nuff fer ter fill a two-bushel baskit, en he look like he dead 'nuff fer ter be skint. Mr. Man druv up, he did, en stop. He look down pun Brer Fox, en den he look all 'roun' fer ter see w'at de 'casion er all deze yer dead Fox is. Mr. Man look all 'roun', he did, but he aint see nothin', en needer do he year nothin'. Den he set dar en study, en bimeby he 'low ter hisse'f, he did, dat he had better 'zamin' w'at kinder kuse zeeze[1] done bin got inter Brer Fox fambly, en wid dat he lit down outer de waggin, en feel er Brer Fox year; Brer Fox year feel right wom. Den he feel Brer Fox neck; Brer Fox neck right wom. Den he feel er Brer Fox in de short ribs; Brer Fox all soun' in de short ribs. Den he feel er Brer Fox lim's; Brer Fox all soun' in de lim's. Den he tu'n Brer Fox over, en, lo en beholes, Brer Fox right limber. W'en Mr. Man see dis, he say ter hisse'f, sezee:

" 'Heyo, yer! how come dis? Dish yer chicken-nabber look lak he dead, but dey aint no bones broked, en I aint see no blood, en needer does I feel no bruise; en mo'n dat he wom en he limber,' sezee. 'Sump'n' wrong yer, sho'! Dish yer pig-grabber *mought* be dead, en den ag'in he moughtent,' sezee; 'but ter make sho' dat he is, I'll des

[1] Disease.

154

gin 'im a whack wid my w'ip-han'le,' sezee; en wid dat, Mr. Man draw back en fotch Brer Fox a clip behime de years—*pow!*—en de lick come so hard en it come so quick dat Brer Fox thunk sho' he's a goner; but 'fo' Mr. Man kin draw back fer ter fetch 'im a n'er wipe, Brer Fox, he scramble ter his feet, he did, en des make tracks 'way fum dar."

Uncle Remus paused and shook the cold ashes from his pipe, and then applied the moral:

"Dat w'at Brer Fox git fer playin' Mr. Smarty en copyin' atter yuther folks, en dat des de way de whole Smarty fambly gwine ter come out."

"I 'speck dat 'uz de reas'n w'at make ole Brer Rabbit git 'long so well, kaze he aint copy atter none er de yuther creeturs," Uncle Remus continued, after a while. "W'en he make his disappearance 'fo' um, hit 'uz allers in some bran new place. Dey aint know wharbouts fer ter watch out fer 'im. He wuz de funniest creetur er de whole gang. Some folks moughter call him lucky, en yit, w'en he git in bad luck, hit look lak he mos' allers come out on top. Hit look mighty kuse now, but 't wa'n't kuse in dem days, kaze hit 'uz done gun up dat, strike 'im w'en you might en whar you would, Brer Rabbit wuz de soopless creetur gwine.

"One time, he sorter tuck a notion, ole Brer Rabbit did, dat he'd pay Brer B'ar a call, en no sooner do de notion strike 'im dan he pick hisse'f up en put out fer Brer B'ar house."

"Why, I thought they were mad with each other," the little boy exclaimed.

"Brer Rabbit make he call w'en Brer B'ar en his fambly wuz off fum home," Uncle Remus explained, with a chuckle which was in the nature of a hearty tribute to the crafty judgment of Brother Rabbit.

"He sot down by de road, en he see um go by—ole Brer B'ar en ole Miss B'ar, en der two twin-chilluns, w'ich one un um wuz name Kubs en de t'er one wuz name Klibs."

The little boy laughed, but the severe seriousness of Uncle Remus would have served for a study, as he continued:

"Ole Brer B'ar en Miss B'ar, dey went 'long ahead, en Kubs en Klibs, dey come shufflin' en scramblin' 'long behime. W'en Brer Rabbit see dis, he say ter hisse'f dat he 'speck he better go see how Brer B'ar gittin' on; en off he put. En 't wa'n't long n'er 'fo' he 'uz ransackin' de premmuses same like he 'uz sho' 'nuff patter-roller. W'iles he wuz gwine 'roun' peepin' in yer en pokin' in dar, he got ter foolin' 'mong de shelfs, en a bucket er honey w'at Brer B'ar got hid in de cubbud fall down en spill on top er Brer Rabbit, en little mo'n he'd er bin drown. Fum head ter heels dat creeter wuz kiver'd wid honey; he wa'n't des only bedobble wid it, he wuz des kiver'd. He hatter set dar en let de natal sweetness drip outen he eyeballs 'fo' he kin see he han' befo' 'im, en den, atter he look 'roun' little, he say to hisse'f, sezee:

"'Heyo, yer! W'at I gwine do now? Ef I go out in de sunshine, de bumly-bees en de flies dey'll swom up'n take me, en if I stay yer, Brer B'ar'll come back en ketch me, en I dunner w'at in de name er gracious I gwine do.'

"Ennyhow, bimeby a notion strike Brer Rabbit, en he tip 'long twel he git in de woods, en w'en he git out dar, w'at do he do but roll in de leafs en trash en try fer ter rub de honey off'n 'im dat a-way. He roll, he did, en de leafs dey stick; Brer Rabbit roll, en de leafs dey stick, en he keep on rollin' en de leafs keep on stickin', twel atter w'ile Brer Rabbit wuz de mos' owdashus-lookin' creetur w'at you ever sot eyes on. En ef Miss Meadows en de gals could er seed 'im den en dar, dey would n't er bin no mo' Brer Rabbit call at der house; 'deed, en dat dey would n't.

"Brer Rabbit, he jump 'roun', he did, en try ter shake de leafs off'n 'im, but de leafs, dey aint gwine ter be shuck off. Brer Rabbit, he shake en he shiver, but de leafs dey stick; en de capers dat creetur cut up out dar in de woods by he own-alone se'f wuz scan'lous—dey wuz dat; dey wuz scan'lous.

"Brer Rabbit see dis wa'n't gwine ter do, en he 'low ter hisse'f dat he better be gittin' on todes home, en off he put. I 'speck you done year talk ez deze yer booggers w'at gits atter bad chilluns," continued Uncle Remus, in a tone so seriously confidential as to be altogether

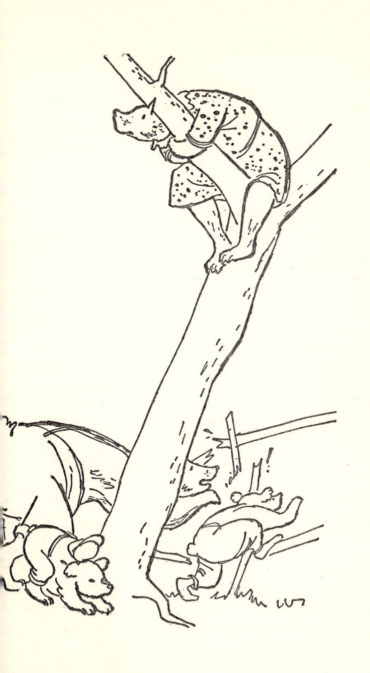

depressing; "well, den, des 'zactly dat a-way Brer Rabbit look, en ef you'd er seed 'im you'd er made sho' he de gran'-daddy er all de booggers. Brer Rabbit pace 'long, he did, en ev'y motion he make, de leafs dey'd go *swishy-swushy*, *splushy-splishy*, en, fum de fuss he make en de way he look, you'd er tuck 'im ter be de mos' suvvigus varment w'at disappear fum de face er de yeth sence ole man Noah let down de draw-bars er de ark en tu'n de creeturs loose; en I boun' ef you'd er struck up long wid 'im, you'd er been mighty good en glad ef you'd er got off wid dat.

"De fus' man w'at Brer Rabbit come up wid wuz ole Sis Cow, en no sooner is she lay eyes on 'im dan she h'ist up 'er tail in de elements, en put out like a pack er dogs wuz atter 'er. Dis make Brer Rabbit laff, kaze he know dat w'en a ole settle' 'oman like Sis Cow run 'stracted in de broad open day-time, dat dey mus' be sump'n' mighty kuse 'bout dem leafs en dat honey, en he keep on a-rackin' down de road. De nex' man w'at he meet wuz a black gal tollin' a whole passel er plantation shotes, en w'en de gal see Brer Rabbit come prancin' 'long, she fling down 'er basket er corn en des fa'rly fly, en de shotes, dey tuck thoo de woods, en sech n'er racket ez dey kick up wid der runnin', en der snortin', en der squealin' aint never bin year in dat settlement needer befo' ner since. Hit keep on dis a-way long ez Brer Rabbit meet anybody—dey des broke en run like de Ole Boy wuz atter um.

"C'ose, dis make Brer Rabbit feel monst'us biggity, en he 'low ter hisse'f dat he 'speck he better drap 'roun' en skummish in de neighborhoods er Brer Fox house. En w'iles he wuz stannin' dar runnin' dis 'roun' in he min', yer come old Brer B'ar en all er he fambly. Brer Rabbit, he git crossways de road, he did, en he sorter sidle todes um. Ole Brer B'ar, he stop en look, but Brer Rabbit, he keep on sidlin' todes um. Ole Miss B'ar, she stan' it long ez she kin, en den she fling down 'er parrysol en tuck a tree. Brer B'ar look lak he gwine ter stan' his groun', but Brer Rabbit he jump straight up in de a'r en gin hisse'f a shake, en, bless yo' soul, honey, ole Brer B'ar make a break, en dey tells me he to' down a whole panel er fence gittin' 'way fum dar! En ez ter Kubs en Klibs, dey tuck der hats in der han's, en dey went skaddlin' thoo de bushes des same ez a drove er hosses."

"And then what?" the little boy asked.

"Brer Rabbit p'raded on down de road," continued Uncle Remus, "en bimeby yer come Brer Fox en Brer Wolf, fixin' up a plan fer ter nab Brer Rabbit, en dey wuz so intents on der confab dat dey got right on Brer Rabbit 'fo' dey seed 'im; but, gentermens, w'en dey is ketch a glimpse un 'im, dey gun 'im all de room he want! Brer Wolf, he try ter show off, he did, kase he wanter play big 'fo' Brer Fox, en he stop en ax Brer Rabbit who is he. Brer Rabbit, he jump up en down in de middle er de road, en holler out:

" 'I'm de Wull-er-de-Wust.[1] I'm de Wull-er-de-Wust, en youer de man I'm atter!'

"Den Brer Rabbit jump up en down en make lak he gwine atter Brer Fox en Brer Wolf, en de way dem creeturs lit out fum dar wuz a caution.

"Long time atter dat," continued Uncle Remus, folding his hands placidly in his lap, with the air of one who has performed a pleasant duty—"long time atter dat, Brer Rabbit come up wid Brer Fox en Brer Wolf, en he git behime a stump, Brer Rabbit did, en holler out:

" 'I'm de Wull-er-de-Wust, en youer de mens I'm atter!'

"Brer Fox en Brer Wolf, dey broke, but 'fo' dey got outer sight en outer year'n', Brer Rabbit show hisse'f, he did, en laugh fit ter kill hisse'f. Atterwuds, Miss Meadows she year 'bout it, en de nex' time Brer Fox call, de gals dey up en giggle, en ax 'im ef he aint feard de Wull-er-de-Wust mought drap in."

[1] Or Wull-er-de-Wuts. Probably a fantastic corruption of "will-o'-the-wisp," though this is not by any means certain.

The rain continued to fall the next day, but the little boy made arrangements to go with 'Tildy when she carried Uncle Remus his supper. This happened to be a waiter full of things left over from dinner. There was so much that the old man was moved to remark:

"I cl'ar ter gracious, hit look lak Miss Sally done got my name in de pot dis time, sho'. I des wish you look at dat pone er co'n-bread, honey, en dem ar greens, en see ef dey aint got Remus writ some'rs on um. Dat ar chick'n fixin's, dey look lak deyer good, yet 'taint familious wid me lak dat ar bile ham. Dem ar sweet-taters, dey stan's fa'r fer dividjun, but dem ar puzzuv,[1] I lay dey fit yo' palate mo' samer dan dey does mine. Dish yer hunk er beef, we kin talk 'bout dat w'en de time come, en dem ar biscuits, I des nat'ally knows Miss Sally put um in dar fer some little chap w'ich his name I aint gwine ter call in comp'ny."

It was easy to perceive that the sight of the supper had put Uncle Remus in rare good-humor. He moved around briskly, taking the plates from the waiter and distributing them with exaggerated carefulness around upon his little pine table. Meanwhile he kept up a running fire of conversation.

"Folks w'at kin set down en have der vittles brung en put down right spang und' der nose—dem kinder folks aint got no needs er no umbrell. Night 'fo' las', w'iles I wuz settin' dar in de do', I year dem Willis-whistlers, en den I des knowed we 'uz gwine ter git a season."[2]

"The Willis-whistlers, Uncle Remus," exclaimed the little boy. "What are they?"

[1] Preserves.
[2] In the South, a rain is called a "season," not only by the Negroes, but by many white farmers.

"Youer too hard fer me now, honey. Dat w'at I knows I don't min' tellin', but w'en you axes me 'bout dat w'at I dunno, den youer too hard fer me, sho'. Deze yer Willis-whistlers, dey bangs my time, en I bin knockin' 'roun' in dish yer low-groun' now gwine on eighty year. Some folks wanter make out deyer frogs, yit I wish dey p'int out unter me how frogs kin holler so dat de nigher you come t'um, de furder you is off; I be mighty glad ef some un 'ud come 'long en tell me dat. Many en many's de time is I gone atter deze yer Willis-whistlers, en, no diffunce whar I goes, deyer allers off yander. You kin put de shovel in de fier en make de squinch-owl hush he fuss, en you kin go out en put yo' han' on de trees en make deze yere locus'-bugs quit der racket, but dem ar Willis-whistlers deyer allers 'way off yander." [3]

Suddenly Uncle Remus paused over one of the dishes, and exclaimed:

"Gracious en de goodness! W'at kinder doin's is dis Miss Sally done gone sont us?"

"That," said the little boy, after making an investigation, "is what mamma calls a floating island."

"Well, den," Uncle Remus remarked, in a relieved tone, "dat's diffunt. I wuz mos' fear'd it 'uz some er dat ar sillerbug, w'ich a whole jugful aint ska'cely 'nuff fer ter make you seem like you dremp 'bout smellin' dram. Ef I'm gwine ter be fed on foam," continued the old man, by way of explaining his position on the subject of syl-labub, "let it be foam, en ef I'm gwine ter git dram, lemme git in reach un it w'ile she got some strenk lef'. Dat's me up and down. W'en it come ter yo' floatin' ilun, des gimme a hunk er ginger-cake en

---

[3] It is a far-away sound that might be identified with one of the various undertones of silence, but it is palpable enough (if the word may be used) to have attracted the attention of the humble philosophers of the old plantation.

a mug er 'simmon-beer, en dey won't fine no nigger w'ats got no slicker feelin's dan w'at I is.

"Miss Sally mighty kuse w'ite 'oman," Uncle Remus went on. "She sendin' all deze doin's en fixin's down yer, en I 'speck deyer monst'us nice, but no longer'n las' Chuseday she had all de niggers on de place, big en little, gwine squallin' 'roun' fer Remus. Hit 'uz Remus yer en Remus dar, en, lo en beholes, w'en I come ter fine out, Miss Sally want Remus fer ter whirl in en cook 'er one er deze yer ole-time ash-cakes. She bleedzd ter have it den en dar; en w'en I git it done, Miss Sally, she got a glass er buttermilk, en tuck'n sot right flat down on de flo', des like she useter w'en she wuz little gal." The old man paused, straightened up, looked at the child over his spectacles, and continued, with emphasis: "En I be bless ef she aint eat a hunk er dat ash-cake mighty nigh ez big ez yo' head, en den she tuck'n make out 't wa'n't cook right.

"Now, den, honey, all deze done fix. You set over dar, and I'll set over yer, en 'twix' en 'tween us we'll sample dish yer truck en see w'at is it Miss Sally done gone en sont us; en w'iles we er makin' 'way wid it, I'll sorter rustle 'roun' wid my 'membunce, en see ef I kin call ter min' de tale 'bout how ole Brer Rabbit got 'im a two-story house widout layin' out much cash."

Uncle Remus stopped talking a little while and pretended to be trying to remember something—an effort that was accompanied by a curious humming sound in his throat. Finally, he brightened up and began:

"Hit tu'n out one time dat a whole lot er de creeturs tuck a notion dat dey'd go in coboots wid buil'n' un um a house. Ole Brer B'ar, he was 'mongs' um, en Brer Fox, en Brer Wolf, en Brer 'Coon, en Brer 'Possum. I won't make sho', but it seem like ter me dat plum down ter ole Brer Mink 'uz 'mongs' um. Leas'ways, dey wuz a whole passel un um, en dey whirl in, dey did, en dey buil' de house in less'n no time. Brer Rabbit, he make lak it make he head swim fer ter climb up on de scaffle, en likewise he say it make 'im ketch de palsy fer ter wuk in de sun, but he got 'im a squar', en he stuck a pencil behime de year, en he went 'roun' medjun[4] en markin'—medjun en markin' —en he wuz dat busy dat de yuther creeturs say ter deyse'f he doin' monst'us sight er wuk, en folks gwine 'long de big road say Brer Rabbit doin' mo' hard wuk dan de whole kit en bilin' un um. Yit all de time Brer Rabbit aint doin' nothin', en he des well bin layin' off in de shade scratchin' de fleas off'n 'im. De yuther creeturs, dey buil' de house, en, gentermens! she 'uz a fine un, too, mon. She'd 'a' bin a fine un deze days, let 'lone dem days. She had er upsta'rs en downsta'rs, en chimbleys all 'roun', en she had rooms fer all de creeturs w'at went inter cahoots en hope make it.

"Brer Rabbit, he pick out one er de upsta'rs rooms, en he tuck'n' got 'im a gun, en one er deze yer brass cannons, en he tuck'n' put um in dar w'en de yuther creeturs aint lookin', en den he tuck'n' got 'im a tub er nasty slop-water, w'ich likewise he put in dar w'en dey aint lookin'. So den, w'en dey git de house all fix, en w'iles dey wuz all a-settin' in de parlor atter supper, Brer Rabbit, he sorter gap en stretch hisse'f, en make his 'skuses en say he b'leeve he'll go ter he room. W'en he git dar, en w'iles all de yuther creeturs wuz a-laughin' en a-chattin' des ez sociable ez you please, Brer Rabbit, he stick he head out er de do' er he room en sing out:

" 'W'en a big man like me wanter set down, wharbouts he gwine ter set?' sezee.

"Den de yuther creeturs dey laugh, en holler back:

" 'Ef big man like you can't set in a cheer, he better set down on de flo'.'

" 'Watch out down dar, den,' sez ole Brer Rabbit, sezee. 'Kaze I'm a gwine ter set down,' sezee.

[4] Measuring.

"Wid dat, *bang!* went Brer Rabbit gun. Co'se, dis sorter 'stonish de creeturs, en dey look 'roun' at one er n'er much ez ter say, W'at in de name er gracious is dat? Dey lissen en lissen, but dey don't year no mo' fuss, en 'twa'n't long 'fo' dey got ter chattin' en jabberin' some mo'. Bimeby, Brer Rabbit stick he head outer he room do', en sing out:

" 'W'en a big man like me wanter sneeze, wharbouts he gwine ter sneeze at?'

"Den de yuther creeturs, dey tuck'n' holler back:

" 'Ef big man like you aint a-gone gump, he kin sneeze anywhar he please.'

" 'Watch out down dar, den,' sez Brer Rabbit, sezee. 'Kase I'm gwine ter tu'n loose en sneeze right yer,' sezee.

"Wid dat, Brer Rabbit let off his cannon—*bulderum-m-m!* De winder-glass dey shuck en rattle, en de house shuck like she gwine ter come down, en ole Brer B'ar, he fell out de rockin'-cheer— *kerblump!* W'en de creeturs git sorter settle, Brer 'Possum en Brer Mink, dey up'n' 'low dat Brer Rabbit got sech a monst'us bad cole, dey b'leeve dey'll step out and git some fresh a'r, but dem yuther creeturs, dey say dey gwine ter stick it out; en atter w'ile, w'en dey git der h'ar smoove down, dey 'gun ter jower 'mongs' deyse'f. 'Bout dat time, w'en dey get in a good way, Brer Rabbit, he sing out:

" 'W'en a big man like me take a chaw terbacker, wharbouts he gwine ter spit?'

"Den de yuther creeturs, dey holler back, dey did, sorter like deyer mad:

" 'Big man er little man, spit whar you please.'

"Den Brer Rabbit, he squall out:

" 'Dis de way a big man spit!' en wid dat he tilt over de tub er slop-water, en w'en de yuther creeturs year it come a-sloshin' down de sta'r-steps, gentermens! Dey des histed deyse'f outer dar. Some un um went out de back do', en some un um went out de front do', en some un um fell out de winders; some went one way en some went n'er way; but dey all went sailin' out."

"But what became of Brother Rabbit?" the little boy asked.

"Brer Rabbit, he des tuck'n' shot up de house en fassen de winders, en den he go ter bed, he did, en pull de coverled up 'roun' he years, en he sleep like a man w'at aint owe nobody nuthin'; en needer do he owe um, kaze ef dem yuther creeturs gwine git skeer'd en run off fum der own house, w'at bizness is dat er Brer Rabbit? Dat w'at I like ter know."

Uncle Remus sighed heavily as he lifted the trivet on the head of his walking-cane, and hung it carefully by the side of the griddle in the cavernous fireplace.

"Folks kin come 'long wid der watchermaycollums," he said presently, turning to the little boy, who was supplementing his supper by biting off a chew of shoemaker's-wax, "en likewise dey kin fetch 'roun' der watziznames. Dey kin walk biggity, en dey kin talk biggity, en, mo'n dat, dey kin feel biggity, but yit all de same deyer gwine ter git kotch up wid. Dey go 'long en dey go 'long, en den bimeby yer come trouble en snatch um slonchways, en de mo' bigger w'at dey is, de wusser does dey git snatched."

The little boy didn't understand this harangue at all, but he appreciated it because he recognized it as the prelude to a story.

"Dar wuz Mr. Lion," Uncle Remus went on; "he tuck'n' sot hisse'f up fer ter be de boss er all de yuther creeturs, en he feel so biggity dat he go ro'in' en rampin' 'roun' de neighborhoods wuss'n dat ar speckle bull w'at you see down at yo' Unk' Jeems Abercrombie place las' year. He went ro'in' 'roun', he did, en eve'ywhar he go he year talk er Mr. Man. Right in de middle er he braggin', some un 'ud up'n' tell 'im 'bout w'at Mr. Man done done. Mr. Lion, he say he done dis, en den he year 'bout how Mr. Man done dat. Hit went on dis a-way twel bimeby Mr. Lion shake he mane, he did, en he up'n' say dat he gwine ter s'arch 'roun' en 'roun', en high en low, fer ter see ef he can't fine Mr. Man, en he 'low, Mr. Lion did, dat w'en he do fine 'im, he gwine ter tu'n in en gin Mr. Man sech n'er larrupin' w'at nobody aint never had yit. Dem yuther creeturs, dey tuck'n' tell Mr. Lion dat he better let Mr. Man 'lone, but Mr. Lion say he gwine ter hunt 'im down spite er all dey kin do.

"Sho' nuff, atter he done tuck some res', Mr. Lion, he put out down de big road. Sun, she rise up en shine hot, but Mr. Lion, he keep on; win', hit come up en blow, en fill de elements full er dust; rain, hit drif' up en drizzle down; but Mr. Lion, he keep on. Bimeby, w'iles he gwine on dis a-way, wid he tongue hangin' out, he come up wid Mr. Steer, grazin' 'long on de side er de road. Mr. Lion, he up'n' ax 'im howdy, he did, monst'us perlite, en Mr. Steer likewise he bow en scrape en show his manners. Den Mr. Lion, he do lak he wanter have some confab wid 'im, en he up'n' say, sezee:

" 'Is dey anybody 'roun' in deze parts name Mr. Man?' sezee.

" 'Tooby sho' dey is,' sez Mr. Steer, sezee; 'anybody kin tell you dat. I knows 'im mighty well,' sezee.

" 'Well, den, he de ve'y chap I'm atter,' sezee.

" 'W'at mought be yo' bizness wid Mr. Man?' sez Mr. Steer, sezee.

" 'I done come dis long ways fer ter gin 'im a larrupin',' sez Mr. Lion, sezee. 'I'm gwine ter show 'im who de boss er deze neighborhoods,' sezee, en wid dat Mr. Lion, he shake he mane, en switch he tail, en strut up en down wuss'n one er deze yer town niggers.

" 'Well, den, ef dat w'at you come atter,' sez Mr. Steer, sezee, 'you des better slew yo'se'f 'roun' en p'int yo' nose todes home, kaze you fixin' fer ter git in sho' 'nuff trouble,' sezee.

" 'I'm gwine ter larrup dat same Mr. Man,' sez Mr. Lion, sezee; 'I done come fer dat, en dat w'at I'm gwine ter do,' sezee.

"Mr. Steer, he draw long breff, he did, en chaw he cud slow, en atter w'ile he say, sezee:

" 'You see me stannin' yer front er yo' eyes, en you see how big I is, en w'at long, sharp hawns I got. Well, big ez my heft is, en sharp dough my hawns be, yit Mr. Man, he come out yer en he ketch me, en he put me und' a yoke, en he hitch me up in a kyart, en he make me haul he wood, en he drive me anywhar he min' ter. He do dat. Better let Mr. Man 'lone,' sezee. 'If you fool 'long wid 'im, watch out dat he don't hitch you up en have you prancin' 'roun' yer pullin' he kyart,' sezee.

"Mr. Lion, he fotch a roar, en put out down de road, en 't wa'n't so mighty long 'fo' he come up wid Mr. Hoss, w'ich he wuz a-nib-blin' en a-croppin' de grass. Mr. Lion make hisse'f know'd, en den he tuck'n' ax Mr. Hoss do he know Mr. Man.

" 'Mighty well,' sez Mr. Hoss, sezee, 'en mo'n dat, I bin a-knowin' 'im a long time. W'at you want wid Mr. Man?' sezee.

" 'I'm a-huntin' 'im up fer ter larrup 'im,' sez Mr. Lion, sezee. 'Dey tels me he mighty stuck up,' sezee, 'en I gwine take 'im down a peg,' sezee.

"Mr. Hoss look at Mr. Lion like he sorry, en bimeby he up'n' say:

" 'I 'speck you better let Mr. Man 'lone,' sezee. 'You see how big I is, en how much strenk w'at I got, en how tough my foots is,' sezee; 'well dish yer Mr. Man, he kin take'n' take me en hitch me up in he buggy, en make me haul 'im all 'roun', en den he kin tak' en' fassen me ter de plow en make me break up all his new groun',' sezee. 'You better go 'long back home. Fus' news you know, Mr. Man'll have you breakin' up his new groun',' sezee.

"Spite er all dis, Mr. Lion, he shake he mane en say he gwine ter larrup Mr. Man anyhow. He went on down de big road, he did, en bimeby he come up wid Mr. Jack Sparrer, settin' up in de top er de tree. Mr. Jack Sparrer, he whirl 'roun' en chirp, en flutter 'bout up dar, en 'pariently make a great 'miration.

" 'Heyo yer!' sezee. 'Who'd er 'speckted fer ter see Mr. Lion 'way down yer in dis neighborhoods?' sezee. 'Whar you gwine, Mr. Lion?' sezee.

"Den Mr. Lion ax ef Mr. Jack Sparrer know Mr. Man, en Mr. Jack Sparrer say he know Mr. Man mighty well. Den Mr. Lion, he ax ef Mr. Jack Sparrer know whar he stay, w'ich Mr. Jack Spar-rer say dat he do. Mr. Lion ax wharbouts is Mr. Man, en Mr. Jack

Sparrer say he right 'cross dar in de new groun', en he up'n' ax Mr. Lion w'at he want wid 'im, w'ich Mr. Lion 'spon' dat he gwine larrup Mr. Man, en wid dat, Mr. Jack Sparrer, he up'n' say, sezee:

"'You better let Mr. Man 'lone. You see how little I is, en likewise how high I kin fly; yit, 'spite er dat, Mr. Man, he kin fetch me down w'en he git good an' ready,' sezee. 'You better tuck yo' tail en put out home,' sez Mr. Jack Sparrer, sezee, 'kaze bimeby Mr. Man'll fetch you down,' sezee.

"But Mr. Lion des vow he gwine atter Mr. Man, en go he would, en go he did. He aint never see Mr. Man, Mr. Lion aint, en he dunner w'at he look lak, but he go on todes de new groun'. Sho' 'nuff, dar wuz Mr. Man, out dar maulin' rails fer ter make 'im a fence. He 'uz rippin' up de butt cut, Mr. Man wuz, en he druv in his wedge en den he stuck in de glut. He 'uz splittin' 'way, w'en bimeby he year rustlin' out dar in de bushes, en he look up, en dar wuz Mr. Lion. Mr. Lion ax 'im do he know Mr. Man, en Mr. Man 'low dat he know 'im mo' samer dan ef he wer' his twin brer. Den Mr. Lion 'low dat he wanter see 'im, en den Mr. Man say, sezee, dat ef Mr. Lion will come stick his paw in de split fer ter hol' de log open twel he git back, he go fetch Mr. Man. Mr. Lion he march up en slap his paw in de place, en den Mr. Man, he tuck'n' knock de glut out, en de split close up, en dar Mr. Lion wuz. Mr. Man, he stan' off en say, sezee:

"'Ef you'd 'a' bin a steer er hoss, you mought er run'd, en ef you'd 'a' bin a sparrer, you mought er flew'd, but yer you is, en you kotch yo'se'f,' sezee.

"Wid dat, Mr. Man sa'nter out in de bushes en cut 'im a hick'ry, en he let in on Mr. Lion, en he frail en frail 'im twel frailin' un 'im wuz a sin. En down ter dis day," continued Uncle Remus, in a tone calculated to destroy all doubt, "you can't git no Lion ter come up whar dey's a Man a-maulin' rails en put he paw in de split. Dat you can't!"

Uncle Remus relapsed into silence again, and the little boy, with nothing better to do, turned his attention to the bench upon which the old man kept his shoemaker's tools. Prosecuting his investigations in this direction, the youngster finally suggested that the supply of bristles was about exhausted.

"I dunner w'at Miss Sally wanter be sendin' un you down yer fer, ef you gwine ter be stirr'n' en bodderin' 'longer dem ar doin's," exclaimed Uncle Remus, indignantly. "Now don't you scatter dem hog-bristle! De time wuz w'en folks had a mighty slim chance fer ter git bristle, en dey aint no tellin' w'en dat time gwine come ag'in. Let 'lone dat, de time wuz w'en de breed er hogs wuz done run down ter one po' little pig, en it look lak mighty sorry chance fer dem w'at was bleedzd ter have bristle."

By this time Uncle Remus's indignation had vanished, disappearing as suddenly and unexpectedly as it came. The little boy was curious to know when and where and how the bristle famine occurred.

"I done tole you 'bout dat too long 'go ter talk 'bout," the old man declared; but the little boy insisted that he had never heard about it before, and he was so persistent that at last Uncle Remus, in self-defence, consented to tell the story of the Pigs.

"One time, 'way back yander, de ole Sow en er chilluns wuz all livin' 'longer de yuther creeturs. Hit seem lak ter me dat de ole Sow wuz a widder 'oman, en ef I don't run inter no mistakes, hit look like ter me dat she got five chilluns. Lemme see," continued Uncle Remus, with the air of one determined to justify his memory by a reference to the record, and enumerating with great deliberation, "dar wuz Big Pig, en dar wuz Little Pig, en dar wuz Speckle Pig, en dar wuz Blunt, en las' en lonesomes' dar wuz Runt.

"One day, deze yer Pig ma she know she gwine kick de bucket, and she tuck'n call up all 'er chilluns en tell um dat de time done come w'en dey got ter look out fer deyse'f, en den she up'n tell um good ez she kin, dough 'er breff mighty scant, 'bout w'at a bad man is ole Brer Wolf. She say, sez she, dat if dey kin make der 'scape from ole Brer Wolf, dey'll be doin' monst'us well. Big Pig 'low she aint skeer'd, Speckle Pig 'low she aint skeer'd, Blunt, he say he mos' big a man ez Brer Wolf hisse'f, en Runt, she des tuck'n root 'roun' in de straw en grunt. But ole Widder Sow, she lay dar, she did, en keep on tellin' um dat dey better keep der eye on Brer Wolf, kaz he mighty mean en 'seetful man.

"Not long atter dat, sho' 'nuff ole Miss Sow lay down en die, en all dem ar chilluns er hern wuz flung back on deyse'f, en dey whirl in, dey did, en dey buil' um all a house ter live in. Big Pig, she tuck'n buil' 'er a house outer bresh; Little Pig, she tuck'n buil' a stick house; Speckle Pig, she tuck'n buil' a mud house; Blunt, he tuck'n buil' a plank house; en Runt, she don't make no great ter-do, en no great brags, but she went ter wuk, she did, en buil' a rock house.

"Bimeby, w'en dey done got all fix, en marters wuz sorter settle, soon one mawnin' yer come ole Brer Wolf, a-lickin' un his chops en a-shakin' un his tail. Fus' house he come ter wuz Big Pig house. Brer Wolf walk ter de do', he did, en he knock sorter saf'—*blim! Blim! Blim!* Nobody aint answer. Den he knock loud—*blam! Blam! Blam!* Dis wake up Big Pig, en she come ter de do', en she ax who dat. Brer Wolf 'low it's a fr'en', en den he sing out:

" 'Ef you'll open de do' en let me in,
   I'll wom my han's en go home ag'in.'

"Still Big Pig ax who dat, en den Brer Wolf, he up'n say, sezee:
" 'How yo' ma?' sezee.
" 'My ma done dead,' sez Big Pig sez she, 'en 'fo' she die she tell

me fer ter keep my eye on Brer Wolf. I see you thoo de crack er de do', en you look mighty like Brer Wolf,' sez she.

"Den ole Brer Wolf, he draw a long breff lak he feel mighty bad, en he up'n say, sezee:

"'I dunner w'at change yo' ma so bad, less'n she 'uz out'n 'er head. I year tell dat ole Miss Sow wuz sick, en I say ter myse'f dat I'd kinder drap 'roun' en see how de ole lady is, en fetch 'er dish yer bag er roas'n'-years. Mighty well does I know dat ef yo' ma wuz yer right now, en in 'er min', she'd take de roas'n'-years en be glad fer ter git um, en mo'n dat, she'd take'n ax me in by de fire fer ter wom my han's,' sez ole Brer Wolf, sezee.

"De talk 'bout de roas'n'-years make Big Pig mouf water, en bimeby, atter some mo' palaver, she open de do' en let Brer Wolf in, en bless yo' soul, honey, dat uz de las' er Big Pig! She aint had time fer ter squeal en needer fer ter grunt 'fo' Brer Wolf gobble 'er up.

"Next day, ole Brer Wolf put up de same game on Little Pig; he go en he sing he song, en Little Pig, she tuck'n let 'im in, en den Brer Wolf he tuck'n 'turn de compelerments[1] en let Little Pig in."

Here Uncle Remus laughed long and loud at his conceit, and he took occasion to repeat it several times.

"Little Pig, she let Brer Wolf in, en Brer Wolf, he let Little Pig in, en w'at mo' kin you ax dan dat? Nex' time Brer Wolf pay a call, he drop in on Speckle Pig, en rap at de do' en sing his song:

"'Ef you'll open de do' en let me in,
    I'll wom my han's en go home ag'in.'

"But Speckle Pig, she kinder 'spicion sump'n', en she 'fuse ter open de do'. Yit Brer Wolf mighty 'seetful man, en he talk mighty saf' en he talk mighty sweet. Bimeby he git he nose in de crack er de

[1] Compliments.

do' en he say ter Speckle Pig, sezee, fer ter des let 'im git one paw in, en den he won't go no furder. He git de paw in, en den he beg fer ter git de yuther paw in, en den w'en he git dat in he beg fer ter git he head in, en den w'en he git he head in, en he paws in, co'se all he got ter do is ter shove de do' open en walk right in; en w'en marters stan' dat way, 't wa'n't long 'fo' he done make fresh meat er Speckle Pig.

"Nex' day, he make way wid Blunt, en de day atter, he 'low dat he make a pass at Runt. Now, den, right dar whar ole Brer Wolf slip up at. He lak some folks w'at I knows. He'd 'a' bin mighty smart, ef he had n't er bin too smart. Runt wuz de littles' one er de whole gang, yit all de same news done got out dat she 'uz pestered wid sense like grown folks.

"Brer Wolf, he crope up ter Runt house, en he got un'need de winder, he did, en he sing out:

" 'Ef you'll open de do' en let me in,
  I'll wom my han's en go home ag'in.'

"But all de same, Brer Wolf can't coax Runt fer ter open de do', en needer kin he break in, kaze de house done made outer rock. Bimeby Brer Wolf make out he done gone off, en den atter while he come back en knock at de do'—*blam, blam, blam!*

"Runt she sot by de fier, she did, en sorter scratch 'er year, en holler out:

" 'Who dat?' sez she.

" 'Hit's Speckle Pig,' sez ole Brer Wolf, sezee, 'twix' a snort en a grunt. 'I fotch yer some peas fer yo' dinner!'

"Runt, she tuck'n laugh, she did, en holler back:

" 'Sis Speckle Pig aint never talk thoo dat many toofies.'

"Brer Wolf go off 'g'in, en bimeby he come back en knock. Runt she sot en rock, en holler out:

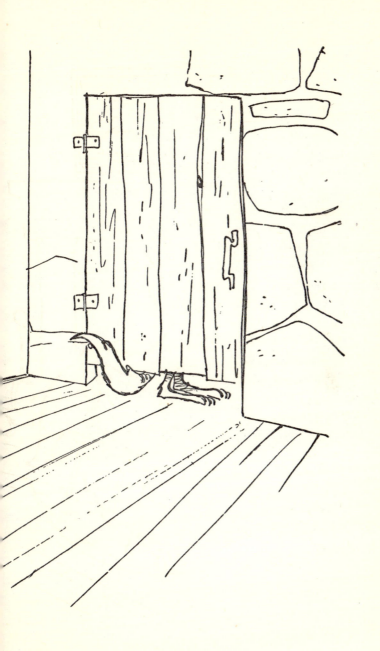

" 'Who dat?'

" 'Big Pig,' sez Brer Wolf. 'I fotch some sweet-co'n fer yo' supper.'

"Runt, she look thoo de crack un'need de do', en laugh en say, sez she:

" 'Sis Big Pig aint had no ha'r on 'er huff.'

"Den ole Brer Wolf, he git mad, he did, en say he gwine come down de chimbley, en Runt, she say, sez she, dat de onliest way w'at he kin git in; en den, w'en she year Brer Wolf clam'in' up on de outside er de chimbley, she tuck'n pile up a whole lot er broom sage front er de h'a'th, en w'en she year 'im clam'in' down on de inside, she tuck de tongs en shove de straw on de fier, en de smoke make Brer Wolf head swim, en he drap down, en 'fo' he know it he 'uz done bu'nt ter a cracklin'; en dat wuz de las' er ole Brer Wolf. Leas'ways," added Uncle Remus, putting in a cautious proviso to fall back upon in case of an emergency, "leas'ways, hit 'uz de las' er dat Brer Wolf."

MR. BENJAMIN RAM
AND HIS WONDERFUL FIDDLE

"I 'speck you done year tell er ole man Benjermun Ram," said Uncle Remus, with a great affectation of indifference, after a pause.

"Old man who?" asked the little boy.

"Ole man Benjermun Ram. I 'speck you done year tell er him too long 'go ter talk 'bout."

"Why, no, I haven't, Uncle Remus!" exclaimed the little boy, protesting and laughing. "He must have been a mighty funny old man."

"Dat's ez may be," responded Uncle Remus, sententiously. "Fun deze days would n't er counted fer fun in dem days; en many's de time w'at I see folks laughin'," continued the old man, with such withering sarcasm that the little boy immediately became serious, "many's de time w'at I sees um laughin' en laughin', w'en I lay dey aint kin tell w'at deyer laughin' at deyse'f. En 'taint der laughin' w'at pesters me, nudder," relenting a little, "hit's dish yer ev'lastin' snickle en giggle, giggle en snickle."

Having thus mapped out, in a dim and uncertain way, what older people than the little boy might have been excused for accepting as a sort of moral basis, Uncle Remus proceeded:

"Dish yer Mr. Benjermun Ram, w'ich he done come up inter my min', wuz one er deze yer ole-timers. Dey tells me dat he 'uz a fiddler fum away back yander—one er dem ar kinder fiddlers w'at can't git de chune down fine 'less dey pats der foot. He stay all by he own-alone se'f way out in de middle un a big new-groun', en he sech a handy man fer ter have at a frolic dat de yuther creeturs like 'im mighty well, en w'en dey tuck a notion fer ter shake der foot, w'ich de notion tuck'n struck um eve'y once in a w'ile, nuthin' 'ud do but dey mus' sen' fer ole man Benjermun Ram en he fiddle; en dey do say," continued Uncle Remus, closing his eyes in a sort of ecstasy, "dat w'en he squar' hisse'f back in a cheer, an git in a weavin' way, he kin des snatch dem ole-time chunes fum who lay de rail.[1] En den, w'en de frolic wuz done, dey'd all fling in, dem yuther creeturs would, en fill up a bag er peas fer ole Mr. Benjermun Ram fer ter kyar home wid 'im.

"One time, des 'bout Christmas, Miss Meadows en Miss Motts en de gals, dey up'n say dat dey'd sorter gin a blowout, en dey got wud ter ole man Benjermun Ram w'ich dey 'speckted 'im fer ter be on han'. W'en de time done come fer Mr. Benjermun Ram fer ter start, de win' blow cole en de cloud 'gun ter spread out 'cross de elements—but no marter fer dat; ole man Benjermun Ram tuck down he walkin'-cane, he did, en tie up he fiddle in a bag, en sot out fer Miss Meadows. He thunk he know de way, but hit keep on gittin' col'er en col'er, en mo' cloudy, twel bimeby, fus' news you know, ole Mr. Benjermun Ram done lose de way. Ef he'd er kep' on down de big road fum de start, it moughter bin diffunt, but he tuck a nigh-cut, en he aint git fur 'fo' he done los' sho' 'nuff. He go dis a-way, en he go dat a-way, en he go de yuther way, yit all de same he wuz done los'. Some folks would er sot right flat down whar dey wuz en study out de way, but ole man Benjermun Ram aint got wrinkle on he hawn fer nothin', kaze he done got de name er ole Billy Hardhead long 'fo' dat. Den ag'in, some folks would er stop right still in der tracks en holler en bawl fer ter see ef dey can't roust up some er de neighbors, but ole Mr. Benjermun Ram, he des stick he jowl in de win', he did, en he march right on des 'zackly like he know he aint gwine de wrong way. He keep on, but 't wa'n't long 'fo' he 'gun ter feel right lonesome, mo' speshually w'en hit come up in he min' how Miss Meadows en de gals en all de comp'ny

[1] That is, from the foundation, or beginning.

be bleedz ter do de bes' dey kin bidout any fiddlin'; en hit kinder make he marrer git cole w'en he study 'bout how he gotter sleep out dar in de woods by hisse'f.

"Yit, all de same, he keep on twel de dark 'gun ter drap down, en den he keep on still, en bimeby he come ter a little rise whar dey wuz a clay-gall. W'en he git dar he stop en look 'roun', he did, en 'way off down in de holler, dar he see a light shinin', en w'en he see dis, ole man Benjermun Ram tuck he foot in he han', en make he way todes it des lak it de ve'y place w'at he bin huntin'. 'T wa'n't long 'fo' he come ter de house whar de light is, en, bless you soul, he don't make no bones er knockin'. Den somebody holler out:

" 'Who dat?'

" 'I'm Mr. Benjermun Ram, en I done lose de way, en I come fer ter ax you ef you can't take me in fer de night,' sezee.

"In common," continued Uncle Remus, "ole Mr. Benjermun Ram wuz a mighty rough-en-spoken somebody, but you better b'leeve he talk monst'us perlite dis time.

"Den some un on t'er side er de do' ax Mr. Benjermun Ram fer ter walk right in, en wid dat he open de do' en walk in, en make a bow like fiddlin' folks does w'en dey goes in comp'ny; but he aint no sooner make he bow en look 'roun' twel he 'gun ter shake en shiver lak he done bin strucken wid de swamp-ager, kaze, settin' right dar 'fo' de fier wuz ole Brer Wolf, wid his toofies showin' up all w'ite en shiny like dey wuz bran new. Ef ole Mr. Benjermun Ram aint bin so ole en stiff I boun' you he'd er broke en run, but 'mos' 'fo' he had time fer ter study 'bout gittin' 'way, ole Brer Wolf done bin jump up en shet de do' en fassen 'er wid a great big chain. Ole Mr. Benjermun Ram he know he in fer't, en he tuck'n put on a bol' face ez he kin, but he des nat'ally hone[2] fer ter be los' in de

---

[2] To pine or long for anything. This is a good old English word, which has been retained in the plantation vocabulary.

woods some mo'. Den he make n'er low bow, en he hope Brer Wolf and all his folks is well, en den he say, sezee, dat he des drap in fer ter wom hisse'f, en 'quire uv de way ter Miss Meadows', en ef Brer Wolf be so good ez ter set 'im in de road ag'in, he be off putty soon en be much 'blige in de bargains.

" 'Tooby sho', Mr. Ram,' sez Brer Wolf, sezee, w'iles he lick he chops en grin; 'des put yo' walkin'-cane in de cornder over dar, en set yo' bag down on de flo', en make yo'se'f at home,' sezee. 'We aint got much,' sezee, 'but w'at we is got is yone w'iles you stays, en I boun' we'll take good keer un you,' sezee; en wid dat Brer Wolf laugh en show his toofies so bad dat ole man Benjermun Ram come mighty nigh havin' n'er ager.

"Den Brer Wolf tuck'n flung 'n'er lighter'd-knot on de fier, en den he slip inter de back room, en present'y, w'iles ole Mr. Benjermun Ram wuz settin' dar shakin' in he shoes, he year Brer Wolf whispun' ter he ole 'oman:

" 'Ole 'oman! Ole 'oman! Fling 'way yo' smoke meat—fresh meat fer supper! Fling 'way yo' smoke meat—fresh meat fer supper!'

"Den ole Miss Wolf, she talk out loud, so Mr. Benjermun Ram kin year:

" 'Tooby sho' I'll fix 'im some supper. We er 'way off yer in de woods, so fur fum comp'ny dat goodness knows I'm mighty glad ter see Mr. Benjermun Ram.'

"Den Mr. Benjermun Ram year ole Miss Wolf whettin' 'er knife on a rock—*shirrah! shirrah! shirrah!*—en ev'y time he year de knife say *shirrah!* he know he dat much nigher de dinner-pot. He know he can't git 'way, en w'iles he settin' dar studyin', hit come 'cross he min' dat he des mought ez well play one mo' chune on he fiddle 'fo' de wuss come ter de wuss. Wid dat he ontie de bag en take out de fiddle, en 'gun ter chune 'er up—*plink, plank, plunk, plink! Plunk, plank, plink, plunk!*"

Uncle Remus's imitation of the tuning of a fiddle was marvellous enough to produce a startling effect upon a much less enthusiastic listener than the little boy. It was given in perfect good faith, but the serious expression on the old man's face was so irresistibly comic that the child laughed until the tears ran down his face. Uncle Remus very properly accepted this as a tribute to his wonderful resources as a story-teller, and continued, in great good-humor:

"W'en ole Miss Wolf year dat kinder fuss, co'se she dunner w'at is it, en she drap 'er knife en lissen. Ole Mr. Benjermun Ram aint know dis, en he keep on chunin' up—*plank, plink, plunk, plank!* Den ole Miss Wolf, she tuck'n hunch Brer Wolf wid 'er elbow, en she say, sez she:

" 'Hey, ole man! W'at dat?'

"Den bofe un um cock up der years en lissen, en des 'bout dat time ole Mr. Benjermun Ram he sling de butt er de fiddle up und' he chin, en struck up one er dem ole-time chunes."

"Well, what tune was it, Uncle Remus?" the little boy asked, with some display of impatience.

"Ef I aint done gone en fergit dat chune off'n my min'," continued Uncle Remus; "hit sorter went like dat ar song 'bout 'Sheep shell co'n wid de rattle er his ho'n,' en yit hit mout er been dat ar yuther one 'bout 'Roll de key, ladies, roll dem keys.' Brer Wolf en ole Miss Wolf, dey lissen en lissen, en de mo' w'at dey lissen de skeerder dey git, twel bimeby dey tuck ter der heels en make a break fer de swamp at de back er de house des lak de patter-rollers wuz atter um.

"W'en ole man Benjermun Ram sorter let up wid he fiddlin', he don't see no Brer Wolf, en he don't year no ole Miss Wolf. Den he look in de back room; no Wolf dar. Den he look in de back po'ch; no Wolf dar. Den he look in de closet en de cubberd: no Wolf aint dar yit. Den ole Mr. Benjermun Ram, he tuck'n shot all de do's en lock um, en he s'arch 'roun' en he fine some peas en fodder in de lof', w'ich he et um fer he supper, en den he lie down front er de fier en sleep soun' ez a log.

"Nex' mawnin' he 'uz up en stirrin' monst'us soon, en he put out fum dar, en he fine de way ter Miss Meadows' time 'nuff fer ter play at de frolic. W'en he git dar, Miss Meadows en de gals, dey run ter de gate fer ter meet 'im, en dis un tuck he hat, en dat un tuck he cane, en t'er'n tuck he fiddle, en den dey up'n say:

"Law, Mr. Ram! Whar de name er goodness is you bin? We so glad you come. Stir 'roun' yer, folks, en git Mr. Ram a cup er hot coffee.'

"Dey make a mighty big ter-do 'bout Mr. Benjermun Ram, Miss Meadows en Miss Motts en de gals did, but 'twix' you en me en de bedpos', honey, dey'd er had der frolic wh'er de ole chap 'uz dar er not, kaze de gals done make 'rangerments wid Brer Rabbit fer ter pat fer um, en in dem days Brer Rabbit wuz a patter, mon. He mos' sho'ly wuz."

"Could Brother Rabbit pat a tune, sure enough, Uncle Remus?" asked the little boy, his thoughts apparently dwelling upon the new accomplishment of Brother Rabbit at which the old man had hinted in his story of Mr. Benjamin Ram. Uncle Remus pretended to be greatly surprised that any one could be so unfamiliar with the accomplishments of Brother Rabbit as to venture to ask such a question. His response was in the nature of a comment:

"Name er goodness! W'at kinder pass dish yer we comin' ter w'en a great big grow'd up young un axin' 'bout Brer Rabbit? Bless yo' soul, honey! Dey wa'n't no chune gwine dat Brer Rabbit can't pat. Let 'lone dat, w'en dey wuz some un else fer ter do de pattin', Brer Rabbit kin jump out inter de middle er de flo' en des nat'ally shake de eyel'ds off'en dem yuther creeturs. En 't wa'n't none er dish yer bowin' en scrapin', en slippin' en slidin', en han's all 'roun', w'at folks does deze days. Hit uz dish yer up en down kinder dancin', whar dey des lips up in de a'r fer ter cut de pidjin-wing, en lights on de flo' right in de middle er de double-shuffle. *Shoo!* Dey aint no dancin' deze days; folks' shoes too tight, en dey aint got dat limber-someness in de hips w'at dey useter is. Dat dey aint.

"En yit," Uncle Remus continued, in a tone which seemed to imply that he deemed it necessary to apologize for the apparent frivolity of Brother Rabbit, "en yit de time come w'en ole Brer Rabbit 'gun ter put dis en dat tergedder, en de notion strak 'im dat he better be home lookin' atter de intruss er he fambly, 'stidder trapesin' en trollopin' 'roun' ter all de frolics in de settlement. He tuck'n study dis in he min' twel bimeby he sot out 'termin' fer ter 'arn he own livelihoods, en den he up'n lay off a piece er groun' en plant 'im a tater-patch.

"Brer Fox, he see all dish yer gwine on, he did, en he 'low ter hisse'f dat he 'speck Brer Rabbit rashfulness done bin supjued kaze he skeer'd, en den Brer Fox make up his min' dat he gwine ter pay Brer Rabbit back fer all he 'seetfulness. He start in, Brer Fox did, en fum dat time forrerd he aggervate Brer Rabbit 'bout he tater-patch. One night he leave de draw-bars down, 'n'er night he fling off de top rails, en nex' night he t'ar down a whole panel er fence, en he keep on dis a-way twel 'pariently Brer Rabbit dunner w'at ter do. All dis time Brer Fox keep on foolin' wid de tater-patch, en w'en he see w'ich Brer Rabbit aint makin' no motion, Brer Fox 'low dat he done skeer'd sho' 'nuff, en dat de time done come fer ter gobble him up bidout lief er license. So he call on Brer Rabbit, Brer Fox did, en he ax 'im will he take a walk. Brer Rabbit, he ax wharbouts. Brer Fox say, right out yander. Brer Rabbit, he ax w'at is dey right out yander? Brer Fox say he know whar dey some mighty fine peaches, en he want Brer Rabbit fer ter go 'long en climb de tree en fling um down. Brer Rabbit say he don't keer ef he do, mo' speshually fer ter 'blige Brer Fox.

"Dey sot out, dey did, en atter w'ile, sho' 'nuff, dey come ter de peach-orchud, en Brer Rabbit, w'at do he do but pick out a good tree, en up he clum. Brer Fox, he sot hisse'f at de root er de tree, kaze he 'low dat w'en Brer Rabbit come down he hatter come down backerds, en den dat 'ud be de time fer ter nab 'im. But, bless yo' soul, Brer Rabbit dun see w'at Brer Fox atter 'fo' he clum up. W'en he pull de peaches, Brer Fox say, sezee:

" 'Fling um down yer, Brer Rabbit—fling um right down yer so I kin ketch um,' sezee.

"Brer Rabbit, he sorter wunk de furdest eye fum Brer Fox, en he holler back, he did:

" 'Ef I fling um down dar whar you is, Brer Fox, en you misses um, dey'll git squshed,' sezee, 'so I'll des sorter pitch um out yander in de grass whar dey won't git bus',' sezee.

"Den he tuck'n flung de peaches out in de grass, en w'iles Brer Fox went atter um, Brer Rabbit, he skint down outer de tree, en hustle hisse'f twel he git elbow-room. W'en he git off little ways, he up'n holler back ter Brer Fox dat he got a riddle he want 'im ter read. Brer Fox, he ax w'at is it. Wid dat, Brer Rabbit, he gun it out ter Brer Fox lak a man sayin' a speech:

" 'Big bird rob en little bird sing,
   De big bee zoon en little bee sting,
   De little man lead en big hoss foller—
   Kin you tell w'at's good fer a head in a holler?'

"Ole Brer Fox scratch he head en study, en study en scratch he head, but de mo' he study de wuss he git mix up wid de riddle, en atter w'ile he tuck'n tell Brer Rabbit dat he dunno how in de name er goodness ter onriddle dat riddle.

" 'Come en go 'longer me,' sez ole Brer Rabbit, sezee, 'en I boun' you I show you how ter read dat same riddle. Hit's one er dem ar kinder riddle,' sez ole man Rabbit, sezee, 'w'ich 'fo' you read 'er you got ter eat a bait er honey, en I done got my eye sot on de place whar we kin git de honey at,' sezee.

"Brer Fox, he ax wharbouts is it, en Brer Rabbit, he say up dar in ole Brer B'ar cotton-patch, whar he got a whole passel er bee-gums. Brer Fox, he 'low, he did, dat he aint got no sweet-toof much, yit he wanter git at de innerds er dat ar riddle, en he don't keer ef he do go 'long.

"Dey put out, dey did, en 't wa'n't long 'fo' dey come ter ole Brer B'ar bee-gums, en ole Brer Rabbit, he up'n gun um a rap wid he walkin'-cane, des lak folks thumps water-millions fer ter see ef dey er ripe. He tap en he rap en bimeby he come ter one un um w'ich she soun' like she plum full, en den he go 'roun' behime it, ole Brer Rabbit did, en he up'n say, sezee:

"'I'll des sorter tilt 'er up, Brer Fox,' sezee, 'en you kin put yo' head und' dar en git some er de drippin's,' sezee.

"Brer Rabbit, he tilt her up, en, sho' 'nuff, Brer Fox, he jam he head un'need de gum. Hit make me laugh," Uncle Remus continued, with a chuckle, "fer ter see w'at a fresh man is Brer Fox, kaze he aint no sooner stuck he head un'need dat ar bee-gum, dan Brer Rabbit turnt 'er aloose, en down she come—*ker-swosh!*—right on Brer Fox neck, en dar he wuz. Brer Fox, he kick; he squeal; he jump; he squall; he dance; he prance; he beg; he pray; yit dar he wuz, en w'en Brer Rabbit git way off, en tu'n 'roun' fer ter look back, he see Brer Fox des a-wigglin' en a-squ'min', en right den en dar Brer Rabbit gun one ole-time whoop, en des put out fer home.

"W'en he git dar, de fus' man he see wuz Brer Fox gran'daddy, w'ich folks all call 'im Gran'sir' Gray Fox. W'en Brer Rabbit see 'im, he say, sezee:

"'How you come on, Gran'sir' Gray Fox?'

"'I still keeps po'ly, I'm 'blije ter you, Brer Rabbit,' sez Gran'sir' Gray Fox, sezee. 'Is you seed any sign er my gran'son dis mawnin'?' sezee.

"Wid dat Brer Rabbit laugh en say w'ich him en Brer Fox bin a-ramblin' 'roun' wid one er 'n'er havin' mo' fun dan w'at a man kin shake a stick at.

"'We bin a-riggin' up riddles en a-readin' un um,' sez Brer Rabbit, sezee. 'Brer Fox is settin' off some'rs in de bushes right now, aimin' fer ter read one w'at I gun 'im. I'll des drap you one,' sez ole Brer Rabbit, sezee, 'w'ich, ef you kin read it, hit'll take you right spang ter whar yo' gran'son is, en you can't git dar none too soon,' sez Brer Rabbit, sezee.

"Den ole Gran'sir' Gray Fox, he up'n ax w'at is it, en Brer Rabbit, he sing out, he did:

" 'De big bird rob en little bird sing;
   De big bee zoon en little bee sting,
   De little man lead en big hoss foller—
   Kin you tell w'at's good fer a head in a holler?'

"Gran'sir' Gray Fox, he tuck a pinch er snuff en cough easy ter hisse'f, en study en study, but he aint make it out, en Brer Rabbit, he laugh en sing:

" 'Bee-gum mighty big fer ter make Fox collar,
   Kin you tell w'at's good fer a head in a holler?'

"Atter so long a time, Gran'sir' Gray Fox sorter ketch a glimpse er w'at Brer Rabbit tryin' ter gin 'im, en he tip Brer Rabbit good-day, en shuffle on fer ter hunt up he gran'son."

"And did he find him, Uncle Remus?" asked the little boy.

"Tooby sho', honey. Brer B'ar year de racket w'at Brer Fox kickin' up, en he go down dar fer ter see w'at de marter is. Soon ez he see how de lan' lay, co'se he tuck a notion dat Brer Fox bin robbin' de bee-gums, en he got 'im a han'ful er hick'ries, Brer B'ar did, en he let in on Brer Fox en he wom he jacket scannerlous, en den he tuck'n tu'n 'im loose; but 't wa'n't long 'fo' all de neighbors git wud dat Brer Fox bin robbin' Brer B'ar bee-gums."

HOW MR. ROOSTER LOST HIS DINNER

It seemed .that the rainy season had set in in earnest, but the little boy went down to Uncle Remus's cabin before dark. In some mysterious way, it appeared to the child, the gloom of twilight fastened itself upon the dusky clouds, and the great trees without, and the dismal perspective beyond, gradually became one with the darkness. Uncle Remus had thoughtfully placed a tin pan under a leak in the roof, and the *drip-drip-drip* of the water, as it fell in the resonant vessel, made a not unmusical accompaniment to the storm.

The old man fumbled around under his bed, and presently dragged forth a large bag filled with lightwood knots, which, with an instinctive economy in this particular direction, he had stored away for an emergency. A bright but flickering flame was the result of this timely discovery, and the effect it produced was quite in keeping with all the surroundings. The rain, and wind, and darkness held sway without, while within, the unsteady lightwood blaze seemed to rhyme with the *drip-drip-drip* in the pan. Sometimes the shadow of Uncle Remus, as he leaned over the hearth, would tower and fill the cabin, and again it would fade and disappear among the swaying and swinging cobwebs that curtained the rafters.

"W'en bed-time come, honey," said Uncle Remus, in a soothing tone, "I'll des snatch down yo' pa buggy umbrell' fum up dar in de cornder, des lak I bin a-doin', en I'll take'n take you und' my arm en set you down on Miss Sally h'a'th des ez dry en ez wom ez a rat'-nes' inside a fodder-stack."

At this juncture 'Tildy, the house-girl, rushed in out of the rain and darkness with a water-proof cloak and an umbrella, and announced her mission to the little boy without taking time to catch her breath.

"Miss Sally say you got ter come right back," she exclaimed. "Kaze she skeerd lightnin' gwine strak 'roun' in yer 'mongs' deze high trees some'rs."

Uncle Remus rose from his stooping posture in front of the hearth and assumed a threatening attitude.

"Well, is anybody year de beat er dat!" was his indignant exclamation. "Look yer, gal! Don't you come foolin' 'longer me—now, don't you do it. Kaze ef yer does, I'll take'n hit you a clip w'at'll put you ter bed 'fo' bed-time comes. Dat's w'at!"

"Lawdy! W'at I done gone en done ter Unk' Remus now?" asked 'Tildy, with a great affectation of innocent ignorance.

"I'm gwine ter put on my coat en take dat ar umbrell', en I'm gwine right straight up ter de big house en ax Miss Sally ef she sont dat kinder wud down yer, w'en she know dat chil sittin' yer 'longer me. I'm gwine ter ax her," continued Uncle Remus, "en if she aint sont dat wud, den I'm gwine ter fetch myse'f back. Now, you des watch my motions."

"Well, I year Miss Sally say she 'feard lightnin' gwine ter strak some'rs on de place," said 'Tildy, in a tone which manifested her willingness to compromise all differences, "en den I axt 'er kin I come down yer, en den she say I better bring deze yer cloak en pairsol."

"Now you dun brung um," responded Uncle Remus, "you des better put um in dat cheer over dar, en take yo'se'f off. Thunder mighty ap' ter hit close ter whar deze here slick-head niggers is."

But the little boy finally prevailed upon the old man to allow 'Tildy to remain, and after a while he put matters on a peace footing by inquiring if roosters crowed at night when it was raining.

"Dat dey duz," responded Uncle Remus. "Wet er dry, dey flops der wings en wakes up all de neighbors. Law, bless my soul!" he exclaimed suddenly, "w'at make I done gone en fergit 'bout Mr. Rooster?"

"What about him?" inquired the little boy.

"One time, 'way back yander," said Uncle Remus, knocking the ashes off his hands and knees, "dey wuz two plan'ations right 'longside one er 'ne'r, en on bofe er deze plan'ations wuz a whole passel of fowls. Dey wuz mighty sociable in dem days, en it tu'n out dat de fowls on one plan'ation gun a party, w'ich dey sont out der invites ter de fowls on de 't'er plan'ation.

"W'en de day come, Mr. Rooster, he blow his hawn, he did, en 'semble um all tergedder, en atter dey 'semble dey got in line. Mr. Rooster, he tuck de head, en atter 'im come ole lady Hen en Miss Pullet, en den dar wuz Mr. Peafowl, en Mr. Tukkey Gobbler, en Miss Guinny Hen, en Miss Puddle Duck, en all de balance un um. Dey start off sorter raggedy, but 't wa'n't long 'fo' dey all kotch de step, en den dey march down by de spring, up thoo de hoss-lot en 'cross by de gin-house, en 't wa'n't long 'fo' dey git ter whar de frolic wuz.

"Dey dance, en dey play, en dey sing. Mo' 'speshually did dey play en sing dat ar song w'ich it run on lak dis:

" 'Come under, come under.
  My honey, my love, my own true love;
  My heart bin a-weepin'
  Way down in Galilee.'

"Dey wuz gwine on dis a-way, havin' der 'musements, w'en bimeby, ole Mr. Peafowl, he got on de comb er de barn en de dinner-hawn. Dey all wash der face en han's in de back po'ch, en den dey went in ter dinner. W'en dey git in dar, dey don't see nothin' on de table but a great big pile er co'n-bread. De pones was pile up on pones, en on de top wuz a great big ash-cake. Mr. Rooster, he look at dis en he tu'n up he nose, en bimeby, atter aw'ile, out he strut. Ole

Miss Guinny Hen, she watchin' Mr. Rooster motions, en w'en she see dis, she take'n squall out, she did:

" 'Pot-rack! Pot-rack! Mr. Rooster gone back! Pot-rack! Pot-rack! Mr. Rooster gone back!'

"Wid dat dey all make a great ter-do. Miss Hen en Miss Pullet, dey cackle en squall, Mr. Gobbler, he gobble, en Miss Puddle Duck, she shake 'er tail en say, quickity-quack-quack. But Mr. Rooster, he ruffle up he cape, en march on out.

"Dis sorter put a damper on de yuthers, but 'fo' Mr. Rooster git outer sight en year'n dey went ter wuk on de pile w'at wuz 'pariently co'n-bread, en, lo en beholes, un'need dem pone er bread wuz a whole passel er meat en greens, en bake' taters, en bile' turnips. Mr. Rooster, he year de ladies makin' great 'miration, en he stop en look thoo de crack, en dar he see all de doin's en fixin's. He feel mighty bad, Mr. Rooster did, w'en he see all dis, en de yuther fowls dey holler en ax 'im fer ter come back, en he craw, w'ich it mighty empty, likewise, it up'n ax 'im, but he mighty biggity en stuck up, en he strut off, crowin' ez he go; but he 'speunce er dat time done las' him en all er his fambly down ter dis day. En you neenter take my wud fer't, ne'r, kaze ef you'll des keep yo' eye open en watch, you'll ketch a glimse er ole Mr. Rooster folks scratchin' whar dey 'specks ter fine der rations, en mo' dan dat, dey'll scratch wid der rations in plain sight. Since dat time, dey aint none er de Mr. Roosters bin fool' by dat w'at dey see on top. Dey aint res' twel dey see w'at und' dar. Dey'll scratch spite er all creation."

"Dat's de Lord's truth!" said 'Tildy, with unction. "I done seed um wid my own eyes. Dat I is."

This was 'Tildy's method of renewing peaceful relations with Uncle Remus, but the old man was disposed to resist the attempt.

"You better be up yander washin' up dishes, stidder hoppin' down yer wid er whole packet er stuff w'at Miss Sally aint dreamp er sayin'."

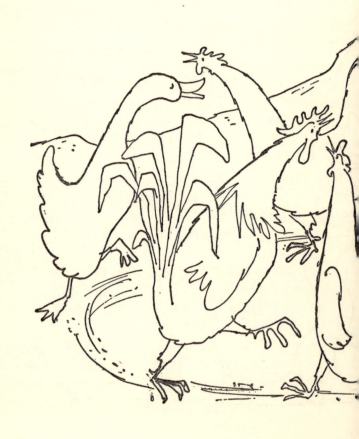

As long as Uncle Remus allowed 'Tildy to remain in the cabin, the little boy was not particularly interested in preventing the perfunctory abuse which the old man might feel disposed to bestow upon the complacent girl. The truth is, the child's mind was occupied with the episode in the story of Mr. Benjamin Ram which treats of the style in which this romantic old wag put Mr. and Mrs. Wolf to flight by playing a tune upon his fiddle. The little boy was particularly struck with this remarkable feat, as many a youngster before him had been, and he made bold to recur to it again by asking Uncle Remus for all the details. It was plain to the latter that the child regarded Mr. Ram as the typical hero of all the animals, and this was by no means gratifying to the old man. He answered the little boy's questions as well as he could, and, when nothing more remained to be said about Mr. Ram, he settled himself back in his chair and resumed the curious history of Brother Rabbit:

"Co'se Mr. Ram mighty smart man. I ain't 'spute dat; but needer Mr. Ram ner yet Mr. Lam is soon creeturs lak Brer Rabbit. Mr. Benjermun Ram, he tuck'n skeer off Brer Wolf en his ole 'oman wid his fiddle, but, bless yo' soul, ole Brer Rabbit he gone en done wuss'n dat."

"What did Brother Rabbit do?" asked the little boy.

"One time," said Uncle Remus, "Brer Fox, he tuck'n ax some er de yuther creeturs ter he house. He ax Brer B'ar, en Brer Wolf, en Brer 'Coon, but he aint ax Brer Rabbit. All de same, Brer Rabbit got win' un it, en he 'low dat ef he don't go, he 'speck he have much fun ez de nex' man.

"De creeturs w'at git de invite, dey tuck'n 'semble at Brer Fox house, en Brer Fox, he ax um in en got um cheers, en dey sot dar en laugh en talk, twel, bimeby, Brer Fox, he fotch out a bottle er dram en lay 'er out on de side-bode, en den he sorter step back en say, sezee:

" 'Des step up, gentermens, en he'p yo'se'f,' en you better b'leeve dey he'p derse'f.

"W'iles dey wuz drinkin' en drammin' en gwine on, w'at you 'speck Brer Rabbit doin'? You des well make up yo' min' dat Brer Rabbit monst'us busy, kase he 'uz sailin' 'roun' fixin' up his tricks. Long time 'fo' dat, Brer Rabbit had been at a bobbycue whar dey was a muster, en w'iles all de folks 'uz down at de spring eatin' dinner, Brer Rabbit he crope up en run off wid one er de drums. Dey wuz a big drum en a little drum, en Brer Rabbit he snatch up de littles' one en run home.

"Now, den, w'en he year 'bout de yuther creeturs gwine ter Brer Fox house, w'at do Brer Rabbit do but git out dis rattlin' drum en make de way down de road todes whar dey is. He tuk dat drum," continued Uncle Remus, with great elation of voice and manner, "en he went down de road todes Brer Fox house, en he make 'er talk like thunner mix up wid hail. Hit talk lak dis:

" *'Diddybum, diddybum, diddybum-bum-bum—diddybum!'*

"De creeturs, dey 'uz a-drinkin', en a-drammin', en a-gwine on at a terrible rate, en dey aint year de racket, but all de same, yer come Brer Rabbit:

" *'Diddybum, diddybum, diddybum-bum-bum—diddybum!'*

"Bimeby Brer 'Coon, w'ich he allers got one year hung out fer de news, he up'n ax Brer Fox w'at dat, en by dat time all de creeturs stop en lissen; but all de same, yer come Brer Rabbit:

" *'Diddybum, diddybum, diddybum-bum-bum— diddybum!'*

"De creeturs dey keep on lis'nin', en Brer Rabbit keep on gittin' nigher, twel bimeby Brer 'Coon retch und' de cheer fer he hat, en say, sezee:

" 'Well, gents, I 'speck I better be gwine. I tole my ole 'oman dat I won't be gone a minnit, on yer 't is 'way 'long in de day.'

"Wid dat Brer 'Coon, he skip out, but he aint git much furder dan de back gate, 'fo' yer come all de yuther creeturs like dey 'uz runnin' a foot-race, en ole Brer Fox wuz wukkin' in de lead."

"Dar, now!" exclaimed 'Tildy, with great fervor.

"Yasser! Dar dey wuz, en dar dey went," continued Uncle Remus. "Dey tuck nigh cuts, en dey scramble over one er 'n'er, en dey aint res' twel dey git in de bushes.

"Ole Brer Rabbit, he came on down de road—*diddybum, diddybum, diddybum-bum-bum*—en bless gracious, w'en he git ter Brer Fox house dey aint nobody dar! Brer Rabbit is dat owdacious, dat he hunt all 'roun' twel he fine de a'r-hole er de drum, en he put his mouf ter dat en sing out, sezee:

" 'Is dey anybody home?' en den he answer hisse'f, sezee, 'Law, no, honey—folks all gone.'

"Wid dat, ole Brer Rabbit break loose en laugh, he did, fit ter kill hisse'f, en den he slam Brer Fox front gate wide open, en march up ter de house. W'en he git dar, he kick de do' open en hail Brer Fox, but nobody aint dar, en Brer Rabbit he walk in en take a cheer, en make hisse'f at home wid puttin' his foots on de sofy en spittin' on de flo'.

"Brer Rabbit aint sot dar long 'fo' he ketch a whiff er de dram——"

"You year dat?" exclaimed 'Tildy, with convulsive admiration.

"—'Fo' he ketch a whiff er de dram, en den he see it on de side-bode, en he step up en drap 'bout a tumbeler full some'rs down in de neighborhoods er de goozle. Brer Rabbit mighty lak some folks I knows. He tuck one tumbeler full, en 't wa'n't long 'fo' he tuck 'n'er'n, en w'en a man do dis a-way," continued Uncle Remus, somewhat apologetically, "he bleedz ter git drammy."

"Truth, too!" said 'Tildy, by way of hearty confirmation.

"All des time de yuther creeturs wuz down in de bushes lissenin' fer de *diddybum,* en makin' ready fer ter light out fum dar at de drop uv a hat. But dey aint year no mo' fuss, en bimeby Brer Fox, he say he gwine back en look atter he plunder, en de yuther creeturs say dey b'leeve dey'll go 'long wid 'im. Dey start out, dey did, en dey crope todes Brer Fox house, but dey crope mighty keerful, en I boun' ef somebody'd 'a' shuck a bush, dem ar creeturs 'ud 'a' nat'ally to' up de ye'th gittin' 'way fum dar. Yit dey still aint year no fuss, en dey keep on creepin' twel dey git in de house.

"W'en dey git in dar, de fus' sight dey see wuz ole Brer Rabbit stannin' up by de dram-bottle mixin' up a toddy, en he wa'n't so stiff-kneed n'er, kase he sorter swage fum side ter side, en he look lak he mighty limbersome, w'ich, goodness knows, a man bleedz ter be limbersome w'en he drink dat kinder licker w'at Brer Fox perwide fer dem creeturs.

"W'en Brer Fox see Brer Rabbit makin' free wid he doin's dat a-way, w'at you 'speck he do?" inquired Uncle Remus, with the air of one seeking general information.

"I 'speck he cusst," said 'Tildy, who was apt to take a vividly practical view of matters.

"He was glad," said the little boy, "because he had a good chance to catch Brother Rabbit."

"Tooby sho' he wuz," continued Uncle Remus, heartily assenting to the child's interpretation of the situation: "tooby sho' he wuz. He stan' dar, Brer Fox did, en he watch Brer Rabbit motions. Bimeby he holler out, sezee:

"'Ah yi![1] Brer Rabbit!' sezee. 'Many a time is you made yo' 'scape, but now I got you!' En wid dat, Brer Fox en de yuther creeturs cloze in on Brer Rabbit.

[1] A corruption of "aye, aye." It is used as an expression of triumph and its employment in this connection is both droll and picturesque.

"Seem like I done tole you dat Brer Rabbit done gone en tuck mo' dram dan w'at 'uz good fer he wholesome. Yit he head aint swim so bad dat he dunner w'at he doin', en time he lay eyes on Brer Fox, he know he done got in close quarters. Soon ez he see dis, Brer Rabbit make like he bin down in de cup mo' deeper dan w'at he is, en he stagger 'roun' like town gal stannin' in a batteau, en he seem lak he des ez limber ez a wet rag. He stagger up ter Brer Fox, he did, en he roll he eyeballs 'roun', en slap 'im on he back en ax 'im how he ma. Den w'en he see de yuther creeturs," continued Uncle Remus, "he holler out, he did:

" 'Vents yo' uppance, gentermens! Vents yo' uppance![2] Ef you'll des gimme han'-roomance en come one at a time, de tussle'll las' longer. How you all come on, nohow?' sezee.

"Ole Brer Rabbit talk so kuse dat de yuther creeturs have mo' fun dan w'at you k'n shake a stick at, but bimeby Brer Fox say dey better git down ter business, en den dey all cloze in on Brer Rabbit, en dar he wuz.

"In dem days, ole man B'ar wuz a jedge 'mongs' de creeturs, en dey all ax 'im w'at dey gwine do 'long wid Brer Rabbit, en Jedge B'ar, he put on his specks, en cle'r up his th'oat, en say dat de bes' way ter do wid a man w'at kick up sech a racket, en run de neighbors outer der own house, en go in dar en level[3] on de pantry, is ter take 'im out en drown 'im; en ole Brer Fox, w'ich he settin' on de jury, he up'n smack he hands togedder, en cry, en say, sezee, dat atter dis he bleedz ter b'leeve dat Jedge B'ar done got all-under holt on de lawyer-books, kase dat 'zackly w'at dey say w'en a man level on he neighbor pantry.

[2] Southern readers will recognize this and "han'-roomance" as terms used by Negroes in playing marbles—a favorite game on the plantations Sunday afternoons. These terms were curt and expressive enough to gain currency among the whites.
[3] Levy.

"Den Brer Rabbit, he make out he skeerd, en he holler en cry, en beg um, in de name er goodness, don't fling 'im in de spring branch, kaze dey all know he dunner how ter swim; but ef dey bleedz fer ter pitch 'im in, den for mussy sake gin' 'im a walkin'-cane, so he kin have sumpin' ter hol' ter w'iles he drownin'.

"Ole Brer B'ar scratch his head en say, sezee, dat, fur ez his 'membunce go back, he aint come 'cross nothin' in de lawyer-book ter de contraries er dat, en den dey all 'gree dat Brer Rabbit kin have a walkin'-cane.

"Wid dat, dey ketch up Brer Rabbit en put 'im in a wheelborrow en kyar 'im down ter de branch, en fling 'im in."

"Eh-eh!" exclaimed 'Tildy, with well-feigned astonishment.

"Dey fling 'im in," continued Uncle Remus, "en Brer Rabbit light on he foots, same ez a tomcat, en pick his way out by de helps er de walkin'-cane. De water wuz dat shaller dat it don't mo'n come over Brer Rabbit slipper, en w'en he git out on t'er side, he holler back, sezee:

" 'So long, Brer Fox!' "

MR. FOX, MR. RABBIT,
AND KING DEER'S DAUGHTER

Notwithstanding Brother Rabbit's success with the drum, the little boy was still inclined to refer to Mr. Benjamin Ram and his fiddle; but Uncle Remus was not, by any means, willing that such an ancient vagabond as Mr. Ram should figure as a hero, and he said that, while it was possible that Brother Rabbit was no great hand with the fiddle, he was a drummer, and a capital singer to boot. Furthermore, Uncle Remus declared that Brother Rabbit could perform upon the quills,[1] an accomplishment to which none of the other animals could lay claim. There was a time, too, the old man pointedly suggested, when the romantic rascal used his musical abilities to win the smiles of a nice young lady of quality—no less a personage, indeed, than King Deer's daughter. As a matter of course, the little boy was anxious to hear the particulars, and Uncle Remus was in nowise loath to give them.

"W'en you come ter ax me 'bout de year en day er de mont'," said the old man, cunningly arranging a defence against criticism, "den I'm done, kaze de almanick w'at dey got in dem times won't pass muster deze days, but, let 'lone dat, I 'speck dey aint had none yit; en ef dey is, dey aint none bin handed down ter Remus.

"Well, den, some time 'long in dar, ole Brer Fox en Brer Rabbit got ter flyin' 'roun' King Deer daughter. Dey tells me she 'uz a monst'us likely gal, en I 'speck may be she wuz; leas'ways, Brer Fox, he hanker atter 'er, en likewise Brer Rabbit, he hanker atter 'er. Ole King Deer look lak he sorter lean todes Brer Fox, kaze ter a settle man like him, hit seem lak dat Brer Fox kin stir 'roun' en keep de pot a-b'ilin', mo' speshually bein 's he de bigges'. Hit go on dis a-way

---

[1] The veritable Pan's pipes. A simple but very effective musical instrument made of reeds, and in great favor on the plantations.

twel hardly a day pass dat one er de yuther er dem creeturs don't go sparklin' 'roun' King Deer daughter, en it got so atter w'ile dat all day long Brer Rabbit en Brer Fox keep de front gate a-skreakin', en King Deer daughter aint ska'cely had time fer ter eat a meal vittels in no peace er min'.

"In dem days," pursued Uncle Remus, in a tone of unmistakable historical fervor, "w'en a creetur go a-courtin' dey wa'n't none er dish yer bokay doin's mix' up 'longer der co'tship, en dey aint cut up no capers like folks does now. Stidder scollopin' 'roun' en bowin' en scrapin', dey des go right straight atter de gal. Ole Brer Rabbit, he mouter had some bubby-blossoms[2] wrop up in his hankcher, but mostly him en Brer Fox 'ud des drap in on King Deer daughter en 'gin ter cas' sheep-eyes at 'er time dey sot down en cross der legs."

"En I bet," said 'Tildy, by way of comment, and looking as though she wanted to blush, "dat dey wa'n't 'shame', nuther."

"Dey went 'long dis a-way," continued Uncle Remus, "twel it 'gun ter look sorter skittish wid Brer Rabbit, kaze ole King Deer done good ez say, sezee, dat he gwine ter take Brer Fox inter de fambly. Brer Rabbit, he 'low, he did, dat dis aint gwine ter do, en he study en study how he gwine ter cut Brer Fox out.

"Las', one day, w'iles he gwine thoo King Deer pastur' lot, he up wid a rock en kilt two er King Deer goats. W'en he git ter de house, he ax King Deer daughter whar'bouts her pa, en she up'n say she go call 'im, en w'en Brer Rabbit see 'im, he az w'en de weddin' tuck place, en King Deer ax w'ich weddin', en Brer Rabbit say de weddin' 'twix' Brer Fox en King Deer daughter. Wid dat, ole King Deer ax Brer Rabbit w'at make he go on so, en Brer Rabbit, he up'n 'spon' dat he see Brer Fox makin' monst'us free wid de fambly, gwine 'roun' chunkin' de chickens en killin' up de goats.

"Ole King Deer strak he walkin'-cane down 'pon de flo', en 'low

[2] A species of sweet-shrub growing wild in the South.

dat he don't put no 'pennunce in no sech tale lak dat, en den Brer Rabbit tell 'im dat ef he'll des take a walk down in de pastur' lot, he kin see de kyarkiss er de goats. Ole King Deer, he put out, en bimeby he come back, en he 'low he gwine ter settle marters wid Brer Fox ef it take 'im a mont'.

"Brer Rabbit say he a good frien' ter Brer Fox, en he aint got no room ter talk 'bout 'im, but yit w'en he see 'im 'stroyin' King Deer goats en chunkin' at his chickens, en rattlin' on de palin's fer ter make de dog bark, he bleedz ter come lay de case 'fo' de fambly.

" 'En mo'n dat,' sez ole Brer Rabbit, sezee, 'I'm de man w'at kin make Brer Fox come en stan' right at de front gate en tell you dat he is kill dem goat; en ef you des wait twel ter-night, I won't ax you ter take my wud,' sezee.

"King Deer say ef Brer Rabbit man 'nuff ter do dat, den he kin git de gal en thanky, too. Wid dat, Brer Rabbit jump up en crack he heels tergedder, en put out fer ter fine Brer Fox. He aint git fur 'fo' he see Brer Fox comin' down de road all primp up. Brer Rabbit, he sing out, he did:

" 'Brer Foxy, whar you gwine?'

"En Brer Fox, he holler back:

" 'Go 'way, Rab; don't bodder wid me. I'm gwine fer ter see my gal.'

"Brer Rabbit, he laugh 'way down in his stomach, but he don't let on, en atter some mo' chat, he up'n say dat ole King Deer done tell 'im 'bout how Brer Fox gwine ter marry he daughter, en den he tell Brer Fox dat he done promise King Deer dat dey'd drap 'roun' ter-night en gin 'im some music.

" 'En I up'n tole 'im,' sez Brer Rabbit, sezee, 'dat de music w'at we can't make aint wuth makin',—me wid my quills, en you wid yo' tr'angle.[3] De nex' motion we makes,' sezee, 'we'll hatter go off

[3] Triangle.

205

some'rs en practise up on de song we'll sing, en I got one yer dat'll tickle um dat bad,' sez Brer Rabbit, sezee, 'twel I lay dey'll fetch out a hunk er dat big chicken-pie w'at I see um puttin' in de pot des now,' sezee.

"In a 'casion lak dis, Brer Fox say he de ve'y man w'at Brer Rabbit huntin', en he 'low dat he'll des 'bout put off payin' he call ter King Deer house en go wid Brer Rabbit fer ter practise on dat song.

"Den Brer Rabbit, he git he quills en Brer Fox he git he tr'angle, en dey went down on de spring branch, en dar dey sing en play, twel dey git it all by heart. Ole Brer Rabbit, he make up de song he own se'f, en he fix it so dat he sing de call, lak de captain er de co'n-pile, en ole Brer Fox, he hatter sing de answer." [4]

At this point Uncle Remus paused to indulge in one of his suggestive chuckles, and then proceeded:

"Don't talk 'bout no songs ter me. Gentermens! Dat 'uz a funny song fum de wud go. Bimeby, w'en dey practise long time, dey gits up en goes 'roun' in de neighborhoods er King Deer house, en w'en night come dey tuck der stan' at de front gate, en atter all got still, Brer Rabbit, he gun de wink, en dey broke loose wid der music. Dey played a chune er two on de quills en tr'angle, en den dey got ter de song. Ole Brer Rabbit, he got de call, en he open up lak dis:

" 'Some folks pile up mo'n dey kin tote,
    En dat w'at de marter wid King Deer goat,'

en den Brer Fox, he make answer:

" 'Dat's so, dat's so, en I'm glad dat it's so!'

Den de quills en de tr'angle, dey come in, en den Brer Rabbit pursue on wid de call:

[4] That is to say, Brother Rabbit sang the air and Brother Fox the refrain.

" 'Some kill sheep en some kill shote,
  But Brer Fox kill King Deer goat,'

en den Brer Fox, he jine in wid de answer:

" 'I did, dat I did, en I'm glad dat I did!'

En des 'bout dat time King Deer, he walk outer de gate en hit Brer Fox a clip wid his walkin'-cane, en he foller it up wid 'n'er'n, dat make Brer Fox fa'rly squall, en you des better b'leeve he make tracks 'way fum dar, en de gal she come out, en dey ax Brer Rabbit in."

"Did Brother Rabbit marry King Deer's daughter, Uncle Remus?" asked the little boy.

"Now, den, honey, you're crowdin' me," responded the old man. "Dey ax 'im in, en dey gun 'im a great big hunk er chicken-pie, but I won't make sho' dat he tuck'n marry de gal. De p'int wid me is de way Brer Rabbit run Brer Fox off fum dar."

MR. TERRAPIN DECEIVES MR. BUZZARD

There was a pause here, which was finally broken by 'Tildy, whose remark was in the shape of a very undignified yawn. Uncle Remus regarded her for a moment with an expression of undisguised scorn, which quickly expressed itself in words:

"Ef you'd er bin outer de house dat whack, you'd er tuck us all in. Pity dey aint some place er 'n'er whar deze yer trollops kin go en l'arn manners."

'Tildy, however, ignored the old man, and, with a toss of her head, said to the little boy in a cool, exasperating tone, employing a pet name she had heard the child's mother use:

"Well, Pinx, I 'speck we better go. De rain done mos' hilt up now, en bimeby de stars'll be a-shinin'. Miss Sally lookin' fer you right now."

"You better go whar you gwine, you triflin' huzzy, you!" exclaimed Uncle Remus. "You better go git yo' Jim Crow kyard en straighten out dem wrops in yo' ha'r. I allers year w'ite folks say you better keep yo' eye on niggers w'at got der ha'r wrop up in strings. Now I done gun you fa'r warnin's."

"Uncle Remus," said the little boy, when the old man's wrath had somewhat subsided, "why do they call them Jim Crow cards?"

"I be bless ef I know, honey, 'ceppin' it's kaze dey er de onliest machine w'at deze yer low-life niggers kin oncomb der kinks wid. Now, den," continued the old man, straightening up and speaking with considerable animation, "dat 'min's me 'bout a riddle w'at been runnin' 'roun' in my head. En dat riddle—it's de outdoin'es' riddle w'at I mos' ever year tell un. Hit go lak dis: Ef he come, he don't come; ef he don't come, he come. Now, I boun' you can't tell w'at is dat."

After some time spent in vain guessing, the little boy confessed that he did n't know.

"Hit's crow en co'n," said Uncle Remus sententiously.

"Crow and corn, Uncle Remus?"

"Co'se, honey. Crow come, de co'n don't come; crow don't come, den de co'n come."

"Dat's so," said 'Tildy. "I done see um pull up co'n, en I done see co'n grow w'at dey don't pull up."

If 'Tildy thought to propitiate Uncle Remus, she was mistaken. He scowled at her, and addressed himself to the little boy:

"De Crow, he mighty close kin ter de Buzzud, en dat puts me in min' dat we aint bin a-keepin' up wid ole Brer Buzzud close ez we might er done.

"W'at de case mout be deze days, I aint a-sayin', but, in dem times, ole Brer Tarrypin love honey mo' samer dan Brer B'ar, but he wuz dat flat-footed dat, w'en he fine a bee-tree, he can't climb it, en he go so slow dat he can't hardly fine um. Bimeby, one day, w'en he gwine 'long down de road des a-honin' atter honey, who should he meet but ole Brer Buzzud.

"Dey shuck han's mighty sociable en ax 'bout de news er de neighborhoods, en den, atter w'ile, Brer Tarrypin say ter ole Brer Buzzud, sezee, dat he wanter go inter cahoots wid 'im 'longer gittin' honey, en 't wa'n't long 'fo' dey struck a trade. Brer Buzzud wuz ter fly 'roun' en look fer de bee-tree, en Brer Tarrypin he wuz ter creep en crawl, en hunt on de groun'.

"Dey start out, dey did, ole Brer Buzzud sailin' 'roun' in de elements, en ole Brer Tarrypin shufflin' en shamblin' on de groun'. 'Mos' de ve'y fus' fiel' w'at he come ter, Brer Tarrypin strak up wid a great big bumbly-bee nes' in de groun'. He look 'roun', ole Brer Tarrypin did, en bimeby he stick he head in en tas'e de honey, en den he pull it out en look all 'roun' fer ter see ef he kin ketch a glimpse er Brer Buzzud; but Brer Buzzud don't seem lak he nowhar. Den Brer Tarrypin say to hisse'f, sezee, dat he 'speck dat bumbly-bee honey aint de kinder honey w'at dey been talkin' 'bout, en dey aint no great shakes er honey dar nohow. Wid dat, Brer Tarrypin crope inter de hole en gobble up de las' drop er de bumbly-bee honey by he own-alone se'f. Atter he done make 'way wid it, he come out, he did, en he whirl in en lick it all off'n his footses, so ole Brer Buzzud can't tell dat he done bin git a mess er honey.

"Den ole Brer Tarrypin stretch out he neck en try ter lick de honey off'n he back, but he neck too short; en he try ter scrape it off up 'g'in' a tree, but it don't come off; en den he waller on de groun', but still it don't come off. Den old Brer Tarrypin jump up, en say ter hisse'f dat he'll des 'bout rack off home, en w'en Brer Buzzud come he kin lie on he back en say he sick, so ole Brer Buzzud can't see de honey.

"Brer Tarrypin start off, he did, but he happen ter look up, en, lo en beholes, dar wuz Brer Buzzud huv'rin' right spang over de spot whar he is. Brer Tarrypin know Brer Buzzud bleedz ter see 'im ef he start off home, en mo'n dat, he know he be fine out ef he don't stir 'roun' en do sump'n' mighty quick. Wid dat, Brer Tarrypin shuffle back ter de bumbly-bee nes' swif' ez he kin, en buil' 'im a fier in dar, en den he crawl out en holler:

" 'Brer Buzzud! O Brer Buzzud! Run yer, fer gracious sake, Brer Buzzud, en look how much honey I done fine! I des crope in a little ways, en it des drip all down my back, same like water. Run yer, Brer Buzzud! Half yone en half mine, Brer Buzzud!'

"Brer Buzzud, he flop down, en he laugh en say he mighty glad, kaze he done git hongry up dar whar he bin. Den Brer Tarrypin tell Brer Buzzud fer ter creep in little ways en tas'e en see how he like um, w'iles he take his stan' on de outside en watch fer somebody. But no sooner is Brer Buzzud crope in de bumbly-bee nes' dan Brer

Tarrypin take'n roll a great big rock front er de hole. Terreckly, de fier 'gun ter bu'n Brer Buzzud, en he sing out like a man in trouble:

"'Sump'n' bitin' me, Brer Tarrypin—sump'n' bitin' me, Brer Tarrypin!'

"Den ole Brer Tarrypin, he holler back:

"'It's de bumbly-bees a-stingin' you, Brer Buzzud; stan' up en flop yo' wings, Brer Buzzud. Stan' up en flop yo' wings, Brer Buzzud, en you'll drive um off,' sezee.

"Brer Buzzud flop en flop he wings, but de mo' w'at he flop, de mo' he fan de fier, en 't wa'n't long 'fo' he done bodaciously bu'n up, all 'ceppin' de big een er his wing-fedders, en dem ole Brer Tarrypin tuck en make inter some quills, w'ich he go 'roun' a-playin' un um, en de chune w'at he play was dish yer:

"'I foolee, I foolee, I foolee po' Buzzud;
Po' Buzzud I foolee, I foolee, I foolee.'"

"That must have been a mighty funny song," said the little boy.

"Fun one time aint fun 'n'er time; some folks fines fun whar yuther folks fines trouble. Pig may laugh w'en he see de rock a-heatin', but dey aint no fun dar fer de pig.[1]

"Yit, fun er no fun, dat de song w'at Brer Tarrypin play on de quills:

" 'I foolee, I foolee, I foolee po' Buzzud;
Po' Buzzud I foolee, I foolee, I foolee.'

"Nobody dunner whar de quills cum fum, kaze Brer Tarrypin, he aint makin' no brags how he git um; yit ev'ybody want um on account er der playin' sech a lonesome[2] chune, en ole Brer Fox, he want um wuss'n all. He beg en he beg Brer Tarrypin fer ter sell 'im dem quills; but Brer Tarrypin, he hol' on t' um tight, en say eh-eh! Den he ax Brer Tarrypin fer ter loan um t' um des a week, so he kin play fer he chilluns, but Brer Tarrypin, he shake he head en put he foot down, en keep on playin':

" 'I foolee, I foolee, I foolee po' Buzzud;
Po' Buzzud I foolee, I foolee, I foolee.'

"But Brer Fox, he aint got no peace er min' on account er dem quills, en one day he meet Brer Tarrypin en he ax 'im how he seem ter segashuate[3] en he fambly en all he chilluns; en den Brer Fox ax Brer Tarrypin ef he can't des look at de quills, kaze he got some

[1] An allusion to the primitive mode of cleaning hogs by heating rocks, and placing them in a barrel or tank of water.
[2] This word "lonesome," as used by the Negroes, is the equivalent of "thrilling," "romantic," etc., and in that sense is very expressive.
[3] An inquiry after his health. Another form is: "How does yo' corporosity seem ter segashuate?"

goose-fedders at he house, en if he kin des get a glimpse er Brer Tarrypin quills, he 'speck he kin make some mighty like um.

"Brer Tarrypin, he study 'bout dis, but he hate ter 'ny small favors like dat, en bimeby he hol' out dem quills whar Brer Fox kin see um. Wid dat, Brer Fox, he tuck'n juk de quills outen Brer Tarrypin han', he did, and dash off des ez hard ez he kin go. Brer Tarrypin, he holler en holler at 'im des loud ez he kin holler, but he know he can't ketch 'im, en he des sot dar, Brer Tarrypin did, en look lak he done los' all de kin-folks w'at he got in de roun' worrul.'

"Atter dis, Brer Fox he strut 'roun' en play mighty biggity, en eve'y time he meet Brer Tarrypin in de road he walk all 'roun' 'im en play on de quills like dis:

" 'I foolee, I foolee, po' Buzzud;
   I foolee ole Tarrypin, too.'

"Brer Tarrypin, he feel mighty bad, but he aint sayin' nothin'. Las', one day w'iles ole Brer Tarrypin was settin' on a log sunnin' hisse'f, yer come Brer Fox playin' dat same old chune on de quills, but Brer Tarrypin, he stay still. Brer Fox, he come up little nigher en play, but Brer Tarrypin, he keep he eyes shot en he stay still. Brer Fox, he come nigher en git on de log; Brer Tarrypin aint sayin' nothin'. Brer Fox still git up nigher en play on de quills; still Brer Tarrypin aint sayin' nothin'.

" 'Brer Tarrypin mighty sleepy dis mawnin',' sez Brer Fox, sezee.

"Still Brer Tarrypin keep he eyes shot en stay still. Brer Fox keep on gittin' nigher en nigher, twel bimeby Brer Tarrypin open he eyes en he mouf bofe, en he make a grab at Brer Fox en miss 'im.

"But hol' on!" exclaimed Uncle Remus, in response to an expression of intense disappointment in the child's face. "You des wait a minnit. Nex' mawnin', Brer Tarrypin take hisse'f off en waller in a mud-hole, en smear hisse'f wid mud twel he look des 'zackly lak a clod er dirt. Den he crawl off en lay down un'need a log whar he know Brer Fox come eve'y mawnin' fer ter freshen[4] hisse'f.

"Brer Tarrypin lay dar, he did, en terreckly yer come Brer Fox. Time he git dar, Brer Fox 'gun ter lip backerds en forerds 'cross de log, and Brer Tarrypin he crope nigher en nigher, twel bimeby he make a grab at Brer Fox en kotch him by de foot. Dey tells me," continued Uncle Remus, rubbing his hands together in token of great satisfaction, "dey tells me dat w'en Brer Tarrypin ketch holt, hit got ter thunder 'fo' he let go. All I know, Brer Tarrypin git Brer Fox by de foot, en he hilt 'im dar. Brer Fox he jump en he r'ar, but Brer Tarrypin done got 'im. Brer Fox, he holler out:

" 'Brer Tarrypin, please lemme go!'

"Brer Tarrypin talk way down in his th'oat:

" 'Gim' my quills!'

" 'Lemme go en fetch um.'

" 'Gim' my quills!'

" 'Do pray lemme go git um.'

" 'Gim' my quills!'

"En, bless gracious! Dis all Brer Fox kin git outer Brer Tarrypin. Las', Brer Fox foot hu't 'im so bad dat he bleedz ter do sump'n', en he sing out fer his ole 'oman fer ter fetch de quills, but he ole 'oman, she busy 'bout de house, en she don't year 'im. Den he call he son, w'ich he name Tobe. He holler en bawl, en Tobe make answer:

" 'Tobe! O Tobe! You Tobe!'

" 'W'at you want, daddy?'

" 'Fetch Brer Tarrypin quills.'

" 'W'at you say, daddy? Fetch de big tray ter git de honey in?'

" 'No, you crazy-head! Fetch Brer Tarrypin quills!'

" 'W'at you say, daddy? Fetch de dipper ter ketch de minners in?'

[4] Exercise himself.

" 'No, you fool! Fetch Brer Tarrypin quills!'

" 'W'at you say, daddy? Water done been spill?'

"Hit went on dis a-way twel atter w'ile ole Miss Fox year de racket, en den she lissen, en she know dat 'er ole man holler'n' fer de quills, en she fotch um out en gun um ter Brer Tarrypin, en Brer Tarrypin, he let go he holt. He let go he holt," Uncle Remus went on, "but long time atter dat, w'en Brer Fox go ter pay he calls, he hatter go *hoppity-fetchity, hoppity-fetchity.*"

The old man folded his hands in his lap, and sat quietly gazing into the lightwood fire. Presently he said:

"I 'speck Miss Sally blessin' us all right now, en fus' news you know she'll h'ist up en have Mars John a-trapesin' down yer; en ef she do dat, den ter-morrer mawnin' my brekkuss'll be col', en lakwise my dinner, en ef dey's sump'n' w'at I 'spizes hit's col' vittels."

Thereupon Uncle Remus arose, shook himself, peered out into the night to discover that the rain had nearly ceased, and then made ready to carry the little boy to his mother. Long before the chickens had crowed for midnight, the child, as well as the old man, had been transported to the land where myths and fables cease to be wonderful,—the land of pleasant dreams.

One night the little boy failed to make his appearance at the accustomed hour, and the next morning the intelligence that the child was sick went forth from the "big house." Uncle Remus was told that it had been necessary during the night to call in two physicians. When this information was imparted to the old man, there was an expression upon his countenance of awe not unmixed with indignation. He gave vent to the latter:

"Dar now! Two un um! W'en dat chile rize up, ef rize up he do, he'll des nat'ally be a shadder. Yer I is, gwine on eighty year, en I aint tuck none er dat ar docter truck yit, ceppin' it's dish yer flas' er poke-root w'at ole Miss Favers fix up fer de stiffness in my j'ints. Dey'll come en dey'll go, en dey'll po' in der jollup yer en slap on der fly-plarster dar, en sprinkle der calomy yander, twel bimeby dat chile won't look like hisse'f. Dat's w'at! En mo'n dat, hit's mighty kuse unter me dat ole folks kin go 'long en stan' up ter de rack en gobble up der 'lowance, en yit chilluns is got ter be strucken down. Ef Miss Sally'll des tu'n dem docter mens loose onter me, I lay I lick up der physic twel dey go off 'stonish'd."

But no appeal of this nature was made to Uncle Remus. The illness of the little boy was severe, but not fatal. He took his medicine and improved, until finally even the doctors pronounced him convalescent. But he was very weak, and it was a fortnight before he was permitted to leave his bed. He was restless, and yet his term of imprisonment was full of pleasure. Every night after supper Uncle Remus would creep softly into the back piazza, place his hat carefully on the floor, rap gently on the door by way of announcement, and so pass into the nursery. How patient his vigil, how tender his ministrations, only the mother of the little boy knew; how comfortable and refreshing the change from the bed to the strong arms of Uncle Remus, only the little boy could say.

Almost the first manifestation of the child's convalescence was the renewal of his interest in the wonderful adventures of Brother Rabbit, Brother Fox, and the other brethren who flourished in that strange past over which this modern Æsop had thrown the veil of fable. "Miss Sally," as Uncle Remus called the little boy's mother, sitting in an adjoining room, heard the youngster pleading for a story, and after a while she heard the old man clear up his throat with a great affectation of formality and begin.

"Dey aint skacely no p'int whar ole Brer Rabbit en ole Brer Fox made der 'greements side wid one er 'n'er; let 'lone dat, dey wuz one p'int 'twix' um w'ich it wuz same ez fier en tow, en dat wuz Miss Meadows en de gals. Little ez you might 'speck, dem same creeturs wuz bofe un um flyin' 'roun' Miss Meadows en de gals. Ole Brer Rabbit, he'd go dar, en dar he'd fine ole Brer Fox settin' up gigglin' wid de gals, en den he'd skuze hisse'f, he would, en gallop down de big road a piece, en paw up de san' same lak dat ar ball-face steer w'at tuck'n tuck off yo' pa' coat-tail las' Feberwary. En lakwise ole Brer Fox, he'd sa'nter in, en fine old man Rab. settin' 'longside er de gals, en den he'd go out down de road en grab a simmon-bush in he mouf, en nat'ally gnyaw de bark off'n it. In dem days, honey," continued Uncle Remus, responding to a look of perplexity on the child's face, "creeturs wuz wuss dan w'at dey is now. Dey wuz dat—lots wuss.

"Dey went on dis a-way twel, bimeby, Brer Rabbit 'gun ter cas' 'roun', he did, fer ter see ef he can't bus' inter some er Brer Fox 'rangerments, en, atter w'ile, one day w'en he wer' settin' down by de side er de road wukkin up de diffunt oggyment w'at strak pun he mine, en fixin' up he tricks, des 'bout dat time he year a clatter up de long green lane, en yer come ole Brer Fox—*too-bookity—bookity—bookity-book*—lopin' 'long mo' samer dan a bay colt in de bolly-patch.

En he wuz all primp up, too, mon, en he look slick en shiny lak he des come outen de sto'. Ole man Rab., he sot dar, he did, en w'en ole Brer Fox come gallopin' 'long, Brer Rabbit, he up'n hail 'im. Brer Fox, he fotch up, en dey pass de time er day wid one er nudder monst'us perlite; en den, bimeby atter w'ile, Brer Rabbit, he up'n say, sezee, dat he got some mighty good news fer Brer Fox; en Brer Fox, he up'n ax 'im w'at is it. Den Brer Rabbit, he sorter scratch he year wid his behime foot en say, sezee:

" 'I wuz takin' a walk day 'fo' yistiddy,' sezee, 'w'en de fus' news I know'd I run up gin de bigges' en de fattes' bunch er grapes dat I ever lay eyes on. Dey wuz dat fat en dat big,' sezee, 'dat de natal juice wuz des drappin' fum um, en de bees wuz a-swawmin' atter de honey, en little ole Jack Sparrer en all er his fambly conneckshun wuz skeetin' 'roun' dar dippin' in der bills,' sezee.

"Right den en dar," Uncle Remus went on, "Brer Fox mouf 'gun ter water, en he look outer he eye like he de bes' frien' w'at Brer Rabbit got in de roun' worl'. He done fergit all 'bout de gals, en he sorter sidle up ter Brer Rabbit, he did, en he say, sezee:

" 'Come on, Brer Rabbit,' sezee, 'en less you 'n me go git dem ar grapes 'fo' deyer all gone,' sezee. En den ole Brer Rabbit, he laff, he did, en up'n 'spon', sezee:

" 'I hungry myse'f, Brer Fox,' sezee. 'but I aint hankerin' atter grapes, en I'll be in monst'us big luck ef I kin rush 'roun' yer some'rs en scrape up a bait er pusley time nuff fer ter keep de breff in my body. En yit,' sezee, 'ef you take'n rack off atter deze yer grapes, w'at Miss Meadows en de gals gwine do? I lay dey got yo' name in de pot,' sezee.

" 'Ez ter dat,' sez ole Brer Fox, sezee, 'I kin drap 'roun' en see de ladies atterwards,' sezee.

" 'Well, den, ef dat's yo' game,' sez ole man Rabbit, sezee, 'I kin squot right flat down yer on de groun' en p'int out de way des de same ez leadin' you dar by de han',' sezee; en den Brer Rabbit sorter chaw on he cud lak he gedder'n up his 'membunce, en he up'n say, sezee:

" 'You know dat ar place whar you went atter sweetgum fer Miss Meadows en de gals t'er day?' sezee.

"Brer Fox 'low dat he know dat ar place same ez he do he own tater-patch.

" 'Well, den,' sez Brer Rabbit, sezee, 'de grapes aint dar. You git ter de sweetgum,' sezee, 'en den you go up de branch twel you come ter a little patch er bamboo-brier—but de grapes aint dar. Den you follow yo' lef' han' en strike 'cross de hill twel you come ter dat big red-oak root—but de grapes aint dar. On you goes down de hill twel you come ter 'n'er branch, en on dat branch dars a dogwood-tree leanin' 'way over, en nigh dat dogwood dars a vine, en in dat vine, dar you'll fine yo' grapes. Deyer dat ripe,' sez ole Brer Rabbit, sezee, 'dat dey look like deyer done melt tergedder, en I speck you'll fine um full er bugs, but you kin take dat fine bushy tail er yone, Brer Fox,' sezee, 'en bresh dem bugs away.'

"Brer Fox 'low he much 'blige, en den he put out atter de grapes in a han'-gallop, en w'en he done got outer sight, en likewise outer year'n, Brer Rabbit, he take'n git a blade er grass, he did, en tickle hisse'f in de year, en den he holler en laff, en laff en holler, twel he hatter lay down fer ter git he breff back 'gin.

"Den, atter so long time, Brer Rabbit he jump up, he do, en take atter Brer Fox, but Brer Fox, he aint look ter de right ner de lef', en needer do he look behime; he des keep a-rackin' 'long twel he come ter de sweetgum-tree, en den he tu'n up de branch twel he come ter de bamboo-brier, en den he tu'n squar ter de lef' twel he come ter de big red-oak root, en den he keep on down he hill twel he come ter de yuther branch, en dar he see de dogwood; en mo'n dat, dar nigh

de dogwood he see de vine, en in dat vine dar wuz de big bunch er grapes. Sho' nuff, dey wuz all kivvud wid bugs.

"Ole Brer Rabbit, he'd bin a-pushin' 'long atter Brer Fox, but he des hatter scratch gravel fer ter keep up. Las' he hove in sight, en he lay off in de weeds, he did, fer ter watch Brer Fox motions. Present'y Brer Fox crope up de leanin' dogwood-tree twel he come nigh de grapes, en den he sorter ballunce hisse'f on a lim' en gun um a swipe wid his big bushy tail, fer ter bresh off de bugs. But, bless yo' soul, honey, no sooner is he done dat dan he fetch a squall w'ich Miss Meadows vow atterwards she year plum ter her house, en down he come—*kerblim!*"

"What was the matter, Uncle Remus?" the little boy asked.

"Law, honey! Dat seetful Brer Rabbit done fool ole Brer Fox. Dem ar grapes all so fine wuz needer mo' ner less dan a great big was'-nes', en dem bugs wuz deze yer red wassies—deze yer speeshy w'at's rank pizen fum een' ter een'. W'en Brer Fox drap fum de tree de wassies dey drap wid 'im, en de way dey wom ole Brer Fox up wuz sinful. Dey aint mo'n tetch 'im 'fo' dey had 'im het up ter de b'ilin' p'int. Brer Fox, he run, en he kick, en he scratch, en he bite, en he scramble, en he holler, en he howl, but look lak dey git wuss en wuss. One time, hit seem lak Brer Fox en his new 'quaintance wuz makin' todes Brer Rabbit, but dey aint no sooner p'int dat way, dan ole Brer Rabbit, he up'n make a break, en he went sailin' thoo de woods wuss'n wunner dese whully-win's, en he aint stop twel he fetch up at Miss Meadows.

"Miss Meadows en de gals, dey ax 'im, dey did, wharbouts wuz Brer Fox, en Brer Rabbit, he up'n 'spon' dat he done gone a-grape-huntin', en den Miss Meadows, she 'low, she did:

"'Law, gals! Is you ever year de beat er dat? En dat, too, w'en Brer Fox done say he comin' ter dinner,' sez she. 'I lay I done wid Brer Fox, kaze you can't put no pennunce in deze yer men-folks,' sez she. 'Yer de dinner bin done dis long time, en we bin a-waitin' lak de quality. But now I'm done wid Brer Fox,' sez she.

"Wid dat, Miss Meadows en de gals dey ax Brer Rabbit fer ter stay ter dinner, en Brer Rabbit, he sorter make like he wanter be skuze, but bimeby he tuck a cheer en sot um out. He tuck a cheer," continued Uncle Remus, "en he aint bin dar long twel he look out en spy ole Brer Fox gwine 'long by, en w'at do Brer Rabbit do but call Miss Meadows en de gals en p'int 'im out? Soon's dey seed 'im dey sot up a monst'us gigglement, kaze Brer Fox wuz dat swell up twel little mo'n he'd a bus'. He head wuz swell up, en down ter he legs, dey wuz swell up. Miss Meadows, she up'n say dat Brer Fox look like he done gone en got all de grapes dey wuz in de neighbor-hoods, en one er de yuther gals, she squeal, she did, en say:

" 'Law, aint you 'shame', en right yer 'fo' Brer Rabbit!'

"En den dey hilt der han's 'fo' der face en giggle des like gals duz deze days."

The next night the little boy had been thoughtful enough to save some of his supper for Uncle Remus, and to this "Miss Sally" had added, on her own account, a large piece of fruit-cake. The old man appeared to be highly pleased.

"Ef ders enny kinder cake w'at I likes de mos', hit's dish yer kine w'at's got reezins strowed 'mongs' it. Wid sick folks, now," he continued, holding up the cake and subjecting it to a critical examination, "dish yer hunk 'ud mighty nigh las' a mont', but wid a well man lak I is, hit won't las' a minnit."

And it didn't. It disappeared so suddenly that the little boy laughed aloud, and wanted Uncle Remus to have some more cake; but the latter protested that he didn't come there "fer ter git founder'd," but merely to see "ef somebody's strenk uz strong 'nuff fer ter stan' 'n'er tale." The little boy said if Uncle Remus meant him, he was sure his health was good enough to listen to any number of stories. Whereupon, the old man, without any tantalizing preliminaries, began:

"Brer Fox done bin fool so much by Brer Rabbit dat he sorter look 'roun' fer ter see ef he can't ketch up wid some er de yuther creeturs, en so, one day, wi'les he gwine long down de big road, who should he strak up wid but old Brer Tarrypin. Brer Fox sorter lick his chops, en 'low dat ef he kin fling ennybody en gin um all-under holt, Brer Tarrypin de man, en he march up, mighty biggity, like he gwine ter make spote un 'im. W'en he git up nigh 'nuff, Brer Fox hail 'im:

"'How you 'speck you fine yo'se'f dis mawnin', Brer Tarrypin?' sezee.

"'Slow, Brer Fox—mighty slow,' sez Brer Tarrypin, sezee. 'Day in

225

en day out I'm mighty slow, en it look lak I'm a-gittin' slower; I'm slow en po'ly, Brer Fox—how you come on?' sezee.

" 'Oh, I'm slanchindickler, same ez I allers is,' sez Brer Fox, sezee. 'W'at make yo' eye so red, Brer Tarrypin?' sezee.

" 'Hit's all 'longer de trouble I see, Brer Fox,' sez Brer Tarrypin, sezee. 'I see trouble en you see none; trouble come en pile up on trouble,' sezee.

" 'Law, Brer Tarrypin!' sez Brer Fox, sezee. 'You aint see no trouble yit. Ef you wanter see sho' 'nuff trouble, you des oughter go 'longer me; I'm de man w'at kin show you trouble,' sezee.

" 'Well, den,' sez ole Brer Tarrypin, sezee, 'ef youer de man w'at kin show me trouble, den I'm de man w'at want a glimpse un it,' sezee.

"Den Brer Fox, he ax Brer Tarrypin is he seed de Ole Boy, en den Brer Tarrypin, he make answer dat he aint seed 'im yit, but he year tell un 'im. Wid dat, Brer Fox 'low de Ole Boy de kinder trouble he bin talkin' 'bout, en den Brer Tarrypin, he up'n ax how he gwine see 'im. Brer Fox, he tak'n lay out de pogrance, en he up'n tell Brer Tarrypin dat ef he'll step up dar in de middle er dat ole broom-sage fiel', en squot dar a spell, 't won't be no time 'fo' he'll ketch a glimpse er de Ole Boy.

"Brer Tarrypin know'd ders sump'n' wrong some'rs, yit he mos' too flat-flooted fer ter have enny scuffle wid Brer Fox, en he say ter hisse'f dat he'll go 'long en des trus' ter luck; en den he 'low dat ef Brer Fox he'p 'im 'cross de fence, he b'leeve he'll go up en resk one eye on de Ole Boy. Co'se Brer Fox hope 'im 'cross, en no sooner is he good en gone, dan Brer Fox, he fix up fer ter make 'im see trouble. He lipt out ter Miss Meadows house, Brer Fox did, en make like he wanter borry a chunk er fier fer ter light he pipe, en he tuck dat chunk, en he run 'roun' de fiel', en he sot de grass a fier, en 't wa'n't

226

long 'fo' it look lak de whole face er de yeth was a-blazin' up."

"Did it burn the Terrapin up?" interrupted the little boy.

"Don't push me, honey; don't make me git de kyart 'fo' de hoss. W'en ole Brer Tarrypin 'gun ter wade thoo de straw, de ve'y fus' man w'at he strak up wid wuz ole man Rabbit layin' dar sleepin' on de shady side uv a tussock. Brer Rabbit, he one er deze yer kinder mens w'at sleep wid der eye wide open, en he wuz 'wake d'reckly he year Brer Tarrypin scufflin' en scramblin' 'long thoo de grass. Atter dey shuck han's en ax 'bout one er n'er fambly, hit aint take long fer Brer Tarrypin fer ter tell Brer Rabbit w'at fotch 'im dar, en Brer Rabbit, he up'n say, sezee.

" 'Hit's des na'tally a born blessin' dat you struck up wid me w'en you did,' sezee, 'kaze little mo' en bofe un us would 'a' bin bobbycu'd,' sezee.

"Dis kinder tarrify Brer Tarrypin, en he say he wanter git out fum dar; but Brer Rabbit he 'low he'd take keer un 'im, en he tuck'n tuck Brer Tarrypin in de middle er de fiel' whar dey wuz a big holler stump. Onter dis stump Brer Rabbit lif' Brer Tarrypin, en den he lip up hisse'f en crope in de holler, en, bless yo' soul, honey, w'en de fier come a-snippin' en a-snappin', dar dey sot des ez safe en ez snug ez you iz in yo' bed dis minnit.

"W'en de blaze blow over, Brer Tarrypin look 'roun', en he see Brer Fox runnin' up'n down de fence lak he huntin' sump'n'. Den Brer Rabbit, he stick he head up outen de hole, en likewise he seed 'im, and den he holler like Brer Tarrypin" (Here Uncle Remus puckered his voice, so to say, in a most amusing squeak):

" 'Brer Fox! Brer Fox! O Brer Fox! Run yer—we done kotch Brer Rabbit!'

"En den Brer Fox, he jump up on de top rail er de fence en fetch a spring dat lan' 'im 'way out in de bu'nin' grass, en it hurted 'im en sting 'im in de footses dat bad, dat he squeal en he roll, en de mo' he roll de wuss it bu'n him, en Brer Rabbit en Brer Tarrypin dey des holler en laff. Bimeby Brer Fox git out, en off he put down de road, limpin' fus' on one foot en den on de yuther."

The little boy laughed, and then there was a long silence—so long, indeed, that Uncle Remus's "Miss Sally," sewing in the next room, concluded to investigate it. An exceedingly interesting tableau met her sight. The little child had wandered into the land of dreams with a smile on his face. He lay with one of his little hands buried in both of Uncle Remus's, while the old man himself was fast asleep, with his head thrown back and his mouth wide open. "Miss Sally" shook him by the shoulder and held up her finger to prevent him from speaking. He was quiet until she held the lamp for him to get down the back steps, and then she heard him say, in an indignantly mortified tone:

"Now den, Miss Sally'll be a-riggin' me 'bout noddin', but stidder dat she better be glad dat I aint bus loose en sno' en 'larm de house— let 'lone dat sick baby. Dat's w'at!"

"I dreamed all about Brother Fox and Brother Rabbit last night, Uncle Remus," exclaimed the little boy when the old man came in after supper and took his seat by the side of the trundle-bed; "I dreamed that Brother Fox had wings and tried to catch Brother Rabbit by flying after him."

"I don't 'spute it, honey, dat I don't!" replied the old man, in a tone which implied that he was quite prepared to believe the dream itself was true. "Manys en manys de time, deze long nights en deze rainy spells, dat I sets down dar in my house over ag'in de chimbley-jam—I sets dar en I dozes, en it seem lak dat ole Brer Rabbit, he'll stick he head in de crack er de do' en see my eye periently shot, en den he'll beckon back at de yuther creeturs, en den dey'll all come slippin' in on der tip-toes, en dey'll set dar en run over de ole times wid one er n'er, en crack der jokes same ez dey useter. En den ag'in," continued the old man, shutting his eyes and giving to his voice a gruesome intonation quite impossible to describe,—"en den ag'in hit look lak dat Brer Rabbit'll gin de wink all 'roun', en den dey'll tu'n in en git up a reg'lar juberlee. Brer Rabbit, he'll retch up en take down de trivet, en Brer Fox, he'll snatch up de griddle, en Brer B'ar, he'll lay holt er de pot-hooks, en ole Brer Tarrypin, he'll grab up de fryin' pan, en dar dey'll have it, up en down, en 'roun' en 'roun'. Hit seem like ter me dat ef I kin git my mine smoove down en ketch up some er dem ar chunes w'at dey sets dar en plays, den I'd lean back yer in dish yer cheer en I'd intrance you wid um, twel, by dis time termorrer night, you'd be settin' up dar at de supper-table 'sputin' 'longer yo' little brer 'bout de 'lasses pitcher. Dem creeturs dey sets dar," Uncle Remus went on, "en dey plays dem kinder chunes w'at moves you fum 'way back yander; en manys de time w'en I gits lonesome kaze dey aint nobody year um 'ceppin' it's me.

Dey aint no tellin' de chunes dey is in dat trivet, en in dat griddle, en in dat fryin'-pan er mine; dat dey aint. W'en dem creeturs walks in en snatches um down, dey lays Miss Sally's pianner in de shade, en Mars John's flute, hit aint nowhars."

"Do they play on them just like a band, Uncle Remus?" inquired the little boy, who was secretly in hopes that the illusion would not be destroyed.

"Dey comes des lak I tell you, honey. W'en I shets my eyes en dozes, dey comes en dey plays, but w'en I opens my eyes dey aint dar. Now, den, w'en dat's de shape er marters, w'at duz I do? I des shets my eyes en hol' um shot, en let um come en play dem ole time chunes twel long atter bed-time done come en gone."

Uncle Remus paused, as though he expected the little boy to ask some question or make some comment, but the child said nothing, and presently the old man resumed, in a matter-of-fact tone:

"Dat dream er yone, honey, 'bout Brer Fox wid wings, fetches up de time w'en Brer Fox en Brer Wolf had der fallin' out wid one er n'er—but I 'speck I done tole you 'bout dat."

"Oh, no, you haven't, Uncle Remus! You know you haven't!" the little boy exclaimed.

"Well, den, one day, atter so long a time, Brer Wolf en Brer Fox dey got ter 'sputin' 'longer one er n'er. Brer Wolf, he tuck'n 'buse Brer Fox kaze Brer Fox let Brer Rabbit fool 'im, en den Brer Fox, he tuck'n quol back at Brer Wolf, kaze Brer Wolf let ole man Rabbit lakwise fool 'im. Dey keep on 'sputin' en 'sputin', twel bimeby dey clinch, en Brer Wolf bein' de bigges' man, 't would n't a bin long 'fo' he'd a wool Brer Fox, but Brer Fox, he watch he chance, he did, en he gin 'im leg bail."

"Gave him what, Uncle Remus?"

"Gin 'im leg bail, honey. He juk loose fum Brer Wolf, Brer Fox did, en, gentermens, he des mosey thoo de woods. Brer Wolf, he tuck atter'm, he did, en dar dey had it, en Brer Wolf push Brer Fox so close, dat de onliest way Brer Fox kin save he hide is ter fine a hole some'rs, en de fus' holler tree dat he come 'cross, inter it he dove. Brer Wolf fetcht a grab at 'im, but he wuz des in time fer ter be too late.

"Den Brer Wolf, he sot dar, he did, en he study en study how he gwine git Brer Fox out, en Brer Fox, he lay in dar, he did, en he study en study w'at Brer Wolf gwine do. Bimeby, Brer Wolf, he tuck'n gedder up a whole lot er chunks, en rocks, en sticks, en den he tuck'n fill up de hole whar Brer Fox went in so Brer Fox can't git out. W'iles dis wuz gwine on, ole Brer Tukky Buzzud, he wuz sailin' 'roun' 'way up in de elements, wid he eye peel fer bizness, en 't wa'n't long 'fo' he glance lit on Brer Wolf, en he 'low ter hisse'f, sezee:

" 'I'll des sorter flop down,' sezee, 'en look inter dis, kaze ef Brer Wolf hidin' he dinner dar wid de expeck'shun er findin' it dar w'en he come back, den he done gone en put it in de wrong place,' sezee.

"Wid dat ole Brer Tukky Buzzud, he flop down en sail 'roun' nigher, en he soon see dat Brer Wolf aint hidin' no dinner. Den he flop down furder, ole Brer Buzzud did, twel he lit on de top er de holler tree. Brer Wolf, he done kotch a glimpse er ole Brer Buzzud shadder, but he keep on puttin' chunks en rocks in de holler. Den, present'y, Brer Buzzud, he open up:

" 'W'at you doin' dar, Brer Wolf?'

" 'Makin' a toom-stone, Brer Buzzud.'

"Co'se Brer Buzzud sorter feel like he got intruss in marters like dis, en he holler back:

" 'Who dead now, Brer Wolf?'

" 'Wunner yo' 'quaintance, w'ich he name Brer Fox, Brer Buzzud.'

" 'W'en he die, Brer Wolf?'

" 'He aint dead yit, but he won't las' long in yer, Brer Buzzud.'

231

"Brer Wolf, he keep on, he did, twel he done stop up de hole good, en den he bresh de trash off'n his cloze, en put out fer home. Brer Tukky Buzzud, he sot up dar, he did, en ontankle his tail fedders, en lissen en lissen, but Brer Fox, he keep dark, en Brer Buzzud aint year nuthin'. Den Brer Buzzud, he flop he wings en sail away.

"Bimeby, nex' day, bright en early, yer he come back, en he sail all 'roun' en 'roun' de tree, but Brer Fox he lay low en keep dark, en Brer Buzzud aint year nuthin'. Atter w'ile, Brer Buzzud he sail 'roun' ag'in, en dis time he sing, en de song w'at he sing is dish yer:

" 'Boo, boo, boo, my filler-mer-loo,
  Man out yer wid news fer you!'

Den he sail all 'roun' en 'roun' n'er time en listen, en bimeby he year Brer Fox sing back:

" 'Go 'way, go 'way, my little jug er beer,
  De news you bring, I yeard las' year.' "

"Beer, Uncle Remus? What kind of beer did they have then?" the little boy inquired.

"Now, den, honey, youer gittin' me up in a close cornder," responded the old man, in an unusually serious tone. "Beer is de way de tale runs, but w'at kinder beer it moughter bin aint come down ter me—en yit hit seem lak I year talk some'rs dat dish yer beer wuz mos' prins'ply 'simmon beer."

This seemed to satisfy the small but exacting audience, and Uncle Remus continued:

"So, den, w'en Brer Buzzud year Brer Fox sing back, he 'low he aint dead, en wid dat, Brer Buzzud, he sail off en 'ten' ter he yuther business. Nex' day back he come, en Brer Fox, he sing back, he did, des ez lively ez a cricket in de ashes, en it keep on dis way twel Brer Fox stomach 'gun ter pinch him, en den he know dat he gotter study

up some kinder plans fer ter git out fum dar. N'er day pass, en Brer Fox, he tuck'n lay low, en it keep on dat a-way twel hit look like ter Brer Fox, pent up in dar, dat he mus' sholy pe'sh. Las', one day Brer Buzzud come sailin' all 'roun' en 'roun' wid dat

" 'Boo, boo, boo, my filler-mer-loo,'

but Brer Fox, he keep dark, en Brer Buzzud, he tuck'n spishun dat Brer Fox wuz done dead. Brer Buzzud, he keep on singin', en Brer Fox he keep on layin' low, twel bimeby Brer Buzzud lit en 'gun ter cle'r 'way de trash en truck fum de holler. He hop up, he did, en tuck out one chunk, en den he hop back en lissen, but Brer Fox stay still. Den Brer Buzzud hop up en tuck out n'er chunk, en den hop back en lissen, en all dis time Brer Fox mouf 'uz waterin' w'iles he lay back in dar en des nat'ally honed atter Brer Buzzud. Hit went on dis a-way, twel des 'fo' he got de hole unkivvud, Brer Fox, he break out he did, en grab Brer Buzzud by de back er de neck. Dey wuz a kinder scuffle 'mongs' um, but 't wa'n't fer long, en dat wuz de las' er ole Brer Tukky Buzzud."

THE MOON IN THE MILL-POND

One night when the little boy made his usual visit to Uncle Remus, he found the old man sitting up in his chair fast asleep. The child said nothing. He was prepared to exercise a good deal of patience upon occasion, and the occasion was when he wanted to hear a story. But, in making himself comfortable, he aroused Uncle Remus from his nap.

"I let you know, honey," said the old man, adjusting his spectacles, and laughing rather sheepishly—"I let you know, honey, w'en I gits my head r'ar'd back dat a-way, en my eyeleds shot, en my mouf open, en my chin p'intin' at de rafters, den dey's some mighty quare gwines on in my min'. Dey is dat, des ez sho' ez youer settin' dar. W'en I fus' year you comin' down de paf," Uncle Remus continued, rubbing his beard thoughtfully, "I 'uz sorter fear'd you mought 'spicion dat I done gone off on my journeys fer ter see ole man Nod."

This was accompanied by a glance of inquiry, to which the little boy thought it best to respond.

"Well, Uncle Remus," he said, "I did think I heard you snoring when I came in."

"Now you see dat!" exclaimed Uncle Remus, in a tone of grieved astonishment. "You see dat! Man can't lean hisse'f 'pun his 'membunce, 'ceppin' dey's some un fer ter come high-primin' 'roun' en 'lowin' dat he done gone ter sleep. *Shoo!* W'en you stept in dat do' dar I 'uz right in 'mungs some mighty quare notions—mighty quare notions. Dey aint no two ways; ef I 'uz ter up en let on 'bout all de notions w'at I gits in 'mungs, folks 'ud hatter come en kyar me off ter de place whar dey puts 'stracted people.

"Atter I sop up my supper," Uncle Remus went on, "I tuck'n year some flutterments up dar 'mungs de rafters, en I look up, en dar wuz a Bat sailin' 'roun'. 'Roun' en 'roun', en 'roun' she go—und' de rafters, 'bove de rafters—en ez she sail she make noise lak she grittin' 'er toofies. Now, w'at dat Bat atter, I be bless ef I kin tell you, but dar she wuz; 'roun' en 'roun', over en under. I ax 'er w'at do she want up dar, but she aint got no time fer ter tell; 'roun' en 'roun', en over en under. En bimeby, out she flip, en I boun' she grittin' 'er toofies en gwine 'roun' en 'roun' out dar, en dodgin' en flippin' des lak de elements wuz full er rafters en cobwebs.

"W'en she flip out I le'nt my head back, I did, en t' wa'n't no time 'fo' I git mix up wid my notions. Dat Bat wings so limber en 'er will so good dat she done done 'er day's work dar 'fo' you could 'er run ter de big house en back. De Bat put me in min' er folks," continued Uncle Remus, settling himself back in his chair, "en folks put me in min' er de creeturs."

Immediately the little boy was all attention.

"Dey wuz times," said the old man, with something like a sigh, "w'en de creeturs 'ud segashuate tergedder des like dey aint had no fallin' out. Dem wuz de times w'en ole Brer Rabbit 'ud 'ten' lak he gwine quit he 'havishness, en dey'd all go 'roun' des lak dey b'long ter de same fambly connexion.

"One time atter dey bin gwine in cohoots dis a-way, Brer Rabbit 'gun ter feel his fat, he did, en dis make 'im git projecky terreckly. De mo' peace w'at dey had, de mo' wuss Brer Rabbit feel, twel bimeby he git restless in de min'. W'en de sun shine he'd go en lay off in de grass en kick at de gnats, en nibble at de mullen stalk en waller in de san'. One night atter supper, w'iles he 'uz romancin' 'roun', he run up wid ole Brer Tarrypin, en atter dey shuck han's dey sot down on de side er de road en run on 'bout ole times. Dey talk en dey talk, dey did, en bimeby Brer Rabbit say it done come ter dat pass whar he bleedz ter have some fun, en Brer Tarrypin 'low dat Brer Rabbit des de ve'y man he bin lookin' fer.

" 'Well den,' sez Brer Rabbit, sezee, 'we'll des put Brer Fox, en

Brer Wolf, en Brer B'ar on notice, en termorrer night we'll meet down by de mill-pon' en have a little fishin' frolic. I'll do de talkin',' sez Brer Rabbit, sezee, 'en you kin set back en say *yea*,' sezee.

"Brer Tarrypin laugh.

"'Ef I aint dar,' sezee, 'den you may know de grasshopper done fly 'way wid me,' sezee.

"'En you neenter bring no fiddle, n'er,' sez Brer Rabbit, sezee, 'kaze dey aint gwineter be no dancin' dar,' sezee.

"Wid dat," continued Uncle Remus, "Brer Rabbit put out fer home, en went ter bed, en Brer Tarrypin bruise 'roun' en make his way todes de place so he kin be dar 'gin de 'p'inted time.

"Nex' day Brer Rabbit sont wud ter de yuther creeturs, en dey all make great 'miration, kaze dey aint think 'bout dis deyse'f. Brer Fox, he 'low, he did, dat he gwine atter Miss Meadows en Miss Motts, en de yuther gals.

"Sho' nuff, w'en de time come dey wuz all dar. Brer B'ar, he fotch a hook en line; Brer Wolf, he fotch a hook en line; Brer Fox, he fotch a dip-net, en Brer Tarrypin, not ter be outdone, he fotch de bait."

"What did Miss Meadows and Miss Motts bring?" the little boy asked.

Uncle Remus dropped his head slightly to one side, and looked over his spectacles at the little boy.

"Miss Meadows en Miss Motts," he continued, "dey tuck'n stan' way back fum de aidge er de pon' en squeal eve'y time Brer Tarrypin shuck de box er bait at um. Brer B'ar ' low he gwine ter fish fer mud-cats; Brer Wolf 'low he gwine ter fish fer horneyheads; Brer Fox 'low he gwine ter fish fer peerch fer de ladies; Brer Tarrypin 'low he gwine ter fish fer minners, en Brer Rabbit wink at Brer Tarrypin en 'low he gwine ter fish fer suckers.

"Dey all git ready, dey did, en Brer Rabbit march up ter de pon' en make fer ter th'ow he hook in de water, but des 'bout dat time hit seem lak he see sump'n'. De t'er creeturs, dey stop en watch his motions. Brer Rabbit, he drap he pole, he did, en he stan' dar scratchin' he head en lookin' down in de water.

"De gals dey 'gun ter git oneasy w'en dey see dis, en Miss Meadows, she up en holler out, she did:

"'Law, Brer Rabbit, w'at de name er goodness de marter in dar?'

"Brer Rabbit scratch he head en look in de water. Miss Motts, she hilt up 'er petticoats, she did, en 'low she monst'us fear'd er snakes. Brer Rabbit keep on scratchin' en lookin'.

"Bimeby he fetch a long bref, he did, en he 'low:

"'Ladies en gentermuns all, we des might ez well make tracks fum dish yer place, kaze dey aint no fishin' in dat pon' fer none er dish yer crowd.'

"Wid dat, Brer Tarrypin, he scramble up ter de aidge en look over, en he shake he head, en 'low:

"'Tooby sho'—tooby sho'! Tut-tut-tut!' en den he crawl back, he did, en do lak he wukkin' he min'.

"'Don't be skeert, ladies, kaze we er boun' ter take keer un you, let come w'at will, let go w'at mus',' sez Brer Rabbit, sezee. 'Accidents got ter happen unter we all, des same ez dey is unter yuther folks; en dey aint nuthin' much de marter, 'ceppin' dat de Moon done drap in de water. Ef you don't b'leeve me you kin look fer yo'se'f,' sezee.

"Wid dat dey all went ter de bank en lookt in; en, sho' nuff, dar lay de Moon, a-swingin' an' a-swayin' at de bottom er de pon'."

The little boy laughed. He had often seen the reflection of the sky in shallow pools of water, and the startling depths that seemed to lie at his feet had caused him to draw back with a shudder.

"Brer Fox, he look in, he did, en he 'low, 'Well, well, well!' Brer Wolf, he look in, en he 'low, 'Mighty bad, mighty bad!' Brer B'ar, he look in, en he 'low, 'Tum, tum, tum!' De ladies dey look in, en Miss Meadows she squall out, 'Aint dat too much?' Brer Rabbit, he look in ag'in, en he up en 'low, he did:

" 'Ladies en gentermuns, you all kin hum en haw, but less'n we gits dat Moon out er de pon', dey aint no fish kin be ketch 'roun' yer dis night; en ef you'll ax Brer Tarrypin, he'll tell you de same.'

"Den dey ax how kin dey git de Moon out er dar, en Brer Tarry-pin 'low dey better lef' dat wid Brer Rabbit. Brer Rabbit he shot his eyes, he did, en make lak he wukkin' he min'. Bimeby, he up'n 'low:

" 'De nighes' way out'n dish yer diffikil is fer ter sen' 'roun' yer to ole Mr. Mud-Turkle en borry his sane, en drag dar Moon up fum dar,' sezee.

" 'I 'clar' ter gracious I mighty glad you mention dat,' says Brer Tarrypin, sezee. 'Mr. Mud-Turkle is setch clos't kin ter me dat I calls 'im Unk Muck, en I lay ef you sen' dar atter dat sane you won't fine Unk Muck so mighty disaccomerdatin'.'

"Well," continued Uncle Remus, after one of his tantalizing pauses, "dey sont atter de sane, en w'iles Brer Rabbit wuz gone, Brer Tarrypin, he 'low dat he done year tell time en time ag'in dat dem w'at fine de Moon in de water en fetch 'im out, lakwise dey ull fetch out a pot er money. Dis make Brer Fox, en Brer Wolf, en Brer B'ar feel mighty good, en dey 'low, dey did, dat long ez Brer Rabbit been so good ez ter run atter de sane, dey ull do de sanein'.

"Time Brer Rabbit git back, he see how de lan' lay, en he make lak he wanter go in atter de Moon. He pull off he coat, en he 'uz fixin' fer ter shuck he wescut, but de yuther creeturs dey 'low dey wa'n't gwine ter let dryfoot man lak Brer Rabbit go in de water. So Brer Fox, he tuck holt er one staff er de sane, Brer Wolf he tuck holt er de yuther staff, en Brer B'ar he wade 'long behime fer ter lif' de sane 'cross logs en snags.

"Dey make one haul—no Moon; n'er haul—no Moon; n'er haul—

no Moon. Den bimeby dey git out furder fum de bank. Water run in Brer Fox year, he shake he head; water run in Brer Wolf year, he shake he head; water run in Brer B'ar year, he shake he head. En de fus' news you know, w'iles dey wuz a-shakin', dey come to whar de bottom shelfed off. Brer Fox he step off en duck hisse'f; den Brer Wolf duck hisse'f; en Brer B'ar he make a splunge en duck hisse'f; en, bless gracious, dey kick en splatter twel it look lak dey 'uz gwine ter slosh all de water outer de mill-pon'.

"W'en dey come out, de gals 'uz all a-snickerin' en a-gigglin', en dey well mought, 'kaze go whar you would, dey wa'n't no wuss lookin' creeturs dan dem; en Brer Rabbit, he holler, sezee:

"'I 'speck you all, gents, better go home en git some dry duds, en n'er time we'll be in better luck,' sezee. 'I hear talk dat de Moon'll bite at a hook ef you take fools fer baits, en I lay dat's de onliest way fer ter ketch 'er,' sezee.

"Brer Fox en Brer Wolf en Brer B'ar went drippin' off, en Brer Rabbit en Brer Tarrypin, dey went home wid de gals."

One night while the little boy was sitting in Uncle Remus's cabin, waiting for the old man to finish his hoe-cake, and refresh his memory as to the further adventures of Brother Rabbit, his friends and his enemies, something dropped upon the top of the house with a noise like the crack of a pistol. The little boy jumped, but Uncle Remus looked up and exclaimed, "Ah-yi!" in a tone of triumph.

"What was that, Uncle Remus?" the child asked, after waiting a moment to see what else would happen.

"News fum Jack Fros', honey. W'en dat hick'y-nut tree out dar year 'im comin' she 'gins ter drap w'at she got. I mighty glad," he continued, scraping the burnt crust from his hoe-cake with an old case-knife, "I mighty glad hick'y-nuts aint big en heavy ez grinestones."

He waited a moment to see what effect this queer statement would have on the child.

"Yasser, I mighty glad—dat I is. 'Kaze ef hick'y-nuts 'uz big ez grinestones dish yer ole callyboose 'ud be a-leakin' long 'fo' Chris'-mus."

Just then another hickory-nut dropped upon the roof, and the little boy jumped again. This seemed to amuse Uncle Remus, and he laughed until he was near to choking himself with his smoking hoe-cake.

"You does des 'zackly lak ole Brer Rabbit done, I 'clar' to gracious ef you don't!" the old man cried, as soon as he could get his breath. "Dez zackly fer de worl'."

The child was immensely flattered, and at once he wanted to know how Brother Rabbit did. Uncle Remus was in such good humor that he needed no coaxing. He pushed his spectacles back on his forehead, wiped his mouth on his sleeve, and began:

"Hit come 'bout dat soon one mawnin' todes de fall er de year, Brer Rabbit wuz stirrin' 'roun' in de woods atter some bergamot fer ter make 'im some ha'r-grease. De win' blow so col' dat it make 'im feel right frisky, en eve'y time he year de bushes rattle he make lak he skeerd. He 'uz gwine on dis a-way, hoppity-skippity, w'en bimeby he year Mr. Man cuttin' on a tree way off in de woods. He fotch up, Brer Rabbit did, en lissen fus' wid one year en den wid de yuther.

"Man, he cut en cut, en Brer Rabbit, he lissen en lissen. Bimeby, w'iles all dis was gwine on, down come de tree—*kubber-lang-bang-blam!* Brer Rabbit, he tuck'n jump des lak you jump, en let 'lone dat, he make a break, he did, en he lipt out fum dar lak de dogs wuz atter 'im."

"Was he scared, Uncle Remus?" asked the little boy.

"Skeerd! Who? *Him?* Shoo! Don't you fret yo'se'f 'bout Brer Rabbit, honey. In dem days dey wa'n't nothin' gwine dat kin skeer Brer Rabbit. Tooby sho', he tuck keer hisse'f, en ef you know de man w'at 'fuse ter take keer hisse'f, I lak mighty well ef you p'int 'im out. Deed'n dat I would!"

Uncle Remus seemed to boil over with argumentative indignation.

"Well, den," he continued, "Brer Rabbit run twel he git sorter het up like, en des 'bout de time he makin' ready fer ter squot en ketch he win', who should he meet but Brer Coon gwine home atter settin' up wid ole Brer Bull-Frog. Brer Coon see 'im runnin', en he hail 'im.

" 'W'at yo' hurry, Brer Rabbit?'

" 'Aint got time ter tarry.'

" 'Folks sick?'

" 'No, my Lord! Aint got time ter tarry!'

" 'Tryin' yo' soopleness?'

" 'No, my Lord! Aint got time ter tarry!'

" 'Do pray, Brer Rabbit, tell me de news!'

" 'Mighty big fuss back dar in de woods. Aint got time ter tarry!'

"Dis make Brer Coon feel mighty skittish, 'kaze he fur ways fum home, en he des lipt out, he did, en went a-b'ilin' thoo de woods. Brer Coon aint gone fur twel he meet Brer Fox.

" 'Hey, Brer Coon, whar you gwine?'

" 'Aint got time ter tarry!'

" 'Gwine at' de doctor?'

" 'No, my Lord! Aint got time ter tarry.'

" 'Do pray, Brer Coon, tell me de news.'

" 'Mighty quare racket back dar in de woods! Aint got time ter tarry!'

"Wid dat, Brer Fox lipt out, he did, en fa'rly split de win'. He aint gone fur twel he meet Brer Wolf.

" 'Hey, Brer Fox! Stop en res' yo'se'f!'

" 'Aint got time ter tarry!'

" 'Who bin want de doctor?'

" 'No'ne, my Lord! Aint got time ter tarry!'

" 'Do pray, Brer Fox, good er bad, tell me de news.'

" 'Mighty kuse fuss back dar in de woods! Aint got time ter tarry!'

"Wid dat, Brer Wolf shuck hisse'f loose fum de face er de yeth, en he aint git fur twel he meet Brer B'ar. Brer B'ar he ax, en Brer Wolf make ans'er, en bimeby Brer B'ar he fotch a snort en run'd off; en, bless gracious! 't wa'n't long 'fo' de las' one er de creeturs wuz a-skaddlin' thoo de woods lak de Ole Boy was atter um—en all 'kaze Brer Rabbit year Mr. Man cut tree down.

"Dey run'd en dey run'd," Uncle Remus went on, "twel dey come ter Brer Tarrypin house, en dey sorter slack up 'kaze dey done mighty nigh los' der win'. Brer Tarrypin, he up'n ax um wharbouts dey gwine, en dey 'low dey wuz a monst'us tarryfyin' racket back dar in de woods. Brer Tarrypin, he ax w'at she soun' lak. One say he dunno, n'er say he dunno, den dey all say dey dunno. Den Brer Tarrypin, he up'n ax who year dis monst'us racket. One say he dunno, n'er say he dunno, den dey all say dey dunno. Dis make ole Brer Tarrypin laff 'way down in he insides, en he up'n say, sezee:

" 'You all kin run 'long ef you feel skittish,' sezee. 'Atter I cook my brekkus en wash up de dishes, ef I gits win' er any 'spicious racket maybe I mought take down my pairsol en foller long atter you,' sezee.

"W'en de creeturs come ter make inquirements 'mungs one er n'er 'bout who start de news, hit went right spang back ter Brer Rabbit, but, lo en beholes, Brer Rabbit aint dar, en it tu'n out dat Brer Coon is de man w'at seed 'im las'. Den dey got ter layin' de blame un it on one er n'er, en little mo' en dey'd er fit dar scan'lous, but ole Brer Tarrypin, he up'n 'low dat ef dey want ter git de straight un it, dey better go see Brer Rabbit.

"All de creeturs wuz 'gree'ble, en dey put out ter Brer Rabbit house. W'en dey git dar, Brer Rabbit wuz a-settin' cross-legged in de front po'ch winkin' he eye at de sun. Brer B'ar, he speak up:

" 'W'at make you fool me, Brer Rabbit?'

" 'Fool who, Brer B'ar?'

" 'Me, Brer Rabbit, dat's who.'

" 'Dish yer de fus' time I seed you dis day, Brer B'ar, en you er mo' dan welcome ter dat.'

"Dey all ax 'im en git de same ans'er, en den Brer Coon put in:

" 'W'at make you fool me, Brer Rabbit?'

" 'How I fool you, Brer Coon?'

" 'You make lak dey wuz a big racket, Brer Rabbit.'

" 'Dey sholy wuz a big racket, Brer Coon.'

" 'W'at kinder racket, Brer Rabbit?'

" '*Ah-yi!* You oughter ax me dat fus', Brer Coon.'

" 'I axes you now, Brer Rabbit.'

" 'Mr. Man cut tree down, Brer Coon.'

"Co'se dis make Brer Coon feel like a nat'al-born Slink, en 't wa'n't long 'fo' all de creeturs make der bow ter Brer Rabbit en mosey off home."

"Brother Rabbit had the best of it all along," said the little boy, after waiting to see whether there was a sequel to the story.

"Oh, he did dat a-way!" exclaimed Uncle Remus. "Brer Rabbit was a mighty man in dem days."

The day and the night before Christmas were full of pleasure for the little boy. There was pleasure in the big house, and pleasure in the humble cabins in the quarters. The peculiar manner in which the Negroes celebrated the beginning of the holidays was familiar to the child's experience, but strange to his appreciation, and he enjoyed everything he saw and heard with the ready delight of his years—a delight, which, in this instance, had been trained and sharpened, if the expression may be used, in the small world over which Uncle Remus presided.

The little boy had a special invitation to be present at the marriage of Daddy Jack and 'Tildy, and he went, accompanied by Uncle Remus and Aunt Tempy. It seemed to be a very curious affair, but its incongruities made small impression upon the mind of the child. 'Tildy wore a white dress and had a wreath of artificial flowers in her hair. Daddy Jack wore a high hat, which he persisted in keeping on his head during the ceremony, and a coat the tails of which nearly dragged the floor. His bright little eyes glistened triumphantly, and he grinned and bowed to everybody again and again. After it was all over, the guests partook of cake baked by Aunt Tempy, and persimmon beer brewed by Uncle Remus.

It seemed, however, that 'Tildy was not perfectly happy; for, in response to a question asked by Aunt Tempy, she said:

"Yes'm, I'm gwine down de country 'long wid my ole man, an' I lay ef eve'ything don't go right, I'm gwineter pick up an' come right back."

"No-no!" exclaimed Daddy Jack, "'e no come bahck no'n 't all. 'E bin stay dey-dey wit' 'e nice ole-a màn."

"You put yo' pennunce in dat!" said 'Tildy, scornfully. "Dey aint nobody kin hol' me w'en I takes a notion, 'cep'n hit's Miss Sally; en, goodness knows, Miss Sally aint gwine ter be down dar."

"Who Miss Sally gwine put in de house?" Aunt Tempy asked.

"Humph!" exclaimed 'Tildy, scornfully, "Miss Sally say she gwine take dat ar Darkess[1] an' put 'er in my place. An' a mighty nice mess Darkess gwine ter make un it! Much she know 'bout waitin' on w'ite folks! Many's an' many's de time Miss Sally'll set down in 'er rockin'-cheer an' wish fer 'Tildy—many's de time."

This was 'Tildy's grievance,—the idea that some one could be found to fill her place; and it is a grievance with which people of greater importance than the humble negro house-girl are more or less familiar.

But the preparations for the holidays went on in spite of 'Tildy's grievance. A large platform, used for sunning wheat and seed cotton, was arranged by the Negroes for their dance, and several wagon-loads of resinous pine—known as lightwood—were placed around about it in little heaps, so that the occasion might lack no element of brilliancy.

At nightfall the heaps of lightwood were set on fire, and the little boy, who was waiting impatiently for Uncle Remus to come for him, could hear the Negroes singing, dancing, and laughing. He was just ready to cry when he heard the voice of his venerable partner.

"Is dey a'er passenger anywhar's 'roun' yer fer Thumptown? De stage done ready en de hosses a-prancin'. Ef dey's a'er passenger 'roun' yer, I lay he des better be makin' ready fer ter go."

The old man walked up to the back piazza as he spoke, held out his strong arms, and the little boy jumped into them with an exclamation of delight. The child's mother gave Uncle Remus a shawl to wrap around the child, and this shawl was the cause of considerable trouble, for the youngster persisted in wrapping it around the

[1] Dorcas.

248

old man's head, and so blinding him that there was danger of his falling. Finally, he put the little boy down, took off his hat, raised his right hand, and said:

"Now, den, I bin a-beggin' un you fer ter quit yo' 'haveishness des long ez I'm a-gwinter, en I aint gwine beg you no mo', 'kaze I'm des teetotally wo' out wid beggin', en de mo' I begs de wuss you gits. Now I'm done! You des go yo' ways en I'll go mine, en my way lays right spang back ter de big house whar Miss Sally is. Dat's whar I'm a-gwine!"

Uncle Remus started to the house with an exaggerated vigor of movement comical to behold; but, however comical it may have been, it had its effect. The little boy ran after him, caught him by the hand, and made him stop.

"Now, Uncle Remus, *please* don't go back. I was just playing."

Uncle Remus's anger was all pretence, but he managed to make it very impressive.

"My playin' days done gone too long ter talk 'bout. When I plays, I plays wid wuk, dat w'at I plays wid."

"Well," said the child, who had tactics of his own, "if I can't play with you, I don't know who I am to play with."

This touched Uncle Remus in a very tender spot. He stopped in the path, took off his spectacles, wiped the glasses on his coat-tail, and said very emphatically:

"Now den, honey, des lissen at me. How de name er goodness kin you call dat playin', w'ich er little mo' en I'd er fell down on top er my head, en broke my neck en yone too?"

The child promised that he would be very good, and Uncle Remus picked him up, and the two made their way to where the Negroes had congregated. They were greeted with cries of "Dar's Unk Remus!" "Howdy, Unk Remus!" "Yer dey is!" "Ole man Remus don't sing; but w'en he do sing—gentermens, des go 'way!"

All this and much more, so that when Uncle Remus had placed the little boy upon a corner of the platform, and made him comfortable, he straightened himself with a laugh and cried out:

"Howdy, boys! Howdy all! I des come up fer ter jine in wid you fer one 'roun' fer de sakes er ole times, ef no mo'."

"I boun' fer Unk Remus!" some one said. "Now des hush en let Unk Remus 'lone!" exclaimed another.

The figure of the old man, as he stood smiling upon the crowd of Negroes, was picturesque in the extreme. He seemed to be taller than all the rest; and, notwithstanding his venerable appearance, he moved and spoke with all the vigor of youth. He had always exercised authority over his fellow-servants. He had been the captain of the corn-pile, the stoutest at the log-rolling, the swiftest with the hoe, the neatest with the plough, and the plantation hands still looked upon him as their leader.

Some Negro from the River place had brought a fiddle, and, though it was a very feeble one, its screeching seemed to annoy Uncle Remus.

"Put up dat ar fiddle!" he exclaimed, waving his hand. "Des put 'er up; she sets my toof on aidje. Put 'er up en less go back ter ole times. Dey aint no room fer no fiddle 'roun' yer, 'kaze w'en you gits me started dat ar fiddle won't be nowhars."

"Dat's so," said the man with the fiddle, and the irritating instrument was laid aside.

"Now, den," Uncle Remus went on, "dey's a little chap yer dat you'll all come ter know mighty well one er deze odd-come-shorts, en dish yer little chap aint got so mighty long fer ter set up 'long wid us. Dat bein' de case we oughter take'n put de bes' foot fo'mus' fer ter commence wid."

"You lead, Unk Remus! You des lead en we'll foller."

Thereupon the old man called to the best singers among the Negroes and made them stand near him. Then he raised his right hand to his ear and stood perfectly still. The little boy thought he was listening for something, but presently Uncle Remus began to slap himself gently with his left hand, first upon the leg and then upon the breast. The other Negroes kept time to this by a gentle motion of their feet, and finally, when the thump—thump—thump of this movement had regulated itself to suit the old man's fancy, he broke out with what may be called a Christmas dance song.

His voice was strong, and powerful, and sweet, and its range was as astonishing as its volume. More than this, the melody to which he tuned it, and which was caught up by a hundred voices almost as sweet and as powerful as his own, was charged with a mysterious and pathetic tenderness.

The fine company of men and women at the big house—men and women who had made the tour of all the capitals of Europe—listened with swelling hearts and with tears in their eyes as the song rose and fell upon the air—at one moment a tempest of melody, at another a heartbreaking strain breathed softly and sweetly to the gentle winds. The song that the little boy and the fine company heard was something like this—ridiculous enough when put in cold type, but powerful and thrilling when joined to the melody with which the Negroes had invested it:

MY HONEY, MY LOVE

"Hit's a mighty fur ways up de Far'well Lane,
     My honey, my love!
  You may ax Mister Crow, you may ax Mr. Crane,
     My honey, my love!
  Dey'll make you a bow, en dey'll tell you de same,
     My honey, my love!

Hit's a mighty fur ways fer to go in de night,
    My honey, my love!
My honey, my love, my heart's delight—
    My honey, my love!

"Mister Mink, he creep twel he wake up de snipe,
    My honey, my love!
Mister Bull-Frog holler, *Come-a-light my pipe,*
    My honey, my love!
En de Pa'tridge ax, *Aint yo' peas ripe?*
    My honey, my love!
Better not walk erlong dar much atter night,
    My honey, my love!
My honey, my love, my heart's delight—
    My honey, my love!

"De Bully-Bat fly mighty close ter de groun',
    My honey, my love!
Mister Fox, he coax 'er, *Do come down!*
    My honey, my love!
Mister Coon, he rack all 'roun' en 'roun',
    My honey, my love!
In de darkes' night, oh, de nigger, he's a sight!
    My honey, my love!
My honey, my love, my heart's delight—
    My honey, my love!

"Oh, flee, Miss Nancy, flee ter my knee,
    My honey, my love!
'Lev'm big fat coons lives in one tree,
    My honey, my love!
Oh, ladies all, won't you marry me?
    My honey, my love!

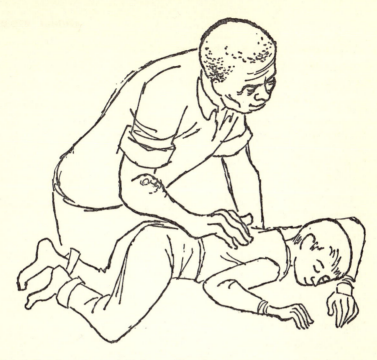

Tu'n lef', tu'n right, we 'ull dance all night,
    My honey, my love!
My honey, my love, my heart's delight—
    My honey, my love!

"De big Owl holler en cry fer his mate,
    My honey, my love!
Oh, don't stay long! Oh, don't stay late!
    My honey, my love!
Hit aint so mighty fur ter de Good-by Gate,
    My honey, my love!
Whar we all got ter go w'en we sing out de night,
    My honey, my love!
My honey, my love, my heart's delight—
    My honey, my love!"

After a while the song was done, and other songs were sung; but it was not long before Uncle Remus discovered that the little boy was fast asleep. The old man took the child in his arms and carried him to the big house, singing softly in his ear all the way; and somehow or other the song seemed to melt and mingle in the youngster's dreams. He thought he was floating in the air, while somewhere near all the Negroes were singing, Uncle Remus's voice above all the rest; and then, after he had found a resting-place upon a soft warm bank of clouds, he thought he heard the songs renewed. They grew fainter and fainter in his dreams until at last (it seemed) Uncle Remus leaned over him and sang